CAPTAIN'S TREASURE

HIS PIRATICAL HAREM - BOOK FOUR

DRAKE LAMARQUE

GREY KELPIE STUDIO

ISBN paperback edition 978-0-473-51322-1

Cover by Sarah Loch of Purple Dragon Design

www.purpledragondesign.com

Printed in United States of America via Kindle Direct Publishing

Published by Grey Kelpie Studio

CHAPTER ONE - IN WHICH A BARGAIN IS MADE

Near the Splintered Isles

The Kelpie's sails were full, the weather was clear and the sky arched overhead as if it would never hold a cloud again.

I had only just managed to stir my bones and force myself out of bed. It was hard to get a restful sleep as we fled from the Royal Navy... and especially since Tate had made the decision to take the supreme risk and use the channel that would take us past the Splintered Isles.

The King's Fleet wouldn't follow us there, of that we could be sure, but it put us into Solomon's territory, and Solomon had been bending his will to take us down for months. He had invaded dreams, worked the Navy against us and his ultimate goal was destruction.

I pulled on a shirt and some trousers, washed my face and combed my hair, trying to ignore the knot of dread that had lodged itself in my stomach several days ago and refused to dissipate.

I spent a quick few moments noting what had happened the day before in the leather bound journal I'd purchased for myself in Nassau - our last port.

Yes, our last port. Our food stores are largely depleted, we had expected to stop off on the way to the Americas and pick up some more stocks of food. Thank Heavens for Ora. We're not in any danger of starving with them doing the lion's share of the fishing.

I set the pen back in its holder and ventured out to deck, looking around. The spires and jutting rocks of the Splintered Isles were far too close for comfort in front of us. To the rear, at least, the Naval fleet wasn't currently visible. It seemed Tate was correct in assuming they wouldn't dare follow us to these cursed waters.

Tate was at the bow of the ship, staring at the Splintered Isles, his eyebrows drawn together and gripping the edge of the ship with both hands. He was utterly still, staring out there as if he'd be able to see the sea witch Solomon if he stared long enough.

Hell, maybe he will be able to... no doubt Solomon knows we're as close as we are. And he'll be trying to get in touch, or... stir up a storm and a great wave to steal me again. Or maybe not me, maybe he'll try for Tate? It didn't go so well with me last time.

I swallowed, hesitating a moment before putting my hand on the small of Tate's back. He startled mightily, gasping and reaching for the sword at his hip. I stepped back hurriedly.

"Sorry! Tate it's just me, sorry, I didn't... I should have warned you."

Tate's hand relaxed on the hilt of his cutlass and his expression relaxed. "Gideon, good God, I almost..." he trailed off, rubbed the bridge of his nose. "I'm too damn tense."

"Yes, we all are," I said, soothingly. "It's all right."

He tugged me close with one hand and I slipped my arms around his neck, pressing myself against him. He wrapped both arms around me and I sighed, soothed by the warmth of him and the hardness of his muscles against mine. His palm rubbed my back and I felt him breathe out heavily.

"I just hate this waiting," Tate said. "I know he's going to try something but I have no idea what or when, and that's what I despise the most."

"I've been thinking much the same thing," I admitted. Tate leaned in and kissed the top of my head. I closed my eyes, savouring this moment of tenderness between us.

"What would I do without you?" Tate murmured and I shook my head.

"Don't talk like that," I said. "I'm not going anywhere at all."

"I hope not," Tate said. I pulled back a little to look up at him.

"Tate, do you..." I swallowed, wondering if I was crossing a line, but knowing I ought to ask him all the same. "Do you want to talk about exactly what happened between the two of you? Maybe it would help to understand what Solomon wants?"

Tate frowned, sighed and shoved a hand through his long, dark, curly hair. He eyed me and then turned his gaze back on the Splintered Isles. We were sailing closer with every moment, the channels here were so narrow, by necessity we had to.

"I don't think so," Tate said. "Feels like I'll summon him up if I say his name too many times."

I shuddered and wrapped my arms around myself. "That's a truly horrible thought," I said. "Maybe... maybe it'd be safer if you went below deck?"

"You're giving me orders now, are you?" Tate's old, cheerful drawl felt like a warm blanket around my shoulders, and I breathed easier, seeing his cheeky smile.

"Well..." I licked my lips. "I have long wanted to try that."

Tate grinned wider and wrapped his arm around my shoulders. "When we're safe again, lad, I'll let you try whatever you want. I assume you've been learning a fair bit from Ezra, after all."

I flushed happily at the thought of that. "Yes, I believe I have."

I went on my tiptoes and kissed his cheek. "Speaking of whom, I should go and say good morning."

"He's with Sagorika, strategising, planning what to do if... when the sea witch strikes. And how best to approach America if we get through this." Tate said. "As if it will help when we have no idea what to expect."

I sighed a little, kissed him once more. "As long as we're all together, I feel like there's nothing we can't overcome," I said. It sounded grand as I said it, like something out of one of my beloved romance stories. Maybe it was a bit too grand though because Tate wrinkled his nose a little, he did smile as well.

"If you say so, Gid."

I went to find Ezra. Zeb was in his now usual place in the crow's nest, keeping an eye on the horizon.

I went below deck to Sagorika's cabin, the largest one on the Grey Kelpie after Tate's. The door stood open, so the sounds of them bickering carried easily to my ears as I approached.

"There's no guarantee that they won't be waiting for us at the other end of the channel," Sagorika said. "Maybe we ought to consider doubling back and sneaking past them."

I got to the door and looked in to see them facing each other across the table, a map laid out on the surface between them. Sagorika wore her favourite plain shift dress and had her arms folded, looking fierce. Her beard was overgrown, getting scruffy on her jawline. It was a testament to how on edge and worried everyone was.

I looked to Ezra, who was also more unshaven than usual on his face and the sides of his head, his hair pulled back into a loose ponytail and not styled at all beyond that. He still looked dashing and handsome, of course, just less groomed than usual.

Ezra shook his head. "We know they're behind us, they're

probably expecting we'd run into trouble here and back out again. Forward is the safest bet."

They glared at each other. I had the distinct feeling this argument had been going in this same circle for some time. I cleared my throat and both looked over at me.

"Gideon, sugar, you need something?" Sagorika said, her voice tinged with a knife's edge of tension.

"Gid, what do you think we should do?" Ezra asked, arching an eyebrow. "America as planned, or double back and try and outrun the British Navy?"

No doubt he expected me to take his side, on account of us being lovers and all, but I shook my head.

"Oh no, I won't be brought into the middle of this, I'm just the cabin boy," I said, smiling. I had no wish at all to take sides. And strategically I had no idea which the best choice would be. "I just wanted to say good morning."

Ezra reached a hand out to me, although he looked mildly irritated still. I went to him, slipped my arm around his waist and kissed him on the lips.

"Good morning," I said, smiling into the kiss.

"Yes, good morning, I'm happy to see you too," he said, although it was largely a grumble. He softened it by squeezing me against him and then kissing me again. I leaned my head against his shoulder and then pulled back, reluctantly.

"I'll leave you to it, I feel like Tate needs the company this morning."

"If only there were something we could do to relieve that tension..." Ezra said.

Sagorika rolled her eyes. "If you and the others could think with the brains in your heads instead of with the contents of your under things perhaps we wouldn't be in this mess in the first place."

That stung, but I couldn't really protest it. Solomon's

vendetta against Tate has been going on for years, but it's definitely my fault that the Navy is close behind us.

"Sorry, Sagorika," I said, looking at the floorboards.

"This isn't your fault," Ezra said, quickly. "Sagorika isn't blaming you."

I looked up at Sagorika, feeling sadness tug at my stomach, and her expression turned from steely to tired. She sighed.

"No, I'm not blaming you," she said. "I'm just exhausted, and there's no easy answer here."

"We'll work something out," I said. "One way or another, I'm sure we'll be all right."

"I hope so." Sagorika collapsed into a chair and eyed the map again. "The sooner we're past these wretched isles, the better."

"You can say that again," Ezra said.

The ship shuddered strangely, as if gently shoved from the port side. Or if there was a huge wave hitting us.

"What was that?" I asked. "I didn't hear a storm or anything...what could it be?"

Ezra's expression clouded. "Nothing good."

The three of us headed up onto the deck as fast as we could manage.

I looked immediately towards the bow, where Tate was still facing the isles, but he wasn't looking at them. Instead, his attention was caught by something that could only have been magically formed.

"What am I looking at?" Ezra asked, drawing his sword as he advanced towards where Tate stood. I hardly knew how to answer him, but as I gazed I started to understand. There was a sheet of mist, or sea spray possibly, standing vertically up from the swells of the waves, several feet from the Grey Kelpie. It moved with the ship, always staying a certain distance from the prow, a few feet ahead like a mystical curtain.

On that mist or sheet of water was a glowing, greenish figure.

Hard to make out in the bright sunshine, but there all the same. I recognised the green light.

"It's Solomon," I said, hurrying close behind Ezra. Sagorika had drawn two throwing knives. "I don't think he's really here," I said. "Don't waste your knives, I think he's somehow projecting his image there."

Sagorika lowered her arms but kept her knives in her hands. I couldn't blame her.

Tate stood transfixed, gazing into the spray, his face pale. He shook his head.

"I don't understand," he said.

"I don't expect you to understand," Solomon - or the illusion of him - said. "I expect you to make a stupid decision and doom your ship."

The crew of the ship had now all gathered behind us. Ezra and Sagorika flanked Tate on either side and I moved behind him, put my hand on the small of his back.

"I'm here," I murmured, although I hardly expected that to be anything but scant comfort to him.

"What decision? What's he talking about Tate?" Ezra asked.

Tate's jaw worked but he didn't respond.

"He's going to doom you all," Solomon's voice got louder, echoing over the ship. I glanced behind to see Zack, his eyes wide, making the sign of the cross. I doubted that would help. James, Anton and the others were all watching in various states of afraid and angry. I turned back towards Solomon.

"He's going to be a coward, and let you all suffer the consequences!" Solomon gloated.

"What is he talking about?" I asked.

"He's offered me a choice," Tate said, his voice low, tight with a brittle tension that shot fear through me. "He says we're close enough now he could sink us. So, either I give myself up to him, or he kills us all."

"It's a trap," Ezra said. "He's bluffing, we have to be closer to the isles for his power to -"

The ship rocked sideways, harder this time. The crew cried out in fear, and I stumbled, grabbing onto Tate's shirt for support. It appeared that the sea itself had surged up against the ship, no doubt Solomon controlling it remotely somehow.

Like when he sent a wave to snatch me off the deck. His powers are vast. How can we fight this?

Tate partially turned to look at me, his eyes sad. My heart thumped, the sick feeling swamping my stomach with dread. I could see in his eyes what he was about to do.

"No, don't - don't do it." My voice broke on the words. "You can't."

"His power has grown, it would seem," Tate said. "And I won't allow him to hurt you," he said it directly to me, but then he looked at Ezra and beyond at the rest of the crew. "I won't allow him to hurt any of you. It's me he wants, and if I go to him, he'll spare the rest of you."

"It's a bluff, it must be," I said, faintly.

"Oh, *Gideon*," Solomon's voice dripped with condescension and spite. "How I've *yearned* to be reunited with you." I flinched back, fearing to look at him, and pressed myself against Tate's back as if I could hide there forever.

"You said it was just me," Tate said, turning back towards the mystical image of Solomon, his eyes darkening.

"I did," Solomon's tone was more serious now. "The bargain is this: Tate comes to me alone and the ship with the rest of the crew may pass."

Tate took a deep breath, his back tensed, and I threw my arms around him as if I could hold him back.

Of course, I couldn't. Besides the simple fact of our size difference, where he could lift me as easily as a cat, and I could barely get my arms all the way around him... his intention was clear and powerful.

Tate and his guilt, his nobleness, his willingness to protect the rest of us, he was going to do as Solomon said.

"I'm sorry, Gid," Tate said, his voice a hoarse whisper. He leaned down and kissed me, and I poured all my sorrow and love into it, returning it as fiercely as I knew how.

There was movement nearby, and I felt Ezra's hand on my back. Tate broke the kiss and turned to Ezra. They had been friends for many years, but lovers only months. Still, they barely hesitated before kissing each other.

Ezra leaned in and whispered something to Tate, who shook his head. "No, Ez, you have to be Captain in my stead, make the decisions that will keep the crew alive, and fed. That's your responsibility now."

I refused to let go of Tate, I simply couldn't make my hands let go of him, although I knew he would leave on some level, I couldn't believe it. Some part of me thought if I kept holding onto him, things would change, that I could keep him in my life.

"Gideon, please," Tate murmured. "I love you. I don't know what's going to happen, but that won't change. All right?"

Ezra moved behind me, put his hand on my shoulder. "Come on, Gid, you know you have to let go," he said. His familiar low rumble was tinged with pain, cracking as he spoke.

Ezra needs me too, and he's right. I'm simply making this harder than it has to be... I don't even have a portrait of Tate to look at, though. I can't let him go...

But I have to.

I breathed out in a rush, dropped my arms from around Tate and stepped back into Ezra's arms. I wished Ora and Zeb could be here, too... but Zeb was still up in the crow's nest and Ora was... in the water somewhere. Maybe close, maybe not.

Ezra's arms closed around me in a reassuringly tight manner, and whether he was trying to hold me back from Tate or trying to protect me from the pain, I wasn't sure, and didn't much care.

"I guess, I guess I'd better use a longboat," Tate said. He

turned towards the boats on our ship, deliberately not looking at me or Ezra.

"No," Solomon said. "I'll give you everything you need, Tate."

Tate turned back, and the rest of us watched, confused as Solomon gestured with one hand, a sort of grab in the air and a slow pull upwards, as if scooping something in his hand.

There was a disturbance in the water near the prow of the ship. A sort of flattening of the waves, and then a swirl that seemed to start of its own accord.

A dark shape, tinged with green light rose up under the swirl and a dark shape surfaced, an ancient looking dinghy from some wreck. Dredged from the bottom of the ocean by Solomon's magic.

The wood was blackened with time, waterlogged and overrun with sea fauna. There was no way it could be seaworthy without magic.

It bobbed on top of the water for a moment and then drifted as if piloted to the side of the Kelpie, bumping gently alongside.

The rope ladder we used for longboats unwound itself with more green sparkles and Tate swallowed hard.

He swung one leg over the side of the ship.

"Don't do it, Cap!" I looked back to see Anton surging forward from where the crew had gathered. "He'll kill you! We can fight him!"

"No." Tate's voice turned to cold steel, carrying over the sounds of the crew. "All of you stay the fuck back!" James grabbed Anton around the chest and pulled him back. "All of you, don't come after me, that's an order. I'm ensuring your safety. Look after each other, especially..." he trailed off and looked at Ezra and me. "Don't come after me," he said, finally.

My eyes blurred with tears and I turned my face into Ezra's chest so I wouldn't have to watch as Tate disappeared from view.

Ezra wrapped his arms tight around me. I could feel the way his chest was moving, shallow breaths that caught each time.

His own feelings largely went unexpressed, but I could feel the pain in him, wracking his body. I squeezed myself tight against him and silently vowed that we would get Tate back.

Solomon's voice rang out again.

"That's it, my boat will bring you to me, that's good... the rest of you, the ship may pass. I will not bother you again."

I looked over in time to see the mist dissipate and the presence of Solomon vanished. The boat holding Tate moved quickly through the water, trailed by strange green sparkles and moving as if it had a full sail and a strong wind, despite it being a dinghy encrusted with barnacles and seaweed.

My knees threatened to give out on me and I leaned more heavily on Ezra, whose arm around my waist seemed strong and ready to take my weight.

"It's all right, Gideon," Ezra murmured to me. "Go to the cabin, I'll be there in a moment."

I took a deep breath, got my legs under me properly and sobbed once. I wanted to hold in the wailing as much as possible in front of the crew, although the tears were flowing down my face regardless.

I nodded at Ezra, hardly daring to trust my voice, and made my way to the Captain's Cabin.

Everything there smelled like him. His coat hung on the hook by the door, his spare pair of boots and his clothes were in the sea chest at the bottom of the bed. My breath hitched and my throat filled with a painful lump.

I crossed the room, threw myself on the bed and sobbed. Within a few minutes, Zeb climbed onto the bed and pulled me into his arms.

CHAPTER TWO - IN WHICH SOLACE IS SOUGHT

*M*y emotions swirled through anger, hate, fear and despair. I was lying on the bed, half on top of Zeb, who was laid back against the pillows much more upright than I was. My head was on his chest and his arms were around me. I was grateful for the comfort, for the solid warmth of him, but I was also lost in more pressing emotions.

Anger at myself for being helpless to stop Solomon, or to hold Tate back. Anger at Tate for being so incredibly foolish and selfless and noble. Of all the times for a pirate to be noble, it had to be now?

Hate for Solomon, because of his anger and his need for revenge, my lover had been taken from me. Hate for my Father, who had encouraged the British fleet to chase us into Solomon's trap.

Fear, because now that Solomon finally had Tate in his clutches, surely he would kill him... I had to stop that, we had to save Tate, there was simply no other choice. And we had to do it fast before he was hurt...

And then despair, because how on Earth could we fight Solomon? Although Sagorika had a little magic, it was nothing compared to his. My own magic was nascent, I didn't know enough about it or how to wield it to be useful, and I had some trouble summoning it in the first place. How could sex magic possibly help in the face of a powerful sea witch?

I slowly became aware that Zeb was purring, a sound he could make in either of his forms, which always managed to soothe me. His hand moved slowly down my back, lifted and settled between my shoulder blades, petting me like I was a kitten.

Zeb had magic of his own, but none of us knew what he was capable of besides changing his form between man and cat - and that power itself had been thrust upon him by Solomon. It was possible there was nothing Zeb could do against Solomon, if his magic had started there.

There's so much I don't understand, still.

And where was Ora? The last time we'd come face to face with Solomon, Ora's siren song had lulled him to sleep...

Oh God, what if something happened to Ora? What if they're blocked from the ship, or... We're close to their clan's home, aren't we? What if they're detaining them somehow?

Tate and Ora have a close bond, and I knew that when they knew what had happened, Ora would be upset to say the least. They'd definitely want to get Tate back from Solomon the way I did.

The door to the cabin opened and I closed my eyes, wishing myself anywhere but here, wishing myself into the past where I had all my lovers around me.

"Gideon," Ezra's voice cut through the wildness of my thoughts and I took a ragged breath. "Gideon, it's all right."

"It's not," I said, against the fabric of Zeb's shirt. "It is very much not all right."

I felt the mattress shift under Ezra's weight and the sigh as he settled in beside Zeb, his leg pushing against mine.

"He needs time to let it out," Zeb said. The first words he'd spoken since joining me in the room. "Give him a minute."

13

"Hm," Ezra said.

Zeb understood. He accepted and understood me. It was enough to warm me a little inside, and push back the tides of my swirling emotions for a moment.

I took another deep breath, sat up a little and wiped my eyes. Zeb kept an arm around me, and I was grateful for that too.

"Thank you, Zeb," I said, leaning forward to kiss his cheek. "I think I'm all right for the moment. I'm so afraid for Tate, and angry at him too, and I don't know where Ora is..." I trailed off and bit my lip.

This was just making me feel worse again. My chest felt squeezed from within, and my mind filled with grey clouds. I sniffed as more tears spilled from my eyes. I flopped down onto Zeb's chest and sobbed some more.

"You could try the thing," Ezra said, after a moment.

"What thing?" Zeb asked.

I felt Ezra's hand on my shoulder, strong, a little insistent. He squeezed it. "When we were in Nassau, you called for me. And... I felt it, from the magic, the uh, connection we have."

I blinked and sat up. "Oh, I'd forgotten... yes, I did do that. Maybe, I could."

I closed my eyes and tried to remember what I'd done that night. I'd stared at the moon and asked her for help, I didn't know if it would work without her influence, but maybe it had been more to do with my incubus powers anyway. It was worth a try, wasn't it?

I took a deep breath and thought of the fire inside me, the strange warmth of my power, which was fuelled by Ezra and Zeb's close proximity. I thought about the places where our bodies were touching, the heat of their bodies against mine, the sexual encounters and my consuming love for them.

Then I pictured Ora. My sweet soul-twin, the gender-ambiguous merfolk with the curious nature, the streak of darkness and their absolute fearlessness. The way they protected me, and sought to draw my own darkness out that I might be fully myself.

I imagined the feel of their cool hand on mine, the softness of their curly hair, the way they could make me laugh even in the midst of love-making.

"My Ora…" I whispered, hoping that would help. It felt natural to say it, so maybe it was part of what I was doing. I thought about them until my heart ached with longing and my throat tightened over a lump. The fire I imagined my magic to be warmed my belly but as far as I could tell nothing else happened.

I opened my eyes and looked at Zeb and Ezra. "I have no idea if that did anything," I said. "We'll have to wait and see."

"I should get back out there," Ezra said, reluctantly. He leaned in to kiss my forehead and I smiled sadly at him. "The crew need a leader right now, they're all… well. You can imagine."

"I'll come, too," I said. "Wallowing in here isn't helping anything."

"It might be helping you," Zeb said, his voice gentle. His arm was still around me and he pulled me a little closer in. I pushed my hair back from my face and gazed into his eyes.

Perhaps he was right.

"Well, maybe just a few more minutes," I said. "We'll be out soon."

Ezra nodded and patted my shoulder, then Zeb's. "Take your time. It's a lot to process. Then we need to get down to planning."

"Planning?" Zeb asked, tilting his head.

"Well, we're not about to sail off and leave Tate to die, are we? We need a plan." Ezra stood and grinned down at me, I felt hope bloom in my chest.

"Oh, thank the Heavens," I said. "I almost thought you'd listened to him and were planning on staying away."

"Don't be an ass, pet," Ezra said. "He's the Captain, and he's Tate. We need him."

"I couldn't agree more."

Ezra winked at us and then left the room, his boot-heels rapping on the wooden floor. I wrapped myself up in Zeb's arms and he started to purr again.

"How do you handle all this so easily?" I murmured to Zeb. "You hardly ever seem upset..."

"Purring soothes me as much as it soothes you," he mumbled into my hair. "And besides, I know it'll all work out in the end. We just have to do all the right things and we'll be back together and happy."

"You make it sound so easy."

"Maybe it is." He shrugged and I felt the movement against my cheek. "We just have to work out what the first right thing to do is and go from there."

CHAPTER THREE - IN WHICH AN APPROACH IS PLANNED

*L*ater, we emerged from the cabin, and I felt a little more centred. Still worried and distressed, but capable of getting up and walking around and talking, which was an improvement.

It was hard to believe it was still a bright, sunshine filled day. The ship was at anchor, announcing our plans to stay and retrieve Tate to anyone watching.

But perhaps Solomon expected this, or perhaps he thought we were mourning... or perhaps he simply hadn't noticed, now that he had Tate as a plaything.

I shivered at the thought of Tate at Solomon's mercy. Who knew what he was doing to him even at this moment? I stared out towards the Splintered Isles and wondered, hoped it wasn't anything too terrible, but I had no way of knowing, of course, so my imagination was free to come up with all sorts of terrible visions.

I turned back to survey the ship. Ezra was in a quiet conversation with Sagorika, no doubt talking about Tate's rescue mission. Zack had a mop and was swabbing the deck, his expression one of absolute fury.

Well, that's... a strange way to look about mopping.

I went to speak to him. Zack was the newest crew member to join the Grey Kelpie, and their only seafaring experience previously had been on a Naval ship under a particularly strict and sour Captain.

"Are you quite all right?" I asked, as I approached. I stopped next to the bucket of soapy water he was using.

"No," Zack said. "I'm furious. This ship is..." he looked up at me, and his expression softened a little. He leaned on the mop and sighed. "This ship is my home, and I know it sounds absolutely idiotic, but if it's my home I sort of think of Tate as my father." His cheeks reddened a little but I shook my head.

"That's not idiotic at all."

"He's always been so kind, so understanding, and this ship I've truly been able to be myself, with everyone knowing my past and not judging me. It's a freedom I honestly never thought to have."

My heart ached and I moved closer, opening my arms to Zack. "That makes so much sense."

Zack propped the mop up in the bucket and hugged me. For a moment we didn't say anything, just squeezed each other. Then something occurred to me.

"Does that mean you think of Sagorika as your mother?" I asked as Zack let go and I stepped back a little.

Zack's blush deepened. "Oh no, I don't think of her like that. In truth, I, uh, well, I think of you like my mother."

My breath caught in my throat and my eyes widened. "You do?"

"Sorry, I know that's sort of strange, but you're so... caring. You're kind and..." he stopped, flustered.

"It's all right," I said, feeling my own cheeks warm. "It's actually quite flattering. My own mother, well, she died when I was younger, but I always thought she was the most wonderful woman in the world. To think I could give you even a little of the same feeling is... well. It makes me happy when I thought I couldn't be."

Zack caught me in another hug and I patted his back.

"I'd be honoured to be your mother, even if I'm not a woman. And well, we don't have a plan yet, but I want you to know we're going to get Tate back. Somehow."

A particular sort of splashing came from the water off the port side and I rushed over to see Ora surface beside the ship. A warm relief washed over me at the sight of them.

Ora waved their fingers at me. "Hello Gideon!"

Another face appeared, breaking the surface of the water beside them. The face was slightly scaled, the way Ora's was in their true form. Behind her, a deep purple fishtail flicked out of the water.

"Another merfolk?" I asked, heart in my mouth.

"Yes, this is Inca of the Coral clan, she's a friend," Ora said. "My people are sort of... well. How about I come up and explain."

Ora turned to Inca and they exchanged some words in a language that had to be some sort of Merfolk dialect. Inca nodded and dove under the water again and Ora swam to the side of the ship, shifting and then climbing the rope ladder.

I retrieved a linen towel and brought it to Ora to dry off with, wrapping it around them as they had absolutely no sense of privacy about their body. I'm certain the crew were used to this, but there was no sense Ora parading themselves in front of them.

"What's going on?" Ora asked, ducking their head as I rubbed their hair with a corner of the towel.

"Solomon," I said, shortly. "He's taken Tate, well. Demanded Tate come to him and Tate went to spare us."

"He went?" Ora grabbed my hand and stared at me, their

eyes wide. "Oh no, you must be so scared. I'm so scared! We have to rescue him."

"Yes, we do," I said. I glanced over my shoulder, Ezra and Sagorika were looking over, so I waved to them. "Your people live around here, maybe they have some insight into what Solomon's been doing."

"They have noticed some things." Ora dropped my hand, took hold of the hem of the towel and wrapped it around their chest so it hung down, tying it off into a makeshift dress. They slipped their arm around my waist and I leaned against them, gratefully.

We walked into the Captain's cabin, Zeb behind us and Ezra and Sagorika behind him.

Anton followed as well but Sagorika pulled herself up to her full height and glared and he backed away, apologising profusely.

Ezra took a deep breath and sighed it out. "Ora, welcome back. We could've used you earlier."

Ora dropped their eyes and I frowned, it seemed harsh of Ezra to say that, but it wasn't exactly untrue either. I leaned against Ora.

"I'm sorry, Ezra," Ora said. "My people... well, they want me to go back to them, I had to argue for some time. The Coral clan and the Kelp clan are at war with some other clans, and they need more fighters. I told them I couldn't help, that I had a new clan that needed me."

I pressed my fingers into Ora's side, trying to wordlessly reassure them. "That can't have been easy," I murmured.

"No, but then I felt your call, and well, they could all sense a trace of it as well. It helped my argument."

That was a good sign. My magic had done what I had asked of it. It had let Ora know that I needed them and they'd felt it and come back to me. Pride set my stomach to butterflies but I squashed it now. It was a good bit of information to have but I had to focus on the task at hand.

"Well, I'm glad they've let you come back to us," Ezra said, gruffly. "Now that we're all here together, we need to plan how we're getting Tate back."

He crossed to the desk and studied the map we'd been navigating by.

"Ora, the detail on the actual land of the Splintered Isles is minimal. Can you perhaps, using your knowledge, make it a bit more detailed for us?"

I let go of them, and Ora crossed to the desk, looking over the map.

"I know where Solomon's lair is," I said, following and pointing at the big central island. "It's over multiple floors, including a cave where the ocean comes in."

I reached over the desk to pick up the pen I used for the log and updating the supplies list, dipped it in the inkwell and sketched the lair as a circle on the island.

"And here's where I found Gideon," Ora said. They took the pen from me and made a careful dot on the tiny islet Solomon had stranded me on. "There's more islands on this side too, and the reef..."

"The reefs are demarcated by these symbols," Ezra said, leaning across Ora and tapping his finger on the key of the map. Ora leaned closer in, squinted and then straightened up, pen in hand to draw on the map again.

"It's bigger over here." Ora started to sketch on the water part of the map, frowning a little. "It's hard to know the exact shape because I'm used to seeing them from closer, under the water, but that's where they are, and the magic place is here, so we'll want to avoid that, of course." They made a little swirly symbol I didn't recognise.

For a moment the only sound was the gentle scratch of the

pen on the map and the ambient creak and sigh of the ship moving up and down on the waves. I cleared my throat.

"The magic place?"

"Yeah." Ora blinked at us all. "You know? Where the isles get their power from."

"Ora," Ezra said. I could see a muscle jumping in his jaw but his voice remained quite calm, if gravelly. "Please assume we know absolutely nothing about any kind of magic place, or magic that... fuels? The island?"

"Ohhhh," Ora's face broke into a wide smile. "Right, because it feels like nothing to you, I understand."

"Well, perhaps you could try and explain it to us?" I suggested, putting my hand on the hollow in Ora's lower back. "Please, it might be useful."

"It's the wellspring, the magic flows out of there and into the water, up through the stones like the veins of iron do. Covering every bit of land, and radiating out with the tides and the currents, but it dies out if it gets too diluted, or uh, too far from the wellspring." Ora wiggled their fingers and gestured outwards, suggesting something being scattered.

"Strongest at the source," Sagorika said, nodding.

"Right, and the sea spray sends it into the air as well, but that's even more diluted." Ora sniffed.

Magic in the water, in the stones, in the very air? That explains why Solomon loved it there so much.

I wonder, would being on or near such a place have an effect on me as well? The little fire of my magic, it was hard to conjure still, and I had no idea of the scope of it. Perhaps the island would work like kindling under the flickering flame.

Then what could I do? What would I have access to? Could I defeat Solomon?

I want to know, I want that power.

My mouth went dry.

"Maybe you should take me there," I said, my voice soft so I didn't betray the sudden urgency rising inside me. My hand on Ora's back twitched, tension causing me to press my fingers against them a little harder.

"I'm not sure that's a good idea, Gideon," Sagorika said. I looked over to see her watching me with a sharp look, her eyebrows arched. I wondered if she had somehow read my sudden yearning to understand what the wellspring of magic could do. "Solomon will know you're close if you take a boat directly to his wellspring." I relaxed, realising she hadn't read my intention, she was simply thinking of logistics and danger.

"I'm not sure Solomon uses the wellspring," Ora said. "When I used to live around there he didn't visit it, I think he gets enough from the stones and the water."

"And I wouldn't need to use a boat," I added. "Ora can swim there, and I can ride on their back. We've done it before."

"Yes, you have," Ezra said. He tapped his chin. As Captain he would be the one to make the final decisions, so we all watched him as he thought. His eyes roving over the map. "But Solomon may still know if you're close, boat or no. And I don't like the idea of you two going in there alone. It's not safe."

I felt my heartbeat increase in speed. I couldn't let Ezra's protectiveness prevent me from participating in the rescue mission. I would not be locked away from the action again.

"Ora's voice put Solomon to sleep," I said.

Ora leaned against me. "I don't know if that will work again. I took him by surprise last time, but now he knows I'm on your side, he'll be expecting me. He may have planned for it, be ready for me. If he's smart, he will have."

I frowned, because of course Ora was right. Solomon was smart, the short time I'd been with him I'd seen plenty of evidence of that.

"We also have no idea what he'll do to you if he catches you," Ezra added. He gazed at me, his expression unreadable, but I sensed his fear. He didn't want to see me in Solomon's clutches again, and I certainly didn't want that either.

"So, you'd rather the crew all approach together?" Sagorika asked.

I sucked my teeth.

My reason for arguing this point was purely selfish - I had to experience the wellspring for myself, I had to know if it would have an effect. But I didn't want to reveal that. Tate should absolutely be my priority, and Ezra's distrust of magic on top of that might make him forbid me from going there.

As if it were a magical vision, I remembered a passage from one of the military strategy textbooks Father had pressed upon me the year before.

"In terms of stealth, smaller groups have more chance of going unnoticed," I said, with a confidence I didn't feel. "He'll be expecting something, we know that much, but if multiple small groups approach from different directions, well..."

"He can't be everywhere at once," Zeb finished for me. I looked up and smiled at him. He gave me a wink of one seaweed green eye. "I think it's a fine idea."

Ezra frowned.

"The call is yours, Captain," Sagorika said.

"I can tell from your tone you agree with the divide and conquer line of attack," Ezra said.

Sagorika shrugged one shoulder. "We simply don't know what will happen. If we all approach together there's a chance Solomon could wipe us all out with one big wave or a sudden squall."

Ezra's eyebrows drew together and the muscles of his jaw twitched again. He must be grinding his teeth. He nodded slowly.

"All right, it makes sense. We split into small groups and approach from different angles. Ora and Gid can swim to the wellspring and go inland from there. He pointed at the gap in the reef on the map. "Sagorika, Anton and I will take the longboat this way, and Zeb, James and Zack, assuming he's up for it, can take the lifeboat around here." He tapped the islet I'd been stranded on, where there was another path through the reefs a small vessel would be able to navigate.

"Which leaves Shem and the others on the Kelpie."

"When?" Ora asked, reaching to take my hand and squeeze it.

"Night is good cover," Sagorika said. "Perhaps very early morning?"

Ezra exhaled through his nose and nodded. "And soon, tonight. The longer we leave Tate with that monster, the more likely he'll be hurt."

"In the meantime, you should get some rest," Sagorika said to Ezra. She hesitated for a moment and then squeezed his shoulder.

"We all should." Ezra rubbed his hand over his eyes.

I sighed. It was barely noon and we'd agreed not to take action for hours. But how could anyone sleep while Tate was gone?

"I'll let the others know what the plan is," Sagorika said. "You lot rest up."

She crossed the room to give me a quick one armed hug, which I returned. "Thank you, Sagorika."

"We'll get him back, try not to worry too much," she said. Then she kissed me on the cheek and left the cabin, closing the door firmly behind her. I went to sit on the bed.

"I don't see how we can possibly sleep," I said.

"Maybe you shouldn't," Ora said. I looked at them and they looked uncharacteristically pensive. "Maybe we should be concentrating on your magic, instead."

"My magic?" I shook my head, unable to follow their reasoning.

Zeb climbed onto the bed behind me and I leaned back into his arms on instinct. He wrapped them around me comfortably.

"Remember what Etta said?" Ora asked, coming closer to the bed.

"Yes, I don't know what you're getting at..." I said. I thought back to the dim, strangely decorated store Etta the moon witch operated, back in Nassau. She'd told me I had fae blood, the inheritance of an incubus ancestor, and that there was a chance I could feed on my lovers until they died. I could hardly forget that.

"What are you talking about Ora?" Ezra asked, sounding tired. He sat at the end of the bed and pulled off his black leather boots.

"Gideon's powers are awakened by us, by his lovers," they said.

"We know that, we've all felt it," Zeb said. He'd pulled me tight against his chest and was idly stroking his fingers over my belly. It was comforting.

"Oh, well now, Ora. You can't possibly be suggesting..." I trailed off when Ora grinned at me. They were absolutely suggesting it.

"I don't think even Gideon can keep it up for twelve hours," Ezra said. "No offence, pet, but you're still human. Mostly."

"No offence taken," I said. "I quite agree with you."

"Well, all right," Ora relented. "But maybe just before we leave the ship? We could all take turns teasing him then once he's had a spectacular orgasm or two, he might be tapped into his magic."

The worst part about that was it sounded plausible. And tempting.

My magic stirred even just thinking about it, even now, feeling half-sick with worry for Tate. But Zeb's body against my back, his hands on my body, it stirred my appetite.

The silence stretched out in the room until I said, almost against my own will. "Maybe it's worth trying."

To think of having pleasure and enjoying my lovers while one of them was in mortal peril? I felt callous and a little sick. But Ora was right, we needed my powers, and I needed to be as protected as possible before we confronted Solomon, and we knew this was how to activate my magic.

Ezra moved up the bed and lay flat on his back. He gazed at me thoughtfully. "Perhaps you could wear your harness on the mission," he said. "It'd remind you of times in the past, maybe keep you a little on edge."

"A little on edge?" I felt myself blush at the thought.

Zeb lay down on the bed beside Ezra, pulling me on top of him.

"Zeb..." I grumbled, so I wouldn't have to answer yes or no to Ezra.

"Would it be all right in the water?" Ora asked. They'd had to discard my beautiful old red coat after wearing it underwater too often and ruining the fabric.

Ezra pulled me by the arm until I was nestled in between him and Zeb. Despite everything, I felt happy at the warm press of their bodies on either side of me.

Ora climbed up on Ezra's other side and settled there.

"Hrm, maybe not," Ezra said. "It's leather after all. Might get a bit looser while it's wet and tighten on his body when it dries, which, it would probably fit him even better afterwards, but the leather will stiffen and go brittle."

"We should try it," Ora said. "It could be like Gid's version of a magical amulet."

"Do I get a say in any of this?" I asked, bemused. It wasn't exactly like I was opposed to the idea, but it was somewhat odd to say the least.

Ora and Ezra shared a laugh, and Zeb turned to face me, threading his fingers through mine.

"Maybe I'll try and put a protection spell on it," Ora said. "I think I can make it so it's protected from the water... maybe."

"I don't want to ruin it," I said, reaching for Ezra with my free hand. "It's important."

"Let me try," Ora said. They sat up, leaned over Ezra's chest and kissed me warmly before sliding off the bed to try the spell.

Zeb wrapped his arms around me and then Ezra, and purred until I started to doze and eventually dropped off.

CHAPTER FOUR - IN WHICH SOLOMON REJOICES

*S*olomon hadn't thought anything could be sweeter than the sight of the sunken boat, green wood glistening in the sun, speeding towards him over the waves with the hunched form of Tate sitting inside it.

Solomon had chosen a prominent rock to stand on, his cloak flowing off his shoulders and billowing in the wind enough to look impressive. His feet were still in the water, he needed the connection to the life force of the island to do this kind of magic, and having started it he could hardly stop it and let the tides wash Tate in as they would.

No, this was his moment of vengeance, his glorious triumph and he was going to enjoy every second of it.

As he watched the ship he inhaled the salt scent of the waves, and riding on it like the high note on a fine glass of wine he scented Tate's fear. The rawness of it. It made Solomon smile even more.

Under the fear there was something else as well...

Narrowing his eyes, Solomon inhaled again.

What was that? Something slippery, something sickly green and unfamiliar. What could it be?

The sensation tugged at Solomon, as if it were something he

should know, but didn't. He shook it off and exhaled, releasing it from his mind. Whatever Tate was feeling, Solomon would coax it out of him with kindness or with cruelty. He had plans for Tate, and not a one of them would be fast to execute.

In the distance he saw the masts of the Grey Kelpie, the masts tied down, bobbing on the waves at anchor. He wasn't sure what they would do.

In true pirate fashion they may simply decide to sail on and abandon their erstwhile Captain, but it was also possible that whelp Gideon and the First Mate, the Shearwater Pirate, would pursue out of some misplaced sense of loyalty.

It didn't matter though, Solomon had set a trap or two in case they attempted a rescue. He had alarms and snares all around the Splintered Isles, and he would deal with them only if he had to.

Tate's boat carried him closer still and Solomon lifted an arm, directing the wind and the ocean to deliver Tate to the cavern under his lair. Let him stew there for a few moments before Solomon made his way through the tunnels and gave him a grand entrance. He waited until the boat had borne Tate past him, tied a knot in the cord he'd been holding to seal the destination of the boat and then went to the tunnels, pocketing the cord.

Inside, where the sunshine couldn't reach, he strode in from the top of the cavern, allowing Tate a view of him from below.

Below me, where he always will be from now on, he thought gleefully.

Tate was climbing out of the dinghy. He made it look infuriatingly easily on the slick stones where the ocean butted up against the cavern floor.

Solomon slowed his steps until he was sure that Tate was watching him, licked his lips and began to speak, words he had practised for weeks, ever since he'd slipped away from him thanks to Gideon and the siren.

"Tate, we meet again. And how pleased I am to welcome you to my home in the Splintered Isles. I'm sure your stay will be entirely pleasurable... For me."

He smirked and approached Tate, who had one hand on the hilt of his cutlass, his eyes never leaving Solomon. He was still a beautiful and powerfully attractive man. A few more tattoos, maybe. Solomon didn't recognise the ones on his forearms. He wore a white shirt, sleeves rolled to his bulging biceps, top of the shirt unlaced. His breeches fit him perfectly, and his hair was a flowing mass of deep brown curls. His personal grooming had suffered though, under the pursuit of the Naval vessels Solomon had conjured. His moustache and goatee were in need of a trim.

"Oh now," Solomon broke from his script to tut his tongue against his teeth and smile indulgently. "You don't think your weapon will save you, do you?"

Tate eyed him and shook his head, although his hand didn't leave the pommel. "No, Solomon, I don't. I assume you're going to do that mind thing on me again, but I have to try. You know I have to try."

Solomon stopped a few feet beyond the range of Tate's cutlass and folded his arms. "You came to me willingly, didn't you?"

"Yes," Tate said, his voice a little lower.

"Then you should lay your weapons at my feet, go to your knees and bow to me, shouldn't you?" Solomon didn't bother to put any magic into this suggestion. He was largely teasing to see how Tate would react.

"That would please you, wouldn't it?" Tate asked. Solomon realised he hadn't met his eyes. He was still afraid.

He thought back many years ago, when the two of them had sailed on the Grey Kelpie as partners in all but marriage law. How Tate had worked to please Solomon. Going to his knees to lick his cock and make him moan. Anything Solomon asked, or ordered of him, he would do.

A younger Tate, looking him in the eyes and asking 'would that please you?' and Solomon free to bind his hands, fuck him hard until both of them were wrecked. Curling up together afterwards, spent and sweaty and utterly lost in each other.

A part of Solomon yearned for it, still, a small reedy voice of a desire that he quelled the instant he felt it.

He nodded. "Yes, Tate, it would please me to have you submit. But if you will not, I will take immense pleasure in breaking you to my will. I've done it before, and I'll happily do it again."

He pulled the cord from his pocket and licked his lips. "Well? What's it to be?"

Tate's shoulders bunched under his shirt and with a sudden cry of anger he rushed at Solomon, drawing his sword and making a broad cutting motion.

Solomon twisted the cord in his fingers and spoke a word of power, the one that would force him to meet Solomon's eyes, allowing him to dominate his mind. Tate met his gaze and Solomon called out "Stop!"

Tate abruptly stopped, staggered to his knees with the momentum of his run. His face went blank and empty. Just how Solomon had hoped it would.

Known it would, rather. He had known that spell would work, of course he had. Tate's will was strong, but it was no match for Solomon's.

"Put your weapons down," he instructed. Without a word, Tate laid his sword at Solomon's feet, drew a dagger from his boot, and another from under his shirt. "Now, put your arms behind your back."

Within mere moments, Solomon had Tate bound with his magical chain, winding it up and down his arms from wrist to bicep. Feeling almost whimsical, he drew the chain around Tate's chest as well, in a large X shape, and fed a long leash of chain off it so he could guide him.

"Now follow," he said. Without waiting to see him obey, he turned and started walking up into the caves making up his home.

It was a disappointment that Tate hadn't taken his chance to apologise to Solomon, or to lovingly submit to him as he once had, but it wasn't exactly a surprise. Solomon may have dreamed idly of those circumstances, but he didn't expect them.

He led Tate to the cell he'd fashioned over the years specifically for this purpose. It was on the opposite side of the cavern to Solomon's workshop and bedroom. Close enough to hear Tate if he should cry out, but far enough that Tate would feel alone.

He hesitated before putting him in it though, now he had him bound it would be nice to do a little more gloating. He cleared his throat and gestured to release the control he had on Tate's mind.

Tate shook his head like a puppy coming out from the ocean and instantly began to struggle against the chains.

White hot heat of pleasure flooded Solomon's veins so fast it made his fingertips prickle and twitch.

This. This is what I wanted. This uselessness in him, taking away his precious freedom. Leaving him nothing but me.

"Do you remember why you left me here, Tate?" He asked, idly, yanking on the chain so that Tate stumbled forward and was forced to look at him.

Tate huffed and tossed his hair back off his face. "Yes, Solomon, I remember. I remember, and," his voice got more gravelly, more defiant. "I'd do it again."

The pleasant feelings evaporated into anger, Solomon's blood pumped fast and hot through him, making him impatient to break Tate. "You won't get the chance. You're mine now, and you'd better get used to that."

Tate narrowed his eyes and didn't reply, perhaps he was biting his tongue.

Solomon regarded him, his mind racing with possible ways to chastise or subdue his captive. Finally, the most obvious solution presented itself and he shoved him inside the cell, closed the door of salvaged iron bars and locked him inside it.

Ignoring his protests, Solomon stalked away.

Let him see how it feels to be left utterly alone for a time.

CHAPTER FIVE - IN WHICH AN OLD
FEAR REARS ITS UGLY HEAD

I woke up to Zeb teasing me from behind and Ezra tracing his fingers over my mouth. Moaning through my bleariness, I pushed my hips back towards Zeb, who was rubbing his cock against me with gentle insistence. His hand on my hip, my trousers removed and gone.

"There you are, pet," Ezra murmured. He pushed a finger inside my mouth and I sucked on it, biting gently at the pad and watching his face. My cock was already hard and throbbing from the attention, and I wondered how long they'd been doing this before I woke?

Imagine if one of them had my cock in his mouth and I'd woken up to that...

My hips bucked at the fantasy and the real contact from my lovers.

Ezra withdrew his finger from my mouth and kissed me instead, pressing his lips to mine insistently. My mouth was still open and his tongue lashed at mine, demanding reciprocation that I willingly gave.

Zeb's fingers, slick with oil, pressed inside me and stretched me open, and I moaned my need into Ezra's mouth. His hand found my cock, stroking gently - too gently for my liking - before he slipped something around it. I groaned with frustration, feeling the thin leather cord wrapped around the base of me, being tied, so that I couldn't orgasm even if I was at the height of my need.

Ezra chuckled into my mouth. "It's all part of the plan, pet, remember? Now, get up on your hands and knees so I can watch Zeb fucking you."

I flushed at his order, but there was nothing I wanted to do more than obey him. I pushed myself up onto my hands and knees, presenting myself to Zeb like an alley cat.

He gripped my hips with both hands and shoved inside of me with a growl, instantly starting to thrust and moan.

"Pace yourself, Zeb," Ezra murmured. He was situated to the side of me, his hands on my chest and caressing my throat, teasing at the idea of a collar I wasn't wearing.

"I can keep this up all day."

"But you don't have to, just... slow down a little. He's already close." Ezra's voice was soothing, and behind me I felt Zeb slow down, changing tack. Instead of thrusting and pounding into me, he was pulling most of the way out, hesitating for a moment and then plunging deep inside me again. It was absolutely tantalising. When he pulled back my instinct was to follow, to push against him, but Ezra's hand closed around my bicep, holding me quite still.

Then Zeb penetrated me deeply again and I moaned. Ezra had been right, I was close to completion. I could feel the blood pumping to my cock and the luscious ache of wanting threatened to consume me.

"That's enough now," Ezra said, and without question Zeb obeyed him, pulling out of me, wrapping an arm around my waist and pulling me against him.

I quivered, feeling used and needy. Every touch seemed to inflame me all over again, and I heard myself whining.

Ezra moved forward on his knees and kissed me, pushing my

head back against Zeb's chest as his hands skittered lightly - far too light a touch for my liking - up and down my sides. The tease was at once delicious and infuriating.

He sat back on his heels, and rested his hands on his thighs. Zeb continued to hold me, but ceased all movement of his hands and hips.

As I panted, I felt the well of my powers deep inside me. The magic was stirring, far out of reach at this point, but there.

"I-I think it's having... an effect," I managed, between heavy breaths. "I feel it."

Ezra smiled with a wickedness that made me shiver - it promised and predicted a lot of pleasure, but no satisfaction for some time to come.

Once a long minute had stretched out and my breathing slowed again, Ezra leaned down and closed his mouth around my hardness. I breathed out a soft sigh of relief, simply from feeling him on me, although I knew I wouldn't get what I wanted in the end.

It continued like this for some time. The both of them had got me to the edge over and over, never quite allowing me to reach completion. Using every trick and technique they knew between them, they teased and retreated, had me begging and whining, pleading for release until my voice strained and my eyes ran with needy tears.

Finally, after an unknowable time had past, Ora rejoined us.

At this point, Ezra had bound my hands behind my back to stop me touching myself or pulling the leather strap off. I had reached some sort of desperate frenzy where I couldn't think clearly, couldn't obey him like I normally would. I was lying on my side, one of my legs held still between Zeb's as he stroked my side and belly, easing me off another close-but-not-close-enough tantalisation.

Ora looked at my flushed and strained expression and smiled, inhaled and turned to Ezra.

"Yes, this is perfect, I can feel it inside him."

Ezra and Zeb had both reached completion themselves, recovered and done it again, during this most divine torture session.

"Maybe it's time to remove this, then?" Ezra's hand closed around the base of my cock, tugging gently on the leather strap there. Some part of me knew it was a gentle touch but it might as well have been a mouth and a sturdy pump of the hand. My back arched and I dissolved into begging once more.

"Please, Ora, please... Ezra, *please* I need to," I begged. "Zeb, have mercy please, I can't..."

Ezra's hand undid the leather strap and I gasped with excitement.

"Hold it just a little longer, pet," Ezra ordered.

Ora sank down on top of me, enclosing my languishing cock with their slick warmth.

"Oh, thank the stars," I muttered.

"Thank me," Ezra said, and leaned in to kiss and bite at my neck. Zeb's hands stroked up my legs, teasing at my balls under where Ora was rocking me in and out of them. Ezra's hand closed around Ora's cock, his other on my throat and soon I was making no noise but a curiously high keening.

"You may come, pet," Ezra whispered in my ear. He bit my earlobe as I let the release take me. I felt the golden light of my magic connecting me to Ora, Ezra and Zeb, their mouths and hands sparking with warmth and glittering light wherever we connected.

The orgasm took me up into the stars, and I fancied I saw a shooting star or some kind of celestial comet fly past me. My sense of being in the correct place - that I had achieved some kind of divine purpose washed over me and I relaxed finally, laughing with hedonistic transcendence as I slowly came back to myself in the cabin of the Grey Kelpie.

When I opened my eyes again I was wrapped in my lovers,

each of them holding and touching me, soothing with words and soft strokes of my skin. I trembled, but I didn't feel worried or lacking in any way. I had three out of my four lovers, and they had transported me with their attention.

Rather than feeling exhausted, I felt curiously energised, and prepared for the task ahead.

"You're amazing." Zeb kissed my shoulder.

"So proud of you, pet," Ezra said, his hand stroking my hair back from my forehead.

"Love you, Gid," Ora added, their head resting on my chest as my breath came back to a normal sort of rhythm.

Once we'd cleaned up, I sat on the bed, wearing just my breeches as Ezra fastened the spelled harness on me. I could even tell it was spelled, not just because it looked strangely shiny when Ora brought it back into the room - although it did. I could sense it somehow. Looking at it, and then touching it, it gave me a strange sensation and made the coppery hairs on my arms stand on end.

I shivered lightly as the leather straps touched my skin and were buckled snug against me. The sensations brought back many memories of time with Ezra, of being restrained and made to orgasm hard enough to leave me trembling.

They'd been right, I could feel my magic within me, stirred up from the teasing and the orgasm, but the excitement from the harness was preventing it from going dormant again.

I swallowed as Ezra fastened the last buckle and grinned at me.

"How's it feel, pet?"

"Like it might work," I said, and gave him a smile that I only partially felt. "My magic is there, near the surface, I don't know if I can do much with it, but I can feel it there."

Soon, we went out onto the deck in the cool air of the early morning. The stars shone overhead, and as I looked up, regarding them, I saw the shape of someone on watch in the crow's nest at the top of the mast. I shuddered and focused instead on the deck itself. I could see quite clearly in the starlight and the light of the lantern Ezra had brought out with him.

Ora stripped off their clothes, kissed Ezra and then Zeb, then jumped overboard and into the water, shifting to their merfolk form as they arced gracefully through the air.

My fears welled up inside me and lodged as a spiky lump in my throat.

I wrapped my arms around Zeb and squeezed him, pressing my cheek to his chest.

"Please be safe, don't... don't run into anything you can't handle, Zeb."

"Don't worry, Gid. I can handle absolutely anything," Zeb said. He rubbed his hand over my back and although his tone was soothing, his words absolutely weren't. My stomach dropped unpleasantly and I pulled back to look Zeb in the eyes.

"Zeb, please. Be careful." I let my concern into my tone, allowing him to see how afraid I was. "Please."

His expression softened and he rubbed his cheek against mine. "Don't fret about me, Gideon. I'll be careful, and I'll watch Ezra's back, too."

I kissed him soundly, hoping the kiss would somehow seal his promise to me.

Then I turned to Ezra, who frowned. I wondered, from the twist of his mouth and the way his eyebrows drew together, if he was finding it as hard as I was to say goodbye.

"I'll... I'll see you soon, pet," he said softly. I swallowed the lump in my throat and lifted my chin.

"Right, soon," I said. I kissed him firmly on the mouth and pulled myself back from him. If I'd let myself hug him, I wasn't at all sure that I'd be able to let go of him again. Or stop myself from crying, come to that. I was afraid and tense, and had a horrible sinking sensation that I would never see him again.

I couldn't think like that.

"We'll get him back," Ezra said. He patted my shoulder encouragingly. "Trust your gut, Gid. It's not led you wrong yet, has it?"

Hadn't it? It didn't feel like I was in the situation I wanted to be in at this exact moment, but I supposed my gut had led me to run away, trust the cat and board the Grey Kelpie.

I stepped back and nodded at him. "You two, watch each other, and stay as safe as you can, please."

It didn't feel like enough, but I didn't want to break down. I walked to the side of the ship and took hold of the railing.

My heart was already racing, so when I looked over the rail and down into the water - several feet below - the vertigo was enhanced by the fear already seizing my body.

Cold sweat drenched my skin and I took a deep breath.

Heights.

I couldn't be undone at this, the very first step in our plan to rescue Tate. It was humiliating and foolish.

Ora's face broke the water and they raised an arm to wave at me, half in the shadow of the ship itself.

They're so far down. I can't possibly...

But I can't possibly just stay on the ship. Tate needs me and I have to... I have to go to him.

"C'mon, Gideon! What're you waiting for?" they called.

I couldn't let go of the ship railing. It had become my anchor to the relatively solid ground of the ship's deck.

It's just the ship, and that's just the ocean below. I have a rope ladder to use, and Ora would catch me if I fell. I know they would. I won't dash myself on any rocks, I'll land in water, quite safe. And it's only a few feet...

I thought this, and knew that logically it was true, and I was safe. But looking down at the waves, my limbs simply refused to take any action allowing me to climb over the rails. I couldn't make myself raise my leg, or even let go of the railings.

"Ah, fuck," I said, under my breath. A word I hardly ever dared use, but now it seemed utterly appropriate to the situation.

"Are you all right?" Zeb asked.

"Need a hand?" I heard Ezra approaching from behind. "I could always toss you over the side if that would help?"

The fear gave way to a sudden and irrational anger and I cried out, terrified that he was going to actually do it.

"NO!"

"That's a no, then," Ezra said, and from his tone this time I was relatively sure he wouldn't do it.

My body shook, but was also not willing to move the way I needed it to. My mind was rattling with logic and fear and the word 'no' seemed to fill most of it. Some terrified part of me was certain that if I climbed over the railing I would fall and die.

I swallowed hard and tried to reason with my racing heart and tense muscles. My hands were white-knuckled where I gripped the railing.

The ocean - and Ora - seemed to be miles away.

Tate needs me. That's the only thing I need to worry about. Tate. Think of Tate and his sweet smile, and the way his eyes flash with mischief. The beautiful geometric patterned tattoos on his shoulders and arms. The feel of his arms around me. His voice, soft and husky first thing in the morning, the way he'd pull me in...

I took a deep, shuddering breath. Feeling my nerves ease off just a little. It was working.

Don't think of anything but Tate. Tate and how much I love him.

I shifted my feet, feeling a wash of relief as my body responded to me finally.

"Can you smell the ocean?" Ora called from below and I took another deep breath in. Yes, of course I could smell the ocean. I thought about that for a moment as well. The salt, the water, the vague smell of seaweed...

My heart was still pounding but I flexed my fingers. I let go of the rails with one hand and with a massive effort of will, I lifted my leg and slung it, shaking, over the rails. I turned, still gripping the rails and stuck my foot into the first rung of the rope ladder.

It wasn't much. And Ezra and Zeb who were watching me, looked worried as I raised my gaze to face them. But it was a start.

"I'm all right," I lied, so that they'd stop looking at me like I was a lunatic, or someone weak who needed to be helped.

Ezra nodded once. "Keep your eyes up, don't look down again if you can help it."

That was surprising. I didn't expect him to be understanding after he'd offered to throw me overboard. Perhaps he'd forgotten how bad my fear of heights was and was sorry now?

It was a helpful suggestion. I kept my eyes on Ezra's face, and then on Zeb when he moved closer. I lowered myself down gingerly, feeling for the rungs with my foot while clinging with all my strength with both hands.

Slowly but surely I lowered myself down the ladder. With that first step taken, the rest was easier. Although the rope ladder moved in the wind and wobbled under my weight, at least I was looking at Ezra - and then at the side of the beloved Grey Kelpie.

My heart was still beating fast but I could breathe normally, and I became aware of Ora's voice nearby as I got down the ladder.

"That's it, love, just one more step." I smiled a little, lowered myself into the water and half turned to see Ora close behind me. Their hands closed on my waist and with a moment's hesitation I let go of the ladder and let Ora and the ocean take my weight.

The water was chilly, and it took my breath as I adjusted to it. Ora kissed my cheek. "All right?"

"Yes, thank you," I said. With a quick movement, Ora turned so that I could put my arms around them, one over their shoulder and the other under their other arm, linking my hands over their chest.

I glanced up at the ship, where Ezra and Zeb were watching. "See you soon!" I called out, with a bright optimism I didn't truly feel.

"Take care," Zeb said, waving a hand.

"Take a breath," Ora said. I did as they said, and with a beat of their powerful tail, we were off.

Ora dived under the water and I closed my eyes and hung on as tight as I could.

CHAPTER SIX - IN WHICH A SOURCE IS DISCOVERED

*T*he trip to shore wasn't as fun as when I usually rode on Ora's back - the last time had been purely for fun, but this time I was still feeling rattled by the climb down, and deeply afraid for Tate.

I took a breath each time Ora surfaced, and each time I opened my eyes to see the tall, dark spires of the Splintered Isles and Solomon's lair rearing up closer and closer still.

Finally Ora's tail slowed, and our progress through the water ceased. In the darkness I couldn't tell how deep the water was, so I just continued to hang onto Ora.

"The source," they said, partially turning to look over their shoulder at me. "You still want to visit it?"

I swallowed the lump of fear in my throat and nodded. "Yes, that was the plan. I want to see what it's like, what it means."

"Right, we might... there might be other merfolk," Ora said. "I'll get you to the air again as soon as I can."

"I appreciate it," I said. I took a deep breath and Ora dove under the water.

It tested my lung capacity - the dive was the longest yet, and I felt myself expelling air without meaning to, my chest starting to ache as I resisted breathing in the water.

My eyes flew open in panic and I was surprised to see a gentle silvery glow where I'd expected to see only brackish darkness. Above us were rocks and tunnels, we'd come into an underwater cavern network of some kind.

"Oh!" I said, or rather, I tried to say and it came out as a garbled blub noise.

Ora glanced at me and shook their head. I closed my mouth and tried to make myself believe that I didn't need oxygen to live.

I was on the verge of inhaling - water or not - when Ora swam up and my head broke the surface of a small cave.

There was an air pocket there, and I drew in the oxygen with a grateful, if rasping, breath.

"You all right?" Ora asked. I took a couple more breaths and the pain in my chest eased. I nodded.

"That was a bit too long without air," I managed to rasp. "But I'm all right now. That glow, what is that?"

The small cave we were in was perhaps only two feet higher than the surface of the water, and the water was all lit by the bizarre light. Although it was undoubtedly strange, the light didn't scare me.

"The source," Ora said. "The place the magic comes from."

I looked down in time to see a large, shadowy shape swim past below my feet. It didn't move like a shark, but it was so fast I didn't get a good look at it. "What was that?"

"A guard," Ora said. "I'll go and talk to them, let them know you won't hurt it. Uh, you can hold on here..." Ora tugged me towards the side of the cave and I took hold of a sort of natural stone ledge.

It wasn't the most secure of spots, but I was confident I could hold on for a while at least. "All right, be quick, maybe? Please?" I coughed a little, I'd swallowed a little sea water at some point and the salt was in my throat. It had likely happened when I'd spoken underwater...

I watched as Ora dove down and out of sight and I

swallowed. I knew Ora wouldn't leave me here - logically I knew that - but the illogical, panicking part of my brain that had almost prevented me from leaving the ship spoke up in the back of my head.

Ora's gone, back to their people and has left you here to be eaten by them.

Or perhaps they intend to come back for you, but the guards will prevent them from doing so. How long can the air in this cave possibly sustain you?

You would lose strength and let go before you ran out of air, perhaps, slip into the deep and be drowned.

I swallowed, tried to distract myself from the thoughts just as I distracted myself climbing over the railing of the Kelpie but it was hopeless. There was nothing to look at but the water and the cave ceiling, and neither of them were comforting sights.

Wait, the harness...I can feel that on me. Focus on that.

I closed my eyes and concentrated on the places the harness was snug against my skin. How did it feel? Good, tight... made me think of Ezra, and then my other lovers as well.

My heart slowed from a panic to a more reasonable pace.

There was a splash and I opened my eyes to see Ora, their eyes wide as they half smiled at me.

"What are you doing?" Ora asked.

"I was just thinking about the harness, and you, and the others," I said. "To calm down."

Ora kissed my cheek and then turned their back to me, so I slipped my arms around them again. "It's worked, I can tell. Your magic is humming at me."

"It is?" I hadn't expected that at all.

"Come on, let's go see the source. Don't pay attention to the guards, they've given us leave to visit. They also said Solomon took one of them, a few days ago. I don't know what that's about. They're concerned, but haven't felt them die."

I swallowed. That sentence raised a few questions to me, but

I focused on the most pressing one. "That sounds bad... I thought you'd said he left your kind alone."

"Yes, this is the first time he's ever done this."

"We'll have to see if we can get them back too, then," I said. "All right, I'm ready to visit the source."

I took a deep breath and braced myself for another dive. Ora dove and within a couple of moments my head broke the surface again.

I opened my eyes, surprised at being in air again and so soon.

We were in another cave, this one a fair bit bigger, more the size of Tate's cabin on the Grey Kelpie, with a curiously evenly domed ceiling to it. As if it had been carved by hand rather than sculpted at random by the elements.

The ocean formed a pool over half of the bottom of the cave, a raised rock floor made up the rest of it. But my attention was all drawn to the source of the glow. My mind couldn't take in exactly what I was seeing, for I had no frame of reference to understand it.

It almost seemed like a glowing rock - as if a lantern of pure white light had been set inside a stone. But that wasn't right, because a rock has defined edges to it, and this object did not.

As I tried to understand it my eyes began to water - how could it be a physical object without defined edges? How could light become solid?

Perhaps it was more akin to looking into a pool of light, where the light acted like water and lapped constantly at the edges of what contained it. I blinked the tears away but more came.

Ora shifted forms and pulled themselves and me up onto the floor.

As we were now closer to the thing, my body started to respond to it, flooded with a soft warmth as if I was bathing in afternoon sunlight. It was most pleasant.

"What does it mean?" I asked Ora.

I pulled my eyes away from the thing to look at them, they seemed a little more merfolk than human, despite being in their human form. Their skin was silvery and their eyes a little larger than normal.

"The source of magic that feeds the Splintered Isles," Ora said. "You can touch it if you like, but... it might hurt if you do."

I heard a sound and looked beyond Ora. I hadn't noticed, with my attention being so drawn to the source - but there were other merfolk in the cave with us. Seated along the cave wall, or bobbing in the water and watching us. They were certainly watching me, and I felt very much the interloper, as if I had entered their church without knowing what the rituals meant.

I swallowed. "Are you sure it's all right for me to touch it?"

Ora nodded. "Yes, they've given permission. Just once, but... it's all right."

It felt wrong to stand in this place. Seated on the edge of the pool I wasn't taller than the source, and I had no desire to be. I went to my knees and crawled to it.

Every inch closer felt like I was getting closer to a fire, or a tidal wave. Like I could burn myself or be swept away if I wasn't careful.

Careful? What did careful even mean in this place? My etiquette teacher never covered this, Mother never warned of how to comfort myself when the merfolk showed me their sacred place...

I kept breathing and crawling and finally came to a stop beside the thing.

My hands were trembling, my breaths coming easier as I inhaled the warmth of it. The feeling of being close to something so obviously emanating magical power surrounded me. I could feel it now, calling to the little flame within me, almost tugging at the harness on my body and making my heart thump louder, with more force than it normally did.

I raised my left hand and reached towards it with my fingers.

The light shone through between my fingers and I felt a force - almost magnetic - drawing me closer.

I touched my fingers to the light and found no resistance, only a tingling sensation over my skin. My breath caught and I found more tears flowing from my eyes but this time they were from joy - touching this thing had filled me with joy and love.

Pushing myself towards it, I plunged my hand deeper inside. And that's when it spoke to me.

"Gideon, my child..."

I choked on my own breath, spluttered and cleared my throat before managing a squeaky word. "Mother?"

It couldn't be, how could she be here? She died, I know she died. But that was her voice!

I cleared my throat and looked around, but all I could see was the light and the cave. I tried closing my eyes. "Mother?"

"I'm here," the voice came from inside my head and also from inside the light somehow. My hand tingled and prickled, but it wasn't in an unpleasant way.

Relaxation and relief flooded through me, as if my mother was here with me and she was going to keep me safe.

I was going to cry again. "You can open your eyes," she said.

Without hesitation, I opened them and then I did weep. She wasn't there, not as I had known her, but the light had formed an image, almost like the illusion Solomon had sent on the sea mist, but this one had no foreboding attached to it, no fear.

My mother's long red hair hung loose about her shoulders in soft waves, her eyes were just as I remembered them, warm and smiling, and her smile was as wide as it had ever been.

I let my hand drop to my knee and took her in, feeling stronger and more full of joy by the second. There were no words to say to her, no questions in my head, I only felt love and hope.

"Gideon, my son, my darling one. Look at all you've done." I felt pride, some of it my own and some of it hers, washing over me, enhancing my own.

"Mother..." I managed to say.

"You don't have to say anything, just listen," she said. "I hear you when you speak to me, I don't know how... or how it can carry to me here, but... I hear you. I love you so much, my darling boy. I am so proud of what you've done, and how far you've come. However, your Father is looking for you." She hesitated, her glowing face growing a little sadder. "He will not rest."

"What should I do?"

"He misses me," she whispered, her eyes filling with grief. "You must help him to move on, somehow."

I swallowed. I couldn't see how I could possibly do anything of the sort, but I wasn't about to argue with her.

"Tate," I started, a little afraid of what she would say. "Solomon has him, and I don't know how to fight him, how to get Tate back. He's so powerful."

My mother nodded and for a moment I didn't think she would respond. Finally she seemed to nod and then spoke again.

"You must do what you always do, listen, respond with your heart. What he needs is hidden, but it's clear as well. You must be the bridge he needs."

"The... I'm sorry, the bridge?"

That didn't sound good at all, I didn't want to allow Solomon a bridge to what he needed... but my mother wouldn't lie to me. I knew that without a doubt, deep in my soul.

I bit my lip and gave voice to my greatest fear. "My lovers, will I hurt them? Mother, I have to know this."

She shook her head, her golden auburn hair flowing around her ghostly shoulders. "Perhaps if you were full blooded, but you're not. Perhaps if you came through into..." she shook her head again, quickly. "But you won't. Your lovers are safe."

I teared up again, relief washing over me like a warm tropical wave. "Thank you."

She nodded. "You must go now, you're soaked in the power of the source, it will make you strong for a time. Choose how you use that time wisely, my darling boy."

"No, don't-" My throat closed on a sob and I reached out, trying to touch her face but my fingers finding only light. Her image was fading. "Please, Mother..."

"You're doing well," she said. "I love you."

"I love you..." I gasped as the light image of her shattered into tiny sparks and all that was left was the source itself.

It had seemed so beautiful and wondrous when we first entered the cave, but my mother had outshone it.

Now I sat back on my heels and sobbed. I was sick of crying so much, of now knowing what to do, and of feeling helpless. Mother had told me she was proud and that I knew what to do, but I truly didn't.

Ora's hand touched my shoulder gently and their cheek nuzzled against mine. "Gideon, it's time to go."

I pressed both my hands over my face and tried to stop the tears flowing. But it wasn't going to happen - seeing my mother, hearing her voice, it had unlocked something. I coughed.

"Ora, was she here? Did you see her?"

"Yes, I did," Ora said. They glanced around the cave and then back to me. "But we have to go, now, the hospitality is about to run out."

"Oh." I let Ora tug me towards the water, waited until they had shifted and then slipped in as well, took a deep breath and put my arms around them.

Ora took us back out from under the caves, and if the swim was too long this time I hardly noticed, because my mind and soul were in such a whirl.

Ora had seen her, she had been there. Her spectre or something like it. And what on Earth did it mean to be a bridge for Solomon?

And beyond that, she had heard all I had told her? And she approved?

I hadn't realised how much I had needed approval from her - or perhaps just from a parent - but now that I had it I felt torn open. The relief was raw, as if a wound had been cleansed in the salt water of the ocean.

CHAPTER SEVEN - IN WHICH GIDEON MEETS A SEA WITCH, AGAIN

*O*ra took me to the nearest shore and held me while I pulled myself together. Although the urge to cry and fall apart was strong, I had to focus on our mission.

Overhead, the stars shone and it almost seemed incredible that scarcely an hour had passed since I left the Grey Kelpie.

"Let the emotions sit at the surface," Ora advised, their hand on the small of my back, pressing gently. "It's your power, your emotions fuel it, remember? Don't swallow it down, let yourself feel it."

"There's a certain sense in what you're saying," I hiccuped. "But I don't want to face Solomon while I'm crying."

"Why not?" Ora asked, but there was hardly a way to answer that. I couldn't form the words.

I took a breath and kissed them quickly. Feeling the love and desire I had for them rise to the surface and imbue my touch with heat. Ora responded with equal enthusiasm, but broke the kiss within a minute.

"That's it, that's what you need to do," they said. They slipped a finger under the central ring of my harness and tugged, pulling a soft moan out of me. "Feel it, near the surface."

Some part of me wished to consummate the desire I felt - the incubus part, surely, empowered by the source perhaps. But we had to focus.

"Thank you." I pressed one chaste kiss to their lips. "For taking me there, for everything."

"Of course," Ora said. "You're my soul's mate, I'd do anything for you."

I wrapped my arms around them and squeezed. "I feel the same way, Ora."

"How sweet," a voice came from up the beach. I startled, hugging Ora closer to me protectively.

Solomon.

Ora began to hum.

It's too soon, I thought wildly, *we're not ready. We were going to meet up with Ezra and the others, get a feel for the layout of the island before...*

Well, none of that mattered now.

Solomon stood up the beach, as if he'd emerged from the rocks, or more realistically, a hidden cave.

He was lit only by the light of the stars and the slim sliver of moon, but I could see him clearly enough. The hardness to his smile, the shining eyes already seemed to be celebrating his success. He wore his salt stained and ancient looking black trousers and ragged cloak, pulled a bit more forward concealing a little more of his chest than I recalled it doing before. His unwashed hair was a spiked black mess, which should have been off-putting but actually added to his uncanny appeal. Because whatever else I felt about him, Solomon was still strikingly attractive.

"Solomon," I said, trying to sound brave and threatening, but the truth was I was huddled on the beach with my merfolk lover and drenched in water, tears running down my face. My voice came out in a strained squeak.

"I had hoped you'd listen to your captain, and stay away,"

Solomon said, lazily. He had something in his hands. A string perhaps, which he was twisting and tangling.

Ora seemed to hiccup and their hum cut off. Alarmed, I moved to put my body between Ora and Solomon, going up to my knees and then standing. There was little point in a weapon - not that I'd brought one. No, if we were to overpower or overcome Solomon it wouldn't be because I'd stabbed him with a knife.

"You knew I wouldn't just leave him," I said. "None of us, we wouldn't just go. He means too much to us, and we won't leave him to die at your hands."

I did wish then for a sword, because my words seemed to require I follow them up with the flourish of a blade. It would have been quite impressive, I imagined.

"Gideon," Ora said, their voice hoarse.

Solomon clicked his tongue against his teeth. "Gideon, what exactly do you expect to achieve, you have no weapon, no support, no magic. How exactly did you think this would play out."

"I do have support, I have..."

Behind me there was a dull thump and I turned, heart in my mouth, to see Ora lying prone on the sand, their chest rising and falling shallowly, but their eyes closed, one hand at the base of his own throat, laying lightly as if there was a pain there.

"Ora!" I turned back to Solomon. "What did you do to them?"

"I tied a knot," Solomon said. He stalked a few steps closer to me, holding up the string in his hands. "I have bound their voice, and when you do that to the merkind, it puts them into a sort of coma, I've discovered. Now, if you don't play along and do what I say, I'll tie the knot that binds their heart. I'm sure you can puzzle out what that would do to your beloved fish."

A coldness washed over me, a dread that whatever I did would be the wrong choice.

I could try and summon my magic, it was fuelled by the source after all, but I was feeling so much terror... and I didn't want Solomon to tie the next knot.

At least if I obeyed him, he would likely take me closer to Tate.

I swallowed hard. "Please, don't hurt them. I'll do as you say, if it will keep them safe."

Solomon's mouth split into an unfriendly smile and I swallowed, hoping this would somehow work out in my favour although in no way trusting that it would. What was I going to do with my magic anyway? Make him feel my love?

I really had no idea how to use my magic, especially not in a combat situation.

"Lovely. Just as you were last time, you're excessively easy to control," Solomon said. I felt my cheeks warm even though there was nothing remotely sexual about the situation. "Bring them along, then."

"I... what?"

"I'm not going to kill you, yet. Or the fish, bring them to my lair, now."

"Right, yes," I said. I turned and gathered Ora into my arms, lifting them off the sand. I was grateful that it was Ora and not Ezra I had to lift, since Ezra was around twice Ora's size and weight.

Ora's body was heavy enough, as they weren't helping at all, their limbs flopping uselessly. I held them to my chest and lifted my chin to look at Solomon. "Ready."

"Not quite," Solomon said. While I lifted Ora he had pocketed the knotted string, and now he held a familiar chain, draped across his hand.

I groaned a little. "I'll follow, you don't have to -"

"Hush." He walked closer, reached over Ora and slipped the chain through the ring at the centre of my chest harness. It fastened itself magically and he turned and walked away, letting the chain play out between us as a leash.

I really wish he wouldn't do things that make me think of Ezra.

I banished the thought and started to follow him, holding Ora securely against me.

It turned out that banishing the thought was all well and good but my body knew what it enjoyed. Even in the circumstances, my cock responded a little to the way the harness straps shifted and tugged against my torso with Solomon tugging on it.

We had made our way into the cave systems and back to a stairway carved out of rock that Solomon had taken me through before, on my last disastrous visit to the Splintered Isles.

As we started to ascend the stairs, Ora's eyelashes fluttered and they made a soft sound against my chest, a faint moan.

"Ora?" I whispered, hardly daring to make a sound louder. Solomon heard all the same. He looked back, his eyebrows drawn together, and shook his head.

"That's not possible," he said. He pulled the chain and strode ahead. I gasped at the severity of the yank and swallowed.

I had to keep an eye on the steps so as not to trip, but I examined Ora's face as well. Their eyes were slightly open and they gazed up at me. I shook my head and Ora closed their eyes again, but subtly, they wound an arm around my neck and distributed their weight a little easier in my arms.

Awake then, despite Solomon saying it's impossible.

My heart thumped with something more like hope than despair.

Solomon led me to the same vast balcony of stone that formed the central landing of the cave lair. I had no idea what to expect from him now. I hoped to see Tate. I hoped he would take me into his inner sanctum again so I could speak with him.

But I had Ora in my arms, and sooner or later, Ora would need ocean water again... and I had no idea of Solomon's plan.

He didn't hesitate. He led me to the right of the landing, the opposite side to the chamber he'd kept me in during my last visit.

There he had a series of cells carved into the stone, small cells, each barely larger than a wardrobe.

We stopped at the first one and Solomon gestured, opening the iron bars of it with a steady hand. "You can lay the merfolk in there," he said.

"They'll need the sea," I said, my voice reedy and timid, humiliating me. "Please, they need to sleep in the salt water."

"Save your fears for your own hide," Solomon snapped, and pointed into the cell.

I swallowed, feeling Ora's fingers pressing against my shoulder blade. I caught their meaning as clearly as if they were speaking to me.

Don't worry about me, I'll be all right.

I stepped into the cell and laid Ora down on the bench carved out of the wall. I turned back and Solomon impatiently yanked on the chain, hurrying me.

He closed the door to Ora's cell and sealed it with a word, then, pushing his hand through the bars he gestured and spoke some words that set my hairs on end. Words in an unknown, mystical language.

From what I could see there was no effect, but I could sense the magic being used.

"What did you do?"

"I bound their tongue further," Solomon said. "There'll be no singing here. No siren song that puts me to sleep or has me obey anything."

I bit my lip.

"Now." With a dramatic turn that caused his cloak to swirl around him, Solomon turned to me, moved closer and glared. I had to tilt my head to look up into his eyes. "You can sit and stew while I devise the best way to deal with a whelp such as yourself."

He pulled me roughly to the next cell and threw the door open, as he pushed me inside I asked, as quickly as I could. "Where's Tate? Is he all right?"

"He is none of your concern!"

A shove in the middle of my back caught me off balance and I fell forwards, scraping my hands and knees and crying out more with the shock of it than any pain.

The bars closed with a clang, and I moved onto my rear to look at Solomon. "Please, just tell me he's unharmed, please," I begged.

Solomon didn't respond, but gestured with his hand, putting me into a deep sleep.

CHAPTER EIGHT - IN WHICH SOLOMON FINDS MORE INTRUDERS

*S*olomon watched Gideon for a moment to be sure that his spell had consumed him. Yes, his breath was even, his body relaxed. He would sleep for some time, lost in a dream he wouldn't wish to wake from. That should keep the pup out of Solomon's hair while he decided the best course of action going forward.

Then he felt one of his alarms go off. The tug at the back of his spine, which was unpleasant enough to wake him if he had been asleep. Closing his eyes he reached out to the island, asking it to tell him where the intrusion had happened. He saw the location in his mind's eye, provided by the magic resonating back to him.

Frowning, he descended the stairs back down to the beach, using the tunnels that took him closest to the beach the alarm had come from.

He saw a rowboat making its slow and steady way to towards shore. A lookout holding a lantern over the water to ensure they didn't run into any of the rocks infesting the waters around the Isles.

There were around five men in the boat. Impatient, Solomon called on the waves and directed them to bring the boat to him.

There were cries of consternation as the boat appeared to move of its own accord. Solomon stepped into the surf and communed with the ocean, then gestured with a word of power to put the passengers of the boat to sleep. He stepped aside and let the waves ground the rowboat on the beach so he could look inside it, picking up the lantern from the lookout to peer at their faces.

He didn't recognise any of the men within the boat, which meant that Tate's First Mate was either still aboard the Kelpie, or getting to the island via another means.

Tiresome, really, to have all these loyal crew determined to steal my prize away.

One of the men gave him a strange feeling, though. His skin was a deep, almost obsidian brown and he had broad shoulders and a muscular frame.

Frowning, Solomon waved a hand over his face, sensing, reaching out with the tendrils of his power to divine what it was that was nagging at him.

My own magic... that's what I can taste on him. But why, and how?

He felt it tangled through the man's body, enabling... a change in form.

"Ah. My old amulet. How interesting that it should have done this particular thing," Solomon said to himself. He pulled a string from his pocket and undid one of the older knots. In the rowboat, the man's form twisted and shrank until he was a black cat, sleeping soundly.

Solomon lifted the cat and tucked it into the crook of his arm. Leaving the boat on the sand, and the rest of its occupants asleep in the boat, he made his way back inside.

Inside his lair, he made his way to the main sanctum, the room he spent much of his time in.

Tate sat on the chaise, his ankle chained to the leg of it, reading a book. He looked up when Solomon came in but didn't say anything, which almost *hurt*. There was a tiny twinge in his chest about it.

And Tate should have still been asleep, which irritated Solomon like a jellyfish sting. Solomon had put him out and his enchantments should definitely last longer than this.

"Here," Solomon said, trying not to sound pettish - that would alert Tate to the possibility that he could hurt Solomon somehow. "I brought you your cat."

Tate sat up quickly and reached his arms out to take the cat. "Zeb?"

"I don't know it's name," Solomon said, dryly. "But he was in human form up until a little while ago."

"What did you do to him?" He cradled the cat to his chest, checking his sides for injury, and trying to open his eyes.

"He's fine," Solomon snapped. "I didn't hurt him, I just put him to sleep and took off the curse."

Tate frowned and tucked the cat inside his shirt, letting it snuggle in against his skin as if it were sick and not merely spelled. Solomon rolled his eyes at the sentimentality.

"What happened to you, Tate?" He asked, folding his arms and looking his ex-lover up and down. "You used to be ruthless, you used to be feared."

"I'm still feared," Tate said.

"You've got a pet cat tucked in your shirt," Solomon said. "You're not the man I knew."

"You're right about that, at least," Tate said. He tossed his hair over his shoulder in the exact manner that had driven Solomon to distraction as a young man. He tamped down on the feelings of lust and focused on his annoyance instead. "Just as you are not the boy who sat in the crow's nest with me and made witchlights dance on the wind."

Solomon had forgotten that. He didn't like being reminded of things he'd forgotten.

Some of his memories from back then were hazed with fog,

he wasn't sure when he'd started to lose memories, but he thought it was when he'd been marooned here. He thought it a small price to pay for the immense power the Splintered Isles had given him, but it was still an unpleasant sensation.

"That boy died when you left me here," Solomon said, putting all the venom and resentment he felt into his words.

"No," Tate said. He tilted his head, regarding Solomon with a sort of scientific interest. "It was before that. You'd already changed from that boy, otherwise I wouldn't have ever left you here."

The very fact that Tate was speaking so frankly enraged Solomon. He was his prisoner, he was supposed to cower, to want to please him. Solomon could barely taste fear on him, in fact. Just a kind of resigned feeling, as if he were almost content.

"What do you want from me?" Solomon cried. He widened his eyes, rubbed his hand over his face. That wasn't at all what he'd planned to say, or how he'd meant to act.

Truth be told, it had felt like nothing was working out the way it should to Solomon. He had got what he wanted - Tate, in his power - but he didn't feel satisfied at all. Tate was a coward, he knew this, so why wasn't he cowering?

"Solomon?" Tate asked, his voice soft, prying. It was tempting - more tempting than Solomon dared to admit to himself, to respond.

Instead he swirled his cape, turned and stalked out of the room. Exiled from his own living space by his frustrating captive. He went to the landing and stared out to sea, his hands on his hips.

He had meant to torture Tate, to make him pay for the years gone by - but now that he had him in his power, Solomon wanted little more than to look at him. Perhaps sit with him...

It was utterly pathetic and not to be borne. One didn't spend years nurturing resentment of a man, to finally capture him and then do nothing more than have tea with him.

Then there were the others - the ones coming for Tate. He couldn't even bring himself to kill the ones in the rowboat, he'd just left them... sleeping.

He was weak, that was the problem. He needed to get over the ridiculous weakness and get down to the business of revenge.

The question was, how would he go about doing either of those things?

CHAPTER NINE - IN WHICH GIDEON SPENDS A PERFECT DAY

*I*t had been a long, lazy day. Sunny and warm with nothing I had to get done. I'd spent the morning writing at the large kitchen table, recollecting a story about our days on the Grey Kelpie with the morning sunshine pouring in the open window.

Ora had been working in the herb garden outside. Tate had kept me company, making tea and reading a book quietly as I worked.

Lunch had been smoked fish that Zeb had caught in the bay at the bottom of the cliffs and then cooked, and fresh greens from the garden. I'd napped much of the afternoon on the verandah with Zeb, cuddled against his chest, listening to the sound of Ezra affixing the storm shutters to the external windows as I drifted in and out of wakefulness.

Soon the Autumn storms would roll up, and the shutters would keep out the worst of it.

In the evening, the sunset lit the kitchen as I prepared dinner alongside Tate, the two of us laughing and joking as we made more than enough food for all the house's inhabitants.

"What shall be our entertainment tonight?" Tate asked, as we ate at the table, sharing a bottle of fine wine.

"Perhaps the last to finish eating is spread on the table so we can all enjoy him for dessert?" Ora suggested, their eyes sparkling.

"There'd be a competition to make the last mouthful of food last the longest," Ezra said, chuckling. "I'm sure Gideon and Zeb would both like to be in that position, but the table's only big enough for one."

I laughed, nodding at the wisdom of this statement. "Indeed, I would eat very slowly."

"Maybe we could play chase and capture, instead?" Ezra said.

I shivered happily. That game was a favourite. Each of us competing with each other.

The ruled were that everyone had the run of the house, if you caught someone unaware, they had to either take off an item of clothing, or put on something like a leather collar, or cuffs, or a harness. The game always ended in a fantastically good time. "I vote for that one."

"Or we could try something totally new?" Tate said. "I learned a few things from a courtesan in Singapore that I've not shown any of you..."

"Sounds intriguing," Ezra leered at Tate and finished the last of his salad. "Zeb, have you any suggestions?"

Zeb stretched his arms over his head and yawned, making the most of everyone's attention being on him. "Chase and capture," he said. "But we can go out into the garden as well. The moon is beautiful tonight, she calls me and I cannot refuse her."

"You and your mistress," Ezra teased, nudging Zeb with his elbow.

"What do you say, Gid?" Tate slipped his arm around my shoulders, pulled me in and kissed the top of my head.

"Yes, chase and capture with outside as well, I said. That's my vote."

"I'm going to catch you," Ora said, lifting their foot to rub against my calf under the table. I chuckled.

"Not if I catch you first," I retorted.

"I'm going to pin Ezra down and make him wear a collar," Zeb said, his voice full of self-assurance.

"Like Hell you are," Ezra said, but he was smiling, too.

"I'll help you Zeb," Tate added. We made quick work of cleaning up from dinner, then it was down into the basement play dungeon Ezra had built, and the old sea chest full of toys and leather straps was opened. Each of us took a handful of supplies. I pocketed the delicate latticework collar that I'd bought for Ora on our last trip to Tortuga and a few lengths of chain and padlocks.

Tate raised his voice into the boom that always took me back to our days sailing the seas on the Kelpie. His Captain-during-a-battle volume.

"Go to your starting positions, count to thirty and then it's begun!"

We all hurried back up the stairs and spread around the ground floor of the house. I slipped out the kitchen door to press against the outside wall and count to thirty.

As I whispered the numbers out loud, I let my gaze lift to the sky. The sun had set less than an hour before, and the stars were plentiful - but the moon was what drew my attention.

Zeb had said it was beautiful, that it called to him. I could see why he'd put it that way.

I looked up at her and smiled, feeling a tug in my heart. The moon was my friend, ever since that day back in Nassau when Etta had spoken to her on my behalf.

I inhaled, enjoying her silver glow, before letting it out in a slow sigh.

Gideon, my darling, what are you doing?

My mother's voice? The moon had never spoken to me in the voice of my mother before. I took a step away from the wall, glancing down to avoid stepping on the catnip and sage, and then turned my face up again.

"What was that?" I asked.

You're wasting time, my darling boy. You must wake up.

Wake? I shook my head. I was awake. I could hear the pounding of running feet from inside the house, someone coming my way. If I wasn't quick - I was about to be tackled to the ground and perhaps stripped, perhaps bound.

I licked my lips. I couldn't be distracted, this was my favourite game, after all. I wanted to put up a fight, whether or not I came out in charge or one of the captives it would be delicious any way it went.

My inner fire demanded to be sated with as many of my lovers as I could be. I hungered for it.

"I'm awake," I muttered.

I turned to look at the kitchen door as it was pushed open, I stepped further back into the shadows, watching Zeb step out, his eyes wide in the darkness.

But something stirred in my belly, a seed of doubt. Did Zeb always look so noble of brow? Was his hair always curled just exactly so? How did his scars only make him look more dashing and not battered and worn?

Licking my lips, I glanced up at the moon again. She looked far too large, too close to be real. Her face close enough to touch if I reached my fingers up...

Perhaps... Perhaps this *was* a dream.

With a growl, Zeb pinned me to the wall with his hands and kissed me hard. Kissed me in just the way I loved, his tongue demanding entrance to my lips, his body shoved against mine with an energetic passion.

I moaned and squirmed against him, shoving back as he gathered my wrists in his hands, pinning them above my head.

If this is a dream, it is a very good dream...

I tipped my head up and his teeth closed on my throat. My hips bucked and I rutted against him, needy and moaning.

Zeb yanked my shirt open and stroked his hand over my chest as I panted.

"That's one thing removed then," I gasped. "You're supposed to let me go again now..."

Not that I wanted him to. He grinned, and his fangs caught the moonlight, sending a shiver through me.

"I'm breaking the rules," he growled. He yanked my trousers open and stroked my cock, which was already rock hard.

"Did I hear rule breaking?" Tate's voice came from somewhere in the darkness. I moaned.

"Yes, help me, Tate," I moaned. "I'm being taken advantage of."

"I can help with that I think..." Tate moved behind Zeb and started kissing the back of his neck, his hands moving to remove Zeb's trousers as well.

Zeb let go of me long enough to fish a leather strap out of his pocket, just before Tate shoved his trousers down his hips.

"Neck or wrists?" Zeb growled, leaning in to nip at my jawline.

What a question. Both. But then I couldn't enjoy touching the two of them. All those muscles...

"Nng, throat," I said. "I want to touch both of you."

He slipped the leather around my neck and buckled it, making me whine with need. I put my hands on his chest, caressing his muscles, tipping my head down to watch as Tate stroked him. Tate leaned forward over Zeb's shoulder and claimed my mouth in a hot kiss.

Zeb leaned back against Tate's chest.

Nearby I could hear footsteps, and I turned my head, breaking the kiss with Tate to see Ezra and Ora, both of them shirtless, approaching from inside the house.

"That was quick," Ora said. "Quicker than normal, usually there's a few rounds of chasing before things get this far along."

"Blame the moon," Zeb said, lifting me into his arms and kissing me hard.

The moon? There was something about the moon...

"Bring him into the lawn," I heard Ezra order. "Let's all have access to Gideon."

"Please," I breathed, and soon we were all of us on the small patch of lawn, under the light of the moon, tearing clothes off each other, catching limbs and torsos with arms and lengths of rope. I wound a piece of chain around Tate's wrist and locked it so I could pull him towards me, guided his hand to my cock, which he stroked with a sure, firm grip.

I leaned back over Ezra's chest and kissed Ora, feeling hands up and down my body.

Ezra's fingers raked through my hair and tugged. I moaned into Ora's mouth, broke the kiss and turned to kiss Ezra instead.

Zeb raked his nails down my back and I arched, hissing a little at the pain as it melted into bliss. Tate's hand tugged on my cock, more insistent and likely to bring me to the edge.

Ora moved to press their mouth between the cheeks of my rear and started to lick me open.

Ezra wound an arm around my chest to hold me down as I writhed and moaned from the attention. Tate and Zeb kissed each other and Tate's hand slowed on my cock as Ora teased me open.

"More, I need more," I gasped. "Please."

Ora shoved their tongue inside me then pulled back and lifted my legs. Ezra's hands went under my arms and lifted me, until I was situated on Ezra's lap. I sank down in his cock, my hands on Ora's shoulders. Zeb's hands on my chest, teasing at my nipples. Tate leaned against Ora from behind and I kissed him over their shoulder, fast losing track of whose hand was where in the tangle of limbs.

Only three thrusts until I was finding release from the cock inside me, all the hands on me, the way each of my lovers seemed to be focusing only on me. It was divine, my orgasm causing me to buck and moan as I reached completion.

The moon above lit the heaving, panting forms of my lovers as I came back to myself, each of us moaning and slowly coming to a stop. I looked up at the light, and found it curious that I hadn't sensed my magic at all during our lovemaking.

That was unusual, and... no, more than unusual. That was unheard of when all of us were together.

This isn't real, then. The moon was right, it is a dream. It has to be. But how do I wake up from it?

"Gideon, ready for another round?" Zeb asked, pulling me forwards into his arms and kissing me wildly. Trying to distract me.

"No," I said. I put my hand on his chest and tried to scramble up. Hands grabbed at me, trying to pull me back into the sweet bliss of their attention...

But this isn't my lovers. This is a dream. I've been in a magical dream before... it was made by... I was witnessing... Solomon.

Solomon has done this.

CHAPTER TEN - IN WHICH FEARS ARE CONFRONTED

$\mathcal{I}$ woke up on the floor of a cell, my head felt thick with sleep and ached with a pounding pain similar to drinking too much rum, or perhaps being sick with a fever.

My mouth was dry and felt sandy, as if it had been a long time since I'd had a drink. When I went to sit up, my elbows seized up and my back ached, making me whine with pain.

"Gideon? Is that you?"

I wiped at my eyes, which were crusted with sleep.

"Mmhm," I replied, coughing a little at the dryness in my throat. I knew that voice. Ezra.

I shuffled towards the bars of my cell and froze when I saw what was beyond.

This wasn't the cell Solomon had initially put me in. No. That one had been on a wider floor... this cell's bars were scant inches from the edge of the flooring. Beyond that was just air. Open air, a long fall and the ocean washing beneath.

I pressed my fingers against the hard stone floor. It was solid - that was good. Solid was safe. It was hard to catch my breath. Keeping my eyes on the drop on the other side of the bars, I moved slowly to one side of the cell. I didn't get up. I stayed sitting, feeling safer with my rear still on the solid floor.

Once I found the wall I pressed my side against it. I was terribly cold, and the wall was colder, but it was solid. I wished it had some kind of handhold I could grip.

"Gideon?" Ezra's voice came again. "Are you all right? Did he hurt you?"

"I'm..." I swallowed as the sentence died on my tongue. I couldn't take my eyes off the tiny strip of ground on the other side of the bars. It was so narrow. How had Solomon got me in here? Had he carried me on the edge of the precipice. Sweat dripped into my eye and I used the back of one hand to wipe it, the other stayed pressed to the wall, anchoring me.

"You're what? Gideon, answer me." That was his in charge voice, his Master voice, and it spoke volumes to how worried he was about me that he hadn't called me pet. He'd used my proper name. Anchoring me there, too.

"I'm not hurt," I said, quickly, in between breaths. "But I'm... he... " I lost track of my words again. If he'd carried me to the cage, parts of me would have been over the edge, dangling. He could have dropped me so easily...

"Close your eyes, don't look at the drop," Ezra said. "Then tell me what happened."

"Right, yes, that makes sense."

My eyes felt wide and strained, like as long as I had my eyes on the drop it couldn't hurt me.

I took a breath in and closed them, feeling relief as the dryness was resolved a little. It was better, with my eyes shut. The danger didn't seem quite as imminent.

"Gideon?"

"Yes, right, uh. I was asleep and I guess it was a magical sleep, and Solomon gave me a dream I wouldn't want to wake up from."

"Are you hurt at all?"

"No, I'm not hurt, just..." I took another breath and let it out as slowly as I could manage, feeling it seem to rattle in my chest with how tense I was. "Terrified."

"That's... well, it's not good but it's good news that he hasn't hurt you," Ezra said. "Did you see Tate?"

"No, I didn't, we didn't. Solomon was ready for us, he ambushed us on the beach, we didn't. Ora? Is Ora with you?"

"No, I think he took Ora down to the water," Ezra said.

That was a bit of good news. I hated the thought of Ora trapped in human form, away from the water. They needed the water.

I opened my eyes and for a moment, was all right with the view. "What did he do to you, Ezra?"

There was a pause and I heard the soft sound of a body moving about. Ezra was in the cell to my left, I thought. I was pressed to the wall on the right side. Perhaps if I could get to the other wall, closer to the bars, I could maybe reach my hand out and find his?

But that was a big if.

"He tried to subdue me with his magic, I think," Ezra said. "It worked enough to get me up here without a fight, he took all my weapons, but..."

"But?" Something in his phrasing stirred an ember of hope in my chest. I glanced down at myself. I was still wearing my harness. I stroked my fingers over it.

"But I sort of got the feeling he meant for me to do more for him. But I refused."

I frowned. The last time we'd been on this island, weeks... or no, months ago now, Solomon had no trouble with controlling the entire crew of the Kelpie with his magic. And Ora had started to wake up when I was carrying them, and I'd realised I was trapped in a dream and got myself out of it... perhaps Solomon's magic was... fading?

I touched my harness again. Or maybe it was my magic, giving my lovers some kind of protection.

"Did you come in with Zeb?" I asked.

"Oh, he's here, hold on." I heard movement and then Ezra's voice. "Come on, wake up, go see Gideon."

I looked at the floor near the bars, instead of looking through to the drop, and shortly the black paws of a familiar cat came padding around and slipped through the space between the bars.

"Zeb..." I breathed, feeling warm relief wash over me. He climbed in my lap, put his front paws on my chest and butted his head against my cheek. I rubbed my cheek on him and smiled to hear his purr, I stroked a hand down his back and felt love well in me, so relieved that he hadn't been hurt.

In an instant, Zeb shifted to human form and I fell back as his weight overwhelmed me. I barked a laugh of surprise and put my arms around him as he kissed my face.

He sat up and looked at his hands. "That was unexpected."

"It was?"

"Zeb? Did you shift? I didn't think you could," Ezra called from the next cell. I frowned, wishing we were all together.

"I did," Zeb said. "Gideon's touch. Seems it broke the spell Solomon put on me."

"Well, that answers that question," I said, softly. I leaned up to kiss Zeb's lips and then gently pushed him off me so I could sit up. "I think my magic is protecting you, like it's meant to."

Zeb moved off my lap but stayed close, slipping his arm around me. "Obviously that's what's happening."

"I wonder if it's doing something with Tate as well... Oh! Zeb, you can transform and go find Tate, can't you?"

He rubbed his cheek on mine. "Yeah, I can." He stood up and shifted back to cat form, then squeezed through the bars and was gone. My stomach turned over unpleasantly. The drop was still there. Whatever happened, I was going to have to deal with it.

I couldn't stay in the cell forever, at some point I was going to be broken out or Solomon would come and take me out, and whichever it was... I'd have to deal with the cliff edge.

I shuffled closer to the bars by a couple of inches.

My heart started to race, and my chest contracted.

"Oh, for the love of God," I whispered. I pressed my fingers against the wall as if I could somehow sink right into the rock and hold on.

"Gideon?" Ezra asked. "What are you doing?"

"Looking at the drop."

I heard him move and then sigh a little. "Why are you torturing yourself?"

"I'm going to have to face it at some point," I said. "I'm not spending the rest of my life in this cell."

"Well, I don't know what to say, really. But I'm here, if you want any help?"

I exhaled slowly, rubbing a hand over my stomach and keeping the other on the wall, then I moved closer to the bars. I heard a roaring noise in my ears.

I swallowed and put my hand on the bars. They weren't as sturdy as I'd expected and my stomach lurched as it shifted under my fingers.

I clung to the mast with both hands as dark clouds flew over the sky, coming closer and closer to the Trinity Royal.

My shipmates crowded the deck at the base of the mast. They were calling my name, yelling at me to come down.

Thornton had ordered me up there to secure the rigging and I was unable to move a muscle.

My fingers were shaking, knuckles aching as I clung to the wood. Lightning flashed and thunder boomed as the storm got closer still, the waves swelled higher.

My body chilled, I shook as the spray and the rain drenched me and still I couldn't move. I was frozen, paralysed with fear of falling. Fear of losing my grip and crashing to the deck.

I desperately wanted to be back on the deck.

My crew mates called to me. "Gideon! Gideon!"

"Ensign Keene!"

"Gideon!"

That last voice snapped me out of my reverie. It was Ezra. I came back to myself a little, although my head was still pounding and I couldn't catch my breath.

"Gideon! Answer me!"

"Y-yes," I murmured.

"What's going on in there?"

How to answer that? I hardly knew. I scrambled backwards, to the back corner of my cell and pressed my back to the wall, pulled my knees up and covered my face with my hands.

"I'm afraid," I said, hoping it was loud enough for Ezra to hear.

"It's all right to be afraid," Ezra said, after a moment. His voice was gentle, the soothing tone he used after a particularly intense session. I felt my body relax ever so slightly. "Everyone has something they're afraid of, everyone is frightened sometimes."

I swallowed. Wished hard that I could be where he was, that I could wrap myself in his strong arms and let the fear wash over me and away. I felt tears leak out between my fingers. I couldn't be with him until we unravelled this whole mess.

What am I doing here? Why did I think I could do anything to help Tate? I can't even look out at a cliff without falling apart.

Ezra's trying to help... saying everyone gets afraid. I can hardly believe that. Ezra's so self-assured, how could he be frightened of anything?

"What are *you* afraid of?" I asked finally, wincing as my voice cracked with fear.

There was a pause, and somewhere in the back of my head, it occurred to me that perhaps he wouldn't want to talk about what he feared while we were locked in cells in a sea witch's lair.

"Losing you," he said, finally. "Losing Tate. Not being able to sail on the Kelpie anymore, or be with any of you. Sometimes, I'm a little afraid of Ora and their teeth."

"Ora would never hurt you," I said softly.

"I know, but still." He went silent.

It took a few minutes for his words to have an effect, but eventually I wiped my face with my hands. With a groan of protest at the stiffness in my back, I stretched my neck and uncurled myself until my back was flat against the wall.

Ezra's words hadn't removed my fear, but they had eased the panic a little. I took my time, adjusting to the new position and enjoying the relief in my joints.

I took a breath and let it out slowly, lifting my head to open my eyes.

I startled to see Solomon outside my cell, looking in.

CHAPTER ELEVEN - IN WHICH SOLOMON AND GIDEON COME TO CONFLICT

J cringed back into the corner as Solomon gestured to the door and said a magical world. Then he put his hand on the iron bars and pulled.

The bars made a horrible shrieking noise against the stone as Solomon pulled it open. It sent shivers down my spine and I swallowed the dryness of my throat.

This is it, he's going to kill me. He's going to take me to the edge of the cliff and push me off.

"Afraid, are you, pup?" Solomon asked, his tone mocking.

I watched him approach, trying to stop my trembling. "Yes."

"I seem to remember how you feel about heights from a dream we shared," he said, slowly. His voice like lantern oil spilled on water - slick, and off putting. "Come on, let's take a look at it, shall we?"

He leaned in and took hold of my arm, just above the elbow and hauled me to my feet. I tried to resist, although there really wasn't any option to get away. I had literally cornered myself and I was in his cell. Besides he was taller and probably stronger than me.

"Please," I said, breathless. "No, I can't look."

"You can and you will," he said. He dragged me towards the cell entrance and the horrible drop beyond it. So close beyond it.

I screwed my eyes shut and tried to contain the raging panic, but it was no good. With my eyes closed I had no idea how close I was to the edge. I opened my eyes to find myself parallel to the bars. I dug my heels in to try and stop the momentum towards the drop.

"No, no no-no no, NO!"

"Yes." Solomon's hand on my arm was firm and I couldn't shake it off. He propelled me closer to the edge.

My heart was in my throat, pounding as fast as a hummingbird's and my eyes felt like they would never shut again. I tried to get away, pulling against Solomon's grip to no avail.

"No! I can't!" I shouted, and inside me I felt something shift. My magic flared briefly and I saw stars. I reached for the bars of the cell to anchor me so I didn't keel over. The last thing I needed was to faint and fall off the edge on my own.

Solomon's fingers dug into my flesh and he stopped moving, stopped tugging me.

I dared a glance at him and saw his eyes had widened, his chest moved as if he were breathing fast.

"Confounded, impossible boy!" He snarled. Turning he marched towards the inner sanctum, dragging me behind him, thankfully to a wider part of the ledge and way from the drop.

I briefly caught a glimpse of Ezra, his legs shackled, seated in the cell beside mine, but Solomon dragged me so fast it was no more than a glimpse.

He took me to the inner sanctum where my heart leapt - there was Tate!

Tate was on his feet, a chain taut between his ankle and the chaise. His hands in fists and his expression stormy, although it softened when he saw me.

"Gideon! What did he do to you? Solomon, I swear if you've hurt him..."

"I didn't hurt him," Solomon snapped, in a far more candid tone than I'd heard from him before. "He's fine. Just... shaken. And *you* are supposed to be asleep."

Tate relaxed a little and shrugged, an insouciant smile sneaking onto his face. "I wasn't sleepy."

Solomon shoved me into a chair. He bit his next words out as if they pained him. "You weren't sleepy? My spells do not care if you feel *sleepy,* they just work."

He went to stand in front of Tate, within grabbing reach, but all Tate did was fold his arms over his chest, one eyebrow raised. "Apparently, not."

Without warning, Solomon slapped Tate, hard enough that the impact of it echoed off the cave walls. Tate's head snapped to one side and then he straightened up and eyed Solomon. They were almost the same height, although Tate had an inch or two on him. Solomon hissed and raked a hand through his hair.

"I don't understand. But it matters not, I don't want to deal with *you* right now, anyway."

He turned to me. I'd been watching, but largely just enjoying the relief of being on solid ground that didn't threaten to drop me. My heart was still racing but it didn't feel like it would choke me, or that I would pass out. The chair was actually quite comfortable.

Solomon stalked past me, went to the desk he had recessed into the wall and picked up an amulet.

I tore my gaze from him to look at Tate - he was tethered far enough away that he couldn't reach me, and I wasn't in a state to get up and defy Solomon. Not yet. The panic had held me for too long.

Tate met my eyes and he raised his eyebrows. "Are you all right, Gid?"

I nodded. "Just... heights. He made me... my cell is at the

edge of a very tall drop," I said and looked him up and down. "Are you well?"

Tate frowned and nodded. "Yeah, he hasn't hurt me. Just... yelled a lot, really."

"The pain is coming," Solomon said, darkly. "Don't worry about that." With those words he turned and approached me again. "Now, boy, you're going to tell me what you're doing. What are you, and what magic you're wielding?" He held up a knife with patterns carved into it, an amulet dangled off his wrist and he caught my eyes. "Tell me or I'll cut pain symbols into your skin."

"What are pain symbols?"

"The sort which hurt even more than the knife itself. I'll take my time, slicing my blade into your tender flesh."

Sort of like how Ora did that time, I thought. Because even through the fear that memory was stirringly hot.

Still, Solomon cutting me won't be for fun or enjoyment, or well. Not mine, anyway...

I cleared my throat. "I'm human," I said, eyeing the knife's blade as he brought it to bear closer to my face than was comfortable. "But I have fae blood."

"Fae blood..." His eyes narrowed and he leaned in, peering into my eyes. "How is that possible?"

"Um, well, as I understand it, it was a few generations back, one of my ancestors, uh, met a member of the fae and... procreated." I tried my best not to stammer, but it was very awkward explaining this with a knife in my face. I swallowed.

"Fae magic shouldn't counteract my own, should it? Unless... hrm. Maybe that explains..." he whirled away from me and strode to Tate. He exhaled, and I felt a wave of anger off him. I licked my lips and concentrated on my own love for Tate.

"Tate, sleep," Solomon said, gesturing with one hand.

Tate tilted his head to the side and shrugged. "I don't feel sleepy."

"It doesn't work." Solomon turned and pointed at me. "What are you doing? What do you know of fae magic?"

"Hardly anything," I said. I felt somewhat empowered by telling him the truth. By just letting him know that I didn't have all the answers. But he had cemented my suspicion and I felt confident to continue. I tipped my chin up as I spoke. "But I believe my lovers are protected somewhat, by my love. Incubus magic is based on sex and love."

For a moment, nothing happened, and then Solomon stalked towards me with quick, heavy steps. He loomed over me, his knife was back in close proximity to my cheek. My earlier confidence about my powers faltered and I took a half step back from him.

"What did you just say?" He snarled.

I heard a noise, Tate trying to get to me and intervene - the clatter of chain and swearing as he was prevented.

Although I didn't want to break eye contact with Solomon, I spared the briefest of glances down to his hand free, which was wreathed in eldritch green light. I swallowed.

"Incubus magic....it's based on sex, and love," I said, my voice far less strong and loud as last time.

"Incubus." Solomon said the word as if it were something revolting, something that tasted foul in his mouth. "That... explains some things, yes. Well, the answer then is simple."

He raised his glowing hand and I flinched, expecting a blow or a swipe of the knife, but instead he very gently pressed his index finger to my forehead. I felt the heat of his fiery magic on my skin not as a burn but as a ticklish tingle. I inhaled.

"What are you doing?" Tate shouted. Solomon ignored him.

I was about to do something rash like push him away with my hands, or fall backwards out of his grasp, when I felt it.

A push inside my head. A green light behind my eyes, nudging at me insistently.

I couldn't see anything but Solomon's eyes and I

remembered how he had controlled me in the past - put a truth onus on me so I couldn't speak a lie, so I had a compulsion to tell him what he wanted to know.

I wondered if it had been like this the last time but I hadn't been able to sense it as I hadn't woken my magic before. Or perhaps I could feel it now because Solomon was trying harder, probing past my defences to do more than put a truth spell on me.

A flare of incandescent pain struck inside my head and I cried out.

Whatever he's trying to do, I should fight back - I shouldn't let him do it. Right, so... summon my magic.

I brought Tate into my mind's eye, picturing him watching, imagined every detail. I couldn't see him, because I couldn't tear my gaze from Solomon's but it didn't matter. I knew Tate, every inch of him, and I brought him to mind and focused on my fierce love for him.

How I loved his laugh, deep from the belly, how I loved the soft way his eyes crinkled when he looked at me. How it felt when he pulled me in against him as he slept, or first thing in the morning when he awoke with his cock hard and wanted relief. I thought of his wide shoulders and his easy going way. His intuition for knowing when to look after me and when to leave me to my own thoughts.

How I would die to protect him.

The probing green light in my head fell away as if it were dry sand being brushed off my arm.

Solomon stepped back and hissed, shaking his hand as if his finger were burned.

"What did you do?"

I shrugged, smiled guilelessly and looked at Tate. "Just thought about Tate."

Solomon's face twisted into an angry snarl and he struck me

across the face, snapping my head to the side, extra power in the blow from the knife's hilt clutched in his hand.

Before I could recover from the blow, he had my wrists, binding them with the magical chain. He shoved me bodily back into the chair, whirled around and approached Tate. He pressed his finger to Tate's head as I struggled more upright, wanting to see what happened.

Tate's expression went from afraid to pained, and then I saw a flash of green and Solomon hissed, pulling his finger away.

"Confounded, cursed wretch! Irksome, irritating canker!" He strode towards me, gathering more magical fire in his hand and raising it. "If I kill you none of this will be relevant, you plaguesome pest!"

I wanted to cower back against the chair, raise my bound hands in front of my face - but if this was to be the end of me, then I had to do something to save myself.

Pushing up onto my feet I tipped my chin up. His flaming hand was coming for my face, I ducked to one side, put my bound hands on his chest and shoved with my magic. "Solomon stop!" I cried. I felt the golden fire of my magic flow up my arms and through my hands into his chest, wishing that somehow my magic could stop him hurting us, stop him trying so hard to get his way and own Tate so no one else could. "Stop it!"

My palms flared with pain. Solomon fell back as if I'd shoved him hard, he sprawled on the floor, the green fire on his hand petered out and the knife clattered onto the floor, sliding out of his reach. He took a ragged breath and sat up slowly, rubbing his forehead.

"What did you do?" Tate asked.

"I don't know," I said, shrugging. "I just... I couldn't let him kill me, so I used my magic to fight him, I didn't know what else to do."

Solomon got to his feet and picked up his knife again. "Well, that was unexpected, but hardly an obstacle." He approached me again, lifting the knife. I backed up until the backs of my knees hit the chair and I sat down. Solomon's hand shook. He tried to lift it over me.

"Solomon, no!" Tate cried, but apparently he needn't have worried. Solomon's arm shook so badly he had to lower it again.

Staring at his own hand, Solomon looked as if he were trying to solve a puzzle.

I felt a wave of anger, a wave of hate and then finally, resignation. Solomon's hands dropped to his sides and I felt an overwhelming sadness.

Perhaps his prodding in my head, or my using my magic on him, opened up a connection between us, some kind of link to his emotions? Could that happen?

How could I know what was possible? I'm in the magical world without any kind of instruction or map.

Solomon pulled out his string of knots and fiddled with it, tying a new one knot and muttering. Tate twitched once, and then shrugged. He met my eyes.

"All right, Gid?"

I nodded, biting my lower lip and wondering what was going to happen next. There was no way to know what he had planned or how he'd lash out next.

Then he threw the knotted cord to the ground.

"Confound it all," Solomon said, and this time his voice didn't sound menacing or passion-fuelled, it sounded weary.

He looked at me, and then at Tate, and then he walked out of the room, his footsteps a dull slap of skin on rock as he retreated.

I waited until I couldn't see him any more, then got up and hurried to Tate's side. I pressed myself against him, wanting to put my arms around him but prevented by the chain. Tate's arms were not fettered and he wrapped them tight around me. I inhaled the delicious, musky scent of him and relaxed, finally.

"You shouldn't have come," Tate said. "You disobeyed your Captain's orders."

"You shouldn't have expected me to obey you," I said, my voice muffled in his shirt. "You're not my Master."

"But I'm your Captain," Tate said, but I could hear the laugh in his voice. He pulled me back, took a look at me and then kissed me. I curled my fingers into his shirt and *wanted* him, but it was not the time or place.

"I love you," I said, by way of response.

"I love you, too," he said. "How are the others?"

I looked up at him and nodded. "I think all right, although I haven't seen Ora since I woke, Ezra's fine, he said he saw Solomon carry Ora down towards the water. And Zeb's around. Solomon thinks he trapped him in cat form but-"

"Yes, I spoke to him earlier, he was going to find some food," Tate said.

I flicked my hair back off my forehead and sighed. "What now?"

"Well, how about we sit down?" Tate tugged me to the chaise and sat down, I settled beside him and leaned into his side, his arm a comforting weight on my shoulder. Technically I could have gone looking for Solomon, he'd chained my hands but not tethered me anywhere, after all. But being reunited with Tate felt too good, I didn't wish to move.

We sat like that, and waited, with no way of knowing what Solomon had planned next.

CHAPTER TWELVE - IN WHICH SOLOMON AND TATE TALK

$\mathcal{S}$olomon stalked back into the room an hour or so later. He looked different. Shorter, somehow, or possibly just his bearing wasn't as upright and correct as before, his shoulders rounded.

He took a look at the two of us cuddled together on the chaise and groaned in irritation.

I moved away from Tate, edged to the end of the chaise and Tate folded his arms across his chest.

"What are you planning, Solomon?"

Solomon dragged a chair over the stone floor to sit opposite the chaise, not seeming to care about the horrible screeching noise the chair's legs made.

"Here's my problem," Solomon said. "I want you, Tate, and just you. But you have him," he nodded at me. "And you care about him. You don't want him hurt, and then the rest of the crew, they're all worried about Gideon as well."

Zeb in cat form came running in on silent paws, glanced at Solomon and leapt onto my lap, where he kneaded for a moment as I scratched under his chin until he started to wash.

Solomon watched and shook his head, sighing. "I simply don't understand it," he said. "Tate, you used to be fearsome, a force to reckon with. Bloodthirsty and angry and fuelled by a desire to conquer."

Tate moved uneasily beside me. I looked at him, but his eyes were fixed on Solomon. "That was before you came into your power," he said. He didn't sound certain though.

"Before I came into this power, yes, before you left me at the Splintered Isles like a piece of refuse."

Tate shook his head. "You got more and more hard," Tate said. "Angry, inflamed with desire to hurt and destroy."

I tried to pretend I wasn't in the room, that I couldn't hear what was going on and wouldn't be affected by it. That I wasn't part of the conversation. Zeb turned in my lap to look at me with his huge green eyes. He seemed to be asking me or suggesting something.

"What?" I whispered.

He nodded his head towards Tate.

"I'm sorry." I lifted my head to look at Tate and Solomon. "I'm not sure I should be a part of this. It feels private."

"It concerns you," Solomon said. "You'll stay because I didn't tell you to leave."

I suppressed the urge to tell him he wasn't my Master either. I had to bite my tongue to keep from saying it.

Tate was looking at me, curious. "You know, I actually think you're helping," Tate said.

"Me?"

"You're influencing him, with your emotions, with your connectedness to your heart and knowing what you want," Tate said.

"He is *not* influencing me," Solomon snapped. He crossed his arms over his chest and then dropped them, one hand moving to rake through his own hair.

Zeb climbed off my lap and hopped onto Tate's, meowing his approval.

"Oh, you sensed that did you, Zeb?" I asked. I reached over to tug gently at his tail.

"Stay out of this," Solomon said, and I had no idea if he meant me or Zeb. "I am trying to talk to Tate."

"You're succeeding at talking because of Gideon's influence," Tate said. "Now, go on. You were talking about the past, when we served together on the HMS Arlingham."

"You and I were going to take on the world, we were going to rule the ocean, and chart our own way through the undiscovered parts of it. You and I, a fearsome duo." Solomon's eyes weren't on any of us now, but focused on something distant, something only he could see.

"The scourge of the seas, undefeatable."

Tate heaved a sigh and shook his head. "I lost my taste for it, even as you gained more," he said. "You became... something I didn't recognise. Your hatred and your desire to kill.."

"You used to share that!" Solomon stood now and started to pace back and forth, shaking his head like a dog worrying at a bone. "You inspired me, you inspired my need to kill. The blood fuelled my power, I could feel the magic growing in me."

Something nagged at the back of my head at Solomon's words, something that felt like the answer, some kind of explanation, although I couldn't put my finger on what exactly.

"The more it grew the less I knew you," Tate sat forward, and Zeb jumped off onto the ground, coming to sit beside my feet, leaning against me a little.

He's caught on to it too, maybe. What am I missing?

The more power Solomon had, the less himself he was... the less Tate felt angry... tied in together somehow?

"You always were a coward," Solomon said, shaking his head. "That hasn't changed, you didn't want to deal with me then and you don't want to deal with me now. I don't know why I spent so many years thinking of you."

I felt something in my chest, something I recognised, so I

spoke up. "That's a lie, I can feel it. You know why you were thinking of him for so many years."

Solomon glanced at me and sighed, shaking his head. "Gideon, be quiet."

I could feel a little magic in his words, but I brushed it aside without even thinking. "You said I'm part of this, that means I can join the conversation. At least when you're lying to Tate, and possibly to yourself."

"I'm not lying."

"You are," I said, feeling bolder by the second. "You love him, you've loved him this entire time, but you're afraid of it. You're afraid of how he hurt you and how he could hurt you again, that's why you kidnapped me, it's why you've captured all of us now. It's why you haven't killed him, even though you said you would." I stopped, sitting back a little on the chair. I had after all, made my point and from the look in Solomon's eyes I shouldn't belabour it.

Tate nudged me with his elbow. "You sure, Gideon?"

I nodded, just as Solomon spoke louder. "No, he's absolutely incorrect."

"Gideon thinks so, and I trust him when it comes to love," Tate said.

Solomon scoffed and rolled his eyes, standing up from his chair. "Don't make me sick. The two of you are clearly deluded, and talking about it won't help clarify things at all. Only one thing will."

He approached and took hold of the chain holding my wrists, gestured with his other hand and the chain on Tate fell away, snaked up his body and bound his wrists in the same manner mine were. "Come on, back to the cells with you. You too, cat."

Zeb wound his way around Solomon's legs, purring, before running ahead towards the cells with his tail up in the air.

I stood quickly, but Tate resisted a little. "Why? Why can't I stay in here, closer to you?" His voice was hard, challenging - trying to provoke him.

Solomon's expression hardened. He gathered both chain leashes in one hand and yanked, pulling the both of us forward.

"Because you are my captives, and my word is the only thing that matters."

He turned and stalked away, tugging the both of us back out to the landing. My breath hitched in my chest. "I can't go back to the cell by the drop-off," I said, my voice strained. "I can't."

"You will," Solomon hissed.

Tate stopped moving and yanked on the chain, perhaps because of the element of surprise, the chains slipped from Solomon's grasp and he turned, gesturing so the chains snaked through the air and back to his hand.

"Solomon, stop it," Tate said. "Just... let him stay in one of the ones that doesn't utterly terrify him. Please. Please, Solomon." His voice went softer, more appealing, and I saw Solomon's shoulders slump a little.

"Fine." Solomon tugged on the chains and led us to the cells. "Wait here."

He went to one knee, pressed his palm to the rock surface, closed his eyes and started to chant. As I watched, the rocky outcrop stretched and grew, making more of a ledge between the cell doors and the drop. My heart appreciated it. The distance eased the anxiety that threatened to bubble over.

And besides that, I couldn't help but think it was a positive sign - that Solomon had acquiesced to Tate's plea, that he had made a change to the layout of his lair in order to accommodate me. It was promising. Of course he couldn't change all at once, that was unreasonable.

He led me to my cell past Ezra's, who was leaning against his cell wall right at the bars, watching the proceedings. "All right, Gid?"

"I'm all right," I said. Zeb was already sitting up inside my cell, and I went inside without making a fuss. I held up my wrists and although he huffed and rolled his eyes, Solomon removed the chains.

"Thank you," I said. He didn't respond, but went back to Tate and brought him to the furthest cell before closing the bars on the three of us.

He said something, and Tate responded softly. Then there was a shout, a word of power, which I felt in my bones - vibrating them in a way that made my teeth rattle and my stomach turn. I sank down onto the ground and pressed my back to the wall. Zeb climbed onto my lap and flopped down into a warm, purring ball.

There was no sound. Then Solomon gave a huge, soul wrenching noise of frustration and stalked away, and I listened to his retreating footsteps.

"What was that?" I asked. "Tate, what did he do to you?"

"Nothing. I think he wanted to hurt me, but nothing happened."

I smiled to myself, enjoying how my magic was thwarting Solomon's attempts to hurt Tate.

"What happened back there, when he took you away?" Ezra asked, and Tate filled him in with as few words as possible.

"Well, you tried, Gid," Tate said, sighing at the end of his tale.

"I think it's going to work," I said. "He's... giving up somehow, something about what he planned isn't what he wants now." The thing in the back of my head that had been nagging at me became more insistent again. There was something more happening - something beyond the love and betrayal. I stroked my hand over Zeb

"Depends what he's going to do now," Ezra said. "He could just go and leave us here to starve."

"I don't think he will," Tate said. "Gid was onto something

when he said Solomon still loves me. I think that's been the problem this whole time."

"You need to apologise to him," I said, suddenly sure of it. I stroked my hand over Zeb's back. "He's still hurt, and you handled it badly. But you also, you also need..."

The two of them are linked, somehow. That's the problem. Solomon got more bloodthirsty and Tate got less... he got more relaxed. Because the emotions leaked through the link, perhaps. The magic Solomon used, it leeched something out of Tate...

And he has more power than ever here, which means it could be leeching more from him, it could be taking my emotions, my compassion as a result. The more we give him of that the better. But we shouldn't stay here. The more he sucks out of all of us the more dangerous it is. Who knows what it would do to him.

We have to save him.

"I think, I think you ... I think we need to take him off the island," I said, slowly. Trying to work out if it sounded irrational as I spoke it out loud. Hoping I was right.

"He'll never leave the island," Tate said.

"He might, if you convince him," Ezra said. "If Gideon's right, and he still wants you, maybe he'd follow you off it. Then he'll be weaker and we can kill him."

I swallowed. The idea of killing turned my stomach at the best of times, but killing Solomon, what with what I had realised about him - or thought I'd realised at least - seemed abhorrent.

"No, don't..." I said, just at the same instant Tate spoke.

"I don't think it will be necessary," Tate said. "He can't hurt any of us."

"Gideon's lovers are protected, but what about the rest of the crew?" Ezra asked.

"I love them too, just... not in the same way, exactly," I said. "I have absolutely no idea if that will work enough to protect them. I don't know how to test that, either."

Tate huffed. "I think getting him off the Isles will help, it will reduce the magic in him, and the magic was what put him on the path of hatred."

"This is all speculation," Ezra said. "What if we trust him, if we put him on the Grey Kelpie and he kills us all in our sleep?"

I couldn't deny it was a concern. My gut instinct was that we didn't have to fear Solomon but it wasn't exactly something I could prove.

CHAPTER THIRTEEN - IN WHICH RECONCILIATION IS ATTEMPTED

*I*t was the early hours of the morning when a small, faintly green light woke Tate up. He'd been curled against the wall he shared with Gideon's cell. The floor was hard underneath him, and he had realised just how pampered he'd become by sleeping all these years in a large bed in his cabin. Back in his days in the Navy he'd been able to sleep anywhere, in any position. Now he was waking up every so often with a crick in his neck or an ache in his side.

I'm getting older, he thought.

But he had been asleep when the light woke him. He sat up, recognising it instantly as one of the witchlights Solomon had used to conjure when they were young.

The light danced in the air before him, and when he reached out a hand to grasp it, it flitted away from his fingers.

It floated towards the door to the cell and Tate saw the bars had gone. Curious, but with a nervous feeling in his stomach, he followed the light out of the cell. It led him not to Solomon's chambers but to a door and a stairway at the back of the cave system. Down the carved stone steps he went and found Solomon on a sandy beach, his legs crossed under him. He was facing away, looking out at the sea where it washed in from the cavern mouth. But Tate thought his shoulders looked relaxed and there was a peaceful sort of air about him.

As he got closer, he realised that Solomon wasn't alone - Ora was half in the water, tail flipping lazily back and forth, elbows propped on the damp sand and chin in their hands as they gazed at Solomon with a soft smile playing at their lips. They weren't speaking out loud, but Tate got the distinct feeling they were communicating all the same.

Tate thought of the bizarre conversation he'd had with Gideon and Ezra.

Ora looked past Solomon and waved, gave him a wink, then looked back to Solomon. Then, with a splash and a flip of their tail, Ora was gone, swimming off into deeper waters.

Solomon turned and smiled, just a tiny touch, at the sight of Tate.

"You saw my light, then?"

"Obviously," Tate said. He regretted his sarcastic tone almost immediately. It didn't seem polite, when Solomon had been so sweet as to send a light and let him out of the cage.

He moved closer and sat near Solomon on the sand, a few feet between them, and waited for Solomon to tell him what he wanted.

Solomon didn't speak right away, instead he partially turned to look at Tate's profile. Tate let him, and kept looking towards the ocean, giving him time and space as he seemed to need it.

Gideon's voice rang in his memory and he took a breath. Maybe Gid had been right, and he did need to apologise.

Gideon was usually right about these things, the boy knew a thing or two about emotions and managing relationships. He would never have slept with Ezra if it hadn't been for Gideon, and if he had, he wouldn't have been able to remain friends. They would have flared bright and hot and then got on each other's nerves. They needed Gideon as an anchor. And then

Gideon had brought in the others, and somehow made all of that work as well. Now, Tate found it hard to imagine being truly happy without Gideon, Ezra, Zeb and Ora in his life. In his bed.

So yes, he trusted Gideon's instincts, which meant he should do as Gideon had advised, and make an apology.

Now was probably the perfect time, and Solomon didn't seem inclined to stab him.

He turned and faced Solomon. "I'm sorry," he said.

There was no sound aside from the gentle wash of the waves on the sand, and a distant drip from some unseen place.

Solomon's face showed many expressions - some Tate could read, such as sadness and anger, and some that flew across his face so fleetingly Tate couldn't follow. Tate didn't breathe, just waited and watched as Solomon processed his words.

"Do you honestly think it's that simple?" Solomon finally said. His voice held none of the usual assuredness or viciousness. It was soft, almost, a little hitch in the word simple, which gave Tate a small spark of hope.

"I think, it could start that simply," Tate said, slowly, choosing his words with the utmost care. "I think, in the past, the two of us may have used each other, may not have taken as much care with our feelings as we could have." He was going to leave it there but he thought of Gideon again. "And I'm very sorry for my part in what happened. I really... I wouldn't have ever wanted to hurt you in the manner I did."

"So formal," Solomon said. He looked away from Tate and gazed at the ocean again. "You sound like him."

There was no need to elaborate on who Solomon meant by 'him', they both knew.

"Well, I'm trying to handle this conversation better than any I've had with you before it," Tate said. "And Gid is very good at these conversations."

Solomon sighed, picked up a round, flat stone from the sand

and turned it over in his hands, letting his eyes drop to it. He didn't speak, and Tate bit his lip before continuing.

"What are you feeling?"

"What am I *feeling*?" Solomon raised an eyebrow and curled his lip. Tate barrelled on.

"Yes, what are you feeling? Right now? Why did you call me down here in the middle of the night? What do you want?"

Solomon rubbed his thumb over the stone and then flung it at the ocean with a flick of his wrist, sending it skipping over the top of the water before it sank into the waves with a small splash.

"I was so focused on my revenge," Solomon said, his voice even lower. Tate shuffled closer to him in order to hear. His hand was close to Solomon's when he set it back down. "It was all I could think of, night and day. And then when I had you, I thought... I thought I could kill you and I would be at peace. But... I can't. I can't bring myself to do it."

"Well, I can't say as I'm sad about that," Tate said.

There was a flash of the old anger, when Solomon glared at him, but the fury in his expression only lasted a moment before fading into a sort of wearied defeat.

"I... I've found that my desire to hurt you has faded, I want revenge, but more than that I've..." he trailed off, his mouth closed and his lips worked - pursing and twisting - unable to express out loud what he was feeling.

Tate took a deep breath, felt something in his stomach similar to when they were about to board an enemy ship, anticipation, nervousness, hope, all rolled in together.

"It's all right, Solomon," Tate said. "Whatever you want to say, it's all right."

Once again, the silence stretched between them. Tate could see Solomon wrestling with something. His eyes narrowed and his eyebrows drew together, his mouth twisted and relaxed.

When he spoke again his voice was as Tate had remembered

it, back on the Naval ship they had both served on. A younger man's voice, far more vulnerable and fearful.

"Why wasn't I enough for you?"

Tate sucked in his breath and shook his head. "I thought I wasn't enough for you. You always wanted more power, to be more impressive and I didn't... I didn't know how to compete with that, how to make it so I was enough."

Solomon turned and looked Tate in the eyes. "That's a lie, you've always been perfect."

Tate barked out a laugh with no mirth in it. "Not hardly. I'm making mistakes every day. I do my best, and most of the time I can muddle through, the crew helps, but me? I'm not perfect. I can be petty and mean, I can be foolish. I can make huge mistakes, like becoming afraid of my lover because he has magic and leaving him on the shores of a godforsaken rock because I wanted the gold for myself... these are mistakes, and I am sorry for them."

On impulse, Tate took Solomon's hand and squeezed it gently. Solomon's back stiffened and he inhaled. Green fire sparked in his eyes and Tate had the urge to let go, to run for his life.

He was afraid, but he resisted. He held tight to Solomon's hand.

The green fire flickered and faltered, Solomon's expression softened, and he took a deep breath. For a moment, the eldritch grey cast to his skin faded and Tate saw the echo of the boy he had been as he smiled.

"Thank you," he said. "Thank you for apologising. I'm sorry as well, I know I've been... a monster."

Tate nodded and laced his fingers through Solomon's. "Thank you for your apology. I forgive you." Although it seemed impossible to say such a thing, Tate found his heart was swelling with happiness. The simple fact of a conversation, of being honest and open with each other, and having such success as a result seemed like a magic in and of itself.

Solomon shuffled closer again to Tate and leaned his shoulder against his. Again, they let the silence fill the space left between them.

CHAPTER FOURTEEN - IN WHICH THE FUTURE IS CONSIDERED

I woke in the morning to an open cell door. I was deliciously warm, and realised it was because Zeb was in human form, his chest pressed against my back and his arm across me, holding me close against him. This was a usual sleeping position for us, and the comfort was beyond compare.

The open cell door was a large question mark in my mind though, so with a little cajoling I managed to extract myself from his embrace and get to my feet. I padded out of the cave with a jittery sort of optimism, uncertain what the open bars meant.

I checked the far side where Tate had been imprisoned and found an empty cell, bars removed. Uncertain if that was a good or bad sign, I went further to see Ezra still asleep in his cell, with the bars removed as well. Unable to stop myself, I went to him and kissed his forehead. He stirred awake with a soft grumble, and his hand gripped my hip, pulling me in for a proper kiss.

It was a sleepy, confused sort of kiss but very much appreciated. Ezra's scent filled me with happiness, but the question mark continued to tug at my attention.

I pulled back a little. Ezra sat up. "Wait, what are you doing in here?"

"The bars are gone," I said, softly, unsure if it was wise to be overheard. "I'm going to see if I can find Tate."

Ezra got to his feet and tugged me to standing as well. "Right, yes, let's find our Captain."

The two of us left the cells. I led the way and when I got to the stone landing, I hesitated - uncertain if it was wise to go into Solomon's private quarters, such as they were, but then... the bars had been removed. That was an indication that I was free to move around, that I could explore as I wished. I couldn't hear any voices, which would have been a good guideline for what to do next.

There was a sound of quiet footsteps and I turned to see that Zeb had joined us.

"Morning," Zeb said, smiling at Ezra sleepily.

"Maybe we should try in there," Ezra said, pointing towards the inner sanctum that Solomon used.

As we walked towards it, I felt a fluttering of hope in my stomach, although I couldn't have told you why I felt that and not more fear. Perhaps I was picking up on emotions from those around me?

Ezra was on my right, Zeb to the left, as I led the way inside. I swallowed, half excited and half fearful of what I was about to see.

For a moment, I caught my breath, fearing the worst as I saw Tate sprawled on the bed, prone and shirtless. Then I realised that there was no blood beneath him, and I could see his chest rising and falling with each breath.

He's alive, just sleeping. And where is Solomon?

I moved a little closer to the bed and saw that the bunched up blanket I could see Tate partially leaning on, his arm flung out over it, was actually Solomon. He was mostly concealed under his cloak, using it as a blanket as he slept, peaceful and softly smiling, beside Tate.

Ezra strode up next to me, a large knife in his hand, and I had to half turn to put my hand on his chest.

"Don't. Look, he's not chained up, I think this is a good thing."

Tate stirred at the sounds of our voices and his eyes flicked open. He gave me a brief smile and then partially turned to press his hand down on the bundle that made up Solomon. He chuckled when Solomon pulled the cloak tighter around himself and turned over to face the wall.

Tate sat up and ran a hand through his hair, his eyes sparkling with amusement. "Right, guess we'd better all have a talk," he said.

Ezra pushed past me and went to touch Tate on the cheek, then looked past him to Solomon, a question in his eyes.

"We've made a sort of peace," Tate said. "But we all need to talk." He squeezed Ezra's wrist briefly and then dropped his hand, turning to shake Solomon's shoulder. "That means you, too."

"I'll go and find Ora," Zeb said and turned to head out of the room. He shifted into cat form as he went and was gone.

Ezra kept hold of the knife and looked to me. I nodded at the chaise and we both sat down on it, dragging it across the stone floor a little so it wasn't too far from the bed. Tate was leaning over Solomon, murmuring to him, and slowly Solomon pushed the cloak back off his shoulders and sat up, one hand rubbing his eyes.

He turned to look at me and I saw a flicker of annoyance, but none of the malice or hatred I was used to seeing in his eyes. My flutter of hope spread wings to be a full-fledged butterfly in my stomach. I took Ezra's hand and squeezed it, excitedly.

Solomon got up and went to the bench where he prepared food. Without a word he started to make some sort of potion, using the fire to heat something and rattling jars.

Tate smiled genially at Ezra and me. I noticed that Ezra

hadn't set the knife down and was holding it on his lap, ready to spring into action, I had no doubt.

"You're all right, then?" Ezra asked, looking at Tate. Tate nodded.

"Yes, I'm completely fine."

Ora and Zeb walked into the room, neither of them with a stitch of clothing on them. I was used to this, of course, but given the circumstances, it didn't seem quite appropriate. I looked around for something to clothe them with. Tate noticed, picked up his shirt from the floor and tossed it to Ora, who caught it and pulled it on. The size difference between them had the shirt hanging down, dress-like on Ora's slim frame.

Zeb - apparently utterly unconcerned about boundaries, picked up Solomon's cloak from the bed and wrapped it around himself, sitting down beside Tate.

"I haven't any milk," Solomon said, from behind us. There was a rattle that sounded uncannily like a tea tray, and I turned to see that was exactly what it was. Mismatched teacups balanced on a tray with a large, stout teapot. He carried it over and set it on a small table before busying himself with pouring cups and handing one to Tate, and then offering them to me and Ezra.

I took it happily. "Thank you, it's been an age since I had proper tea."

Ezra eyed it and then shook his head, his expression stony. Solomon turned and offered the cup to Zeb instead, who took it with a smile.

"Right, so," Tate said, as Ora and Zeb accepted cups of tea from Solomon and he himself sat down as well. "Solomon and I are reconciled. He's not going to hurt any of you, or keep you here any more."

"And I woke up your crew mates," Solomon said. "They know it's safe for them back on the ship and I believe they've all returned there for now."

"What about you, Tate?" I asked, suddenly fearing that Tate intended to stay with Solomon. My heart ached at the thought of Tate choosing to stay with Solomon and not being in my life anymore. Terribly greedy of me, really. I'd still have the other three lovers... But it still scared me.

"Well, uh," Tate said. He glanced at Solomon, who met his gaze and then looked down, almost shyly. "We were wondering how everyone would feel about Solomon joining the crew of the Kelpie."

"Absolutely not," Ezra said, immediately. "He's tried to kill us, multiple times."

"And I'm sorry for that," Solomon said.

"He's... I think if we get him off the Splintered Isles, it'll be easier on him," Tate said.

"Away from the source," I said, nodding. Ora looked between Ezra, Solomon, and Tate and then nodded as well.

"I agree with that, it's not for humans to know the source, not really," they said. "My people have guarded it for centuries."

Solomon's head tilted to the side and his expression turned hungry. "Show it to me."

Tate put a hand on Solomon's knee and they exchanged a look. "I don't think it's a safe idea for you to see it," Tate said.

Ora shook his head at Solomon. "It's not for you."

Solomon frowned and leaned his shoulder against Tate's a little.

"Obviously, I'd like for us all to agree," Tate said. "I would like to take Solomon away from the corrupting influence of the islands."

"It's not safe," Ezra said. He sighed and shook his head. "He might be playing like he's a kitten now, but what if he's enchanted all of us? What if he's waiting until we're all on the ship and then he kills us all and takes it for himself?"

"He could have done that already," I said. "He had us all in cages."

"And I didn't," Solomon said. "Besides, all the enchantments have been wearing off, in case you haven't noticed." He sounded particularly spiteful, and I wasn't quite brave enough to meet his eyes, embarrassed somehow that I'd thwarted him without actively doing so.

"Gideon's protection at work. It stopped me being trapped as a cat as well," Zeb said, smiling wide. I met his eyes and we grinned at each other, my embarrassment fading into pride.

"It really shouldn't have," Solomon said. And this time his tone sounded interested, almost academic. I looked up and met his eyes and found something curious there. "I'd like to do some studies, learn more about what you can do. Because Zeb, as I understand, only can shape shift because of my curse. It should be reversible, but somehow it isn't?"

"The only studies you're allowed are the ones that don't include vivisection," Tate said. Solomon huffed his breath out and he looked away.

"I know that."

Ezra sucked his teeth and and smacked his lips. "I don't like it. And what does this mean? Is Solomon becoming one of Gideon's lovers, now?" His eyebrows drew together and I swallowed - uncertain if it was something I wanted. I had a certain attraction to Solomon, but I wasn't at all convinced he wanted me.

"Oh, definitely not," Solomon said, which answered the question quite neatly. "I only want Tate. I'll... adjust to sharing him, to him being part of whatever it is you all have, that's fine, but I won't be partaking in any of the..." He pulled a face before continuing. "Group activities. I have no interest in Gideon, incubus or not, or the rest of you."

My mind raced, trying to think through all of the implications of what Solomon and Tate were suggesting.

"So, it'd be sort of like, Tate was still a part of... this, with me," I said, gesturing to Ezra and then the others. "But he'd also be your lover, Solomon?"

"I won't agree to it unless everyone agrees," Tate said, quickly. "You mean the world to me, Gideon, but there are also feelings for Solomon, and I don't want to lose him again. If I don't have to."

Ezra, his arms crossed over his chest, drummed his fingers on his bicep and sighed again. "I don't like it, I can't trust him," he said.

"He'll be my responsibility," Tate said.

"I'm not a dog," Solomon snapped. "I'm here in the room, you don't have to talk about me like I'm not here."

"None of us trust him," Zeb said, his tone reasonable, appealing to Ezra's logical mind. "So all of us will be watching him. And Tate is under Gid's protection, so we know he can't be bewitched."

"He can't even put me to sleep," Tate said.

"I think it's a fine idea," I said. I stood up and crossed the room to offer my hands to Tate and Solomon. As I approached, I fancied I could feel an echo of the love and longing the two of them had nursed for decades. My stomach flipped with the anticipation they both felt - the edge of something wonderful if they could just get over this last obstacle. It cemented my decision. Tate took my hand readily, Solomon hesitated but I met his eyes and nodded and he took it. "If you two want it to work out, then it will. As Zeb says, we'll all of us be keeping a watchful eye over Solomon, it won't be easy on the crew at all, but over time we'll all adjust. What do you all think? It's not just my decision." I let go of Tate and Solomon and turned to Ora.

Ora smiled and shrugged a shoulder. "Solomon and I had a good talk last night, I think it's a good idea."

Zeb nodded. "Yes, Solomon knows that if he hurts any of you, I'll tear his throat out."

I glanced at Solomon who had paled a little, his mouth

forming a thin line. "Yes, quite," he said.

"And I'd help." Ora bared their teeth in a slightly terrifying smile.

That left Ezra, so I turned to him, but Tate was already appealing to him.

"Ezra, you don't have to trust him. He can't affect me, or the others, and he'll be under watch. We can even lock him up if you like. But you trust *me*, I know you do, and I say this is a workable solution."

Ezra stared into Tate's eyes, his expression hard, demanding, and then rolled his eyes and sighed. "All right, fine, but if I see any proof of abuse from him, of any dark magic that hurts you, then I'll run him through."

"That wouldn't stop me," Solomon muttered.

"You are really not helping your case," I said to him.

"Then we are agreed?" Tate said, brightly. He stood up and wrapped me in his arms. "Thank you, Gideon."

Privately, I didn't think he should be thanking me, as it was him who had made peace with Solomon and somehow bartered this course of action, and besides that, it had taken everyone agreeing. But it seemed ungracious to disagree with him, so I hugged him tight and smiled.

"I love you," I said, instead.

"I just hope you all remember that I said this was a bad idea," Ezra said, getting up. "Well, when do we leave?"

"Tonight," Tate said. "Solomon needs some time to pack the things he wants to bring, and we should talk to the crew before he comes aboard as well."

"While I'm preparing, please help yourself to whatever food you care for, and of course you have the run of the isles. I assume you'll all want to consummate your decision, or something like that."

He kissed Tate chastely on the cheek and got up, walking out of the room with inhuman grace and leaving the five of us alone.

CHAPTER FIFTEEN - IN WHICH GIDEON AND HIS LOVERS ARE REUNITED

I breathed out, feeling my shoulders relax. I hadn't actually realised just how tense my body had been until then, that I'd been half waiting for things to go badly - for Solomon to lash out, perhaps, or for Ezra to snap and attack him.

But none of that had happened, and although I could feel a wave of annoyance, of anger masking fear, from Ezra, the atmosphere in the room relaxed and I did as well.

It felt like the adrenaline was draining out of the group of us. I had imagined some kind of huge magical battle and instead, we'd managed to just sort of talk Solomon down.

Perhaps my magic had been affecting him from when I first got here, making all of it... easier for us? I have no way to know, I suppose.

I went to Ezra and kissed his cheek. "Thank you for looking out for all of us," I said.

"One of us has to be sensible," Ezra grumbled. "And I knew Ora wouldn't, or Zeb."

"I can smell when he does magic," Zeb said, shrugging. "There's no danger to me."

"What now? Shall we do as he suggested?" Ora asked, they raised their eyebrows and smiled at the rest of us, hopefully.

Tate smiled and beckoned to Ora, who was quickly at his side, and snuggled into his side. I felt Ezra's hand on my hip, pulling me towards him. "I'm not sure how I feel about having sex in a sea witch's bedroom," Ezra said. "But I have honestly missed being able to touch you, pet."

I shivered happily. Ezra's annoyance was still present but it was being replaced by a warm affection that I could feel through his hands and through his emotions. I leaned against him and watched as Ora and Tate kissed, slow and lazy.

Zeb crawled onto the bed beside Tate and lay back, one hand on Tate's back until Tate turned, leaned down and kissed him on the mouth.

"I guess we're doing this, then?" Ezra didn't sound too enthusiastic, but I thought I had a way of getting him on board with the idea. I sank down to my knees and went to work on the waistband of his trousers.

"Maybe I can convince you that it's a good idea to celebrate, since we've essentially rescued Tate and are all back together again," I said. Using both hands I tugged his trousers open and off and leaned in to lick at the tip of him.

He was already getting hard, and he leaned back, gently stroking his fingers through my hair.

I heard Tate chuckle behind me and smiled before leaning in and taking all of Ezra's cock in my mouth. I moaned at the taste of him and at the way he groaned softly, as if he didn't want to be heard.

I bobbed my head a few times, slicking his length with my tongue and ensuring his hardness before I pulled back, feeling a marvellous tug in my hair as I pulled it out of his hands, his fingers trying to catch hold.

Feeling mischief bubbling up within me, I got quickly to my feet, darted back out of Ezra's reach and joined the others on the bed, keeping my eyes on Ezra, tempting him to follow me.

It didn't take any more than that - or perhaps his hardness

was enough to convince him - because he was on the bed with the rest of us in a moment.

I slipped onto Tate's lap as Ora turned to kiss Ezra, drawing him in and closer to Zeb.

Tate's trousers had been opened but not removed, so I reached between us to push them down a little more and stroke his cock.

"Gideon," he moaned, burying his face in my neck and rocking against me.

"Is there oil?" I looked around, uncertain where Solomon would keep it, if he had it.

Tate straightened his back, looked me in the eye and then, holding me tightly in one place with one arm, he leaned down and felt under the mattress, his face lighting up with a smile as he withdrew a small vial of coconut oil.

"That was unexpected," I said, as he righted himself and me.

"Some things are habit, I suppose," Tate said. He slipped his fingers into the oil and reached behind me to tease me open. Then he passed the vial to Ezra, who used it on Zeb.

Ora slipped behind Tate, pressing their front against his back to kiss me over his shoulder, one of their hands slipping around to stroke Tate, the other teasing one of my nipples and gently pulling on it.

"I'm ready," I said, after Tate had barely stretched me. "I want it."

Tate removed his fingers and pressed against me with his cock instead. I moaned, leaning my head against Ora's cheek as I felt the stretch and pull of him entering me. Ora tugged Tate down with an arm around his chest, and I saw that Ezra was on his back, Zeb riding him. Ora rested against his side at right angles. Ezra's fingers found Tate's hair and tugged it roughly, causing him to buck into me with a rough thrust.

I gasped and reached for Ora's hand, using it to balance as I sat upright and rode Tate's cock. Zeb's hand found my shoulder from the other side, and as soon as I was touching him as well, my magic flared and shot through me, connecting all of us in a magical matrix of reflected sensations. I could feel my own delight blurring into Tate's joy. Ezra's lust flowing into Zeb's hedonistic exaltations and Ora's confidence in giving and receiving carnal rapture.

I opened my eyes and saw the golden threads linking us, a glowing connection that filled my heart with love and lust, and fed the sensations I was receiving from the others.

It wasn't long at all until all of us were coming, touching each other and crying out as one, each lover's enjoyment heightened beyond imagining by the way the magic filtered each other's love back to one another.

I felt the power of it, not as an overwhelming transportation as it had been on other occasions but a warmth akin to coming home. Each of my lovers was a part of my heart, and knowing I had them all with me, all connected to me physically and emotionally, I felt a deep and abiding peace and contentment.

As we slowly extricated ourselves, and cleaned up as best we could, Tate began to yawn. It had been a rough night, and somewhat stressful few days for all of us.

Without speaking, because we all understood, we settled onto the bed. Tate in the middle, with me pressed against his right side, Ezra on the other side of me, one arm slung over me and his hand resting on Tate's belly. Ora was on Tate's left, their arm draped over his chest and their fingers threaded through mine. Zeb sprawled half on top of Ora, his legs over Tate's, at an odd angle compared to the rest, but in a way that made perfect sense for him.

We dropped off to sleep warm and content, wrapped in the love of each other.

CHAPTER SIXTEEN - IN WHICH SOLOMON LEAVES THE SPLINTERED ISLES

*W*e spent the afternoon ferrying books and various items of alchemical investigation from the underground cavern to the Grey Kelpie.

I was on the first boat over to it and was relieved to see Zack and Sagorika completely well and fine.

They'd been watching the longboat approach, of course, so it wasn't a surprise when I boarded the ship. Zack threw his arms around me and squeezed.

"Thank the good lord that you're all right," he said. "Tate, too?"

"Yes, Tate too," I said. "He's back on the isles still, talking to Solomon. They'll be along shortly, oh uh. So, the plan we have is to bring Solomon with us."

"What?" Zack let go of me and examined my face. "Have you taken leave of your senses, or something?"

"He hasn't," Ezra climbed aboard, tossed a bundle of rolled up maps on the deck and raised his voice to address the crew. "Listen up, everyone. Tate and Solomon have made peace with each other, and we've agreed that Solomon can join us on the Kelpie." As the crew protested, Ezra continued to explain what had happened, how my magic had protected Tate from magical control, and the rest of my lovers. He even speculated that because of my affection for the ship itself, as well as the crew aboard it, we would all be protected from dark magics.

It wasn't often I got to see Ezra in this light - a leader, gifted to be sure, even if he wasn't as natural at it as Tate was. In some ways, I reflected, that it was better to hear this news from the First Mate, because they all knew that he would have expressed concerns and fought if he'd thought it necessary.

If Ezra had accepted this course of events, perhaps the rest of the crew didn't have to worry.

As Ezra ordered the crew to clear out a space below deck for Solomon to stow his things, Sagorika pulled me aside.

"You all right, then? No new scars or broken bones?"

"Not a thing." I smiled, trying to reassure her. "Solomon thought he wanted revenge, but what he really needed was reconciliation. I'll tell you the story someday, but... maybe not quite yet."

"You look good, to be frank. Like something weighing on you's been lifted. I suppose it has, at that?"

I tilted my head, surprised at her words. I certainly felt better since we'd talked with Solomon and negotiated peace, and since sleeping with my lovers, but I hadn't imagined it would show on my physicality in any way.

"I suppose it has. I feel good, and more in touch with my magic than ever before, perhaps that's what you're seeing?"

Sagorika nodded and ruffled her hand through my hair affectionately. I felt a wide smile tug at my lips. I let it happen. It really did feel as if things had been laid to rest here. I had spoken with my Mother, or at least, some phantom presence of her, we'd quelled the sea witch and managed to keep our little coterie of lovers unified. I had used my magic to protect those I loved, and I felt nothing but contentment when I thought of my heritage. The fear of what it could do, what I might be, had vanished. I knew who I was, and I knew I wouldn't hurt my lovers with my magic. I knew it as an absolute truth in my gut.

Sagorika looked out towards the Splintered Isles. "Blasted eerie sort of place," she said. "It'll be good to get him away from it, I can feel that in my bones."

In my bones, I could feel that the influence of the source was wearing off me, or possibly had worn off already and now I was lacking the proximity to it. I could feel a little echo of the pull Solomon must feel, but thankfully I didn't find it overwhelming to resist. More and more I found I pitied Solomon. I turned back to Sagorika.

"So you're not worried about him joining the crew?"

"What happened, there, on the island, Gideon?" Sagorika asked. I tried to explain it, aware that I didn't have all the details of what had happened between Tate and Solomon.

"His magic stopped working on Tate, because you were there?"

"It seemed like it I was protecting him, without intentionally doing it."

"Maybe your magic broke whatever spell was linking the two of them," Sagorika said. "Whatever thing it was which drew them together and then split them apart again?"

I hadn't considered that, but it made a sort of sense. I resolved to talk to Solomon and Tate about it, maybe in a few days when things had settled down.

"You're not worried at all, then?"

"Not any more worried than when we took on you, or Zack," Sagorika teased.

"You should have been worried about me," I said, only half in jest. "I brought the Royal Navy down on us."

"Not to mention you started fucking the captain," Sagorika said. "But hey, remember what I told you the very first time we met?"

"This ship is a place for people to be themselves." I smiled, genuinely this time. "I've never forgotten that."

"Maybe all Solomon needs is some guidance, and some time with normal people. Well. Relatively normal." On impulse I hugged Sagorika again, feeling my love rise inside me but in a different way than it did with my lovers.

I really did love everyone on the crew, and the ship itself. I didn't truly believe that Solomon would try to sabotage us, but if he did, perhaps my love would be a protection over everyone aboard.

Although I had a little difficulty with the rope ladder, I descended again and went back to the island to ferry back more items.

Solomon had finished directing Tate and Zeb to carry things down to the beach for him, and was now standing with his ankles in the surf, his head turned up to the sky and his eyes closed.

In the bright sunlight his skin looked less silver and a little more natural coloured. A bit more brown than grey. His hair was still a shiny reddish black, the red catching highlights in the sun. He wore tight black trousers, apparently unconcerned that they were being soaked by the waves, and a faded grey shirt that could have at one point been black. He still looked like a being of another world, and certainly sinister in aspect, but he didn't strike fear into my heart.

Tate went to put his hand on his arm after another boat of items had been taken to the ship with Sagorika and Ezra. Ezra rowed the boat back to shore, his muscles shifting under his shirt and making my mouth water.

After a time, Solomon turned to look at Tate and I saw a softness in his expression. I looked away and busied myself with helping Ezra get the longboat into the shallows.

"It's time," Ezra said.

"Are you ready?" Tate asked Solomon, who sighed. He sounded weary.

"As ready as it's possible for me to be, I suppose. It will hurt to leave, I think. These isles have grown used to my presence."

"It existed for many years before you came to its shores, it will do fine without you, too, I'll wager."

Tate smiled softly and offered his arm to Solomon, who laughed - actually laughed, and not in a vindictive way - and took it.

"You are ridiculous."

"Finally, something we can agree on," Ezra said, as Solomon and then Tate climbed into the longboat. I dug my toes into the sand as I held the vessel as still as I could. I fancied I could feel the tug of the magic, and a sudden wild temptation to go down to the source of the magic and speak again to my mother took me. I closed my eyes, breathing out slowly and trying to let go of the temptation.

The source will still be there if I ever return, I told myself. *No need to inconvenience the others with fussing about it now. Not when getting Solomon away from here is our goal and priority.*

"Gideon?" Tate's voice sounded concerned, so I opened my eyes, shook my hair out and shoved the boat off the sand, jumping up and into it as it took the waves. Tate and Ezra sat side by side and started to row as I settled in the back of the boat. Solomon had taken a seat at the front, looking back at me, or rather, back at the island as we moved away from it.

I half turned and looked at the shore as well, chewing my lip as I felt the various mystical forces tug at me like an insistent wind. I thought about the Kelpie, and my lovers, and felt the tug lessen somewhat.

Letting my gaze drop, I noticed shapes in the water - merfolk - I looked for the tails of their fins, but I didn't see the black of Ora's. There was a purple one, though, which could have been Inca, the other merfolk Ora had introduced. Possibly some of them were the ones who had been present when I visited the source, but I had no way of telling.

There was a strangled noise from the front of the boat and I looked up to see Solomon clutching at his head with both hands, bent almost in half at the waist.

"What is it?" Tate asked, his voice tense.

"The Splintered Isles..." Solomon gasped. "They're... there's a force...calling me back, wanting me to stay." He groaned and pressed his head down between his knees.

Tate shored his oar and moved closer to Solomon, kneeling on the bottom of the boat so it didn't rock too much. Ezra stopped rowing and watched, his face unreadable. I moved to take Tate's place, nudging him.

"It's best if we keep rowing, I think," I said. In this case I couldn't see how my magic would help, since I didn't love Solomon, he wouldn't be protected. Perhaps just getting as much distance between us and the islands was what we needed.

"I don't think I can resist," Solomon groaned.

"There now, of course you can. You're the strongest witch on the seas, aren't you?" Tate's hand rubbed Solomon's back as he spoke soothingly.

I swallowed, feeling it tugging at the edges of me, and unable to imagine how much worse it must be for Solomon.

CHAPTER SEVENTEEN - IN WHICH PLANS ARE DISCUSSED AND SETTLED UPON

"You're absolutely sure this is what you want to do?" Tate asked me. I nodded. We were in the Captain's cabin with Ezra, Ora and Zeb.

"Yes, absolutely sure," I said. "If I don't go and talk to him, he'll just keep on trying to find me. Mother said...well, the ghost of Mother, or her spirit or whatever it was, said he won't stop. He misses her, and he won't let me go. Not if he can help it."

"I hate this idea," Ezra said. "Please put me down on record as being against it, and hating everything about it."

"We're not making notes," Ora said. "But I'll remember that you said it, if that helps?"

Ezra was seated on the bed, Zeb sprawled out with his head in Ezra's lap, which was a touchingly tender position for the both of them. Ora was seated on the floor near me, one elbow braced on my knee where I sat on the desk chair. Tate was pacing, looking up at the ceiling and trying to resist telling me yes.

"If we go back to Kingston now, the whole of the King's Navy will be ready and waiting to ensnare us. Especially after we humiliated the Trinity Royal and snatched you and Zack away from them."

I smiled a little at the thought of Tate and the others kidnapping me. It was more of an arousing game than a truth, but it had been a good cover when we escaped from the Trinity. I shook my head rather than follow down that particular thought path, or this conversation was likely to become an orgy, and we had other work to do before the day was done.

"I don't know what to do to avoid the Navy," I said. I cleared my throat. "But perhaps Solomon could help. He was doing interesting illusions with mist. Perhaps there's something he can do to mask our arrival?"

Solomon had told us that the ships we'd been running from were merely illusions, and the potential of that trick had sat in the back of my head ever since. Ezra tilted his head to the side, considering.

"Could that work?"

"He did all that was when he was on the Isles, with all the magic," Tate said. He chewed his lip. "Maybe we should get him up here and ask, though?"

"I should be able to help," Ora said, from my lap. They wrapped an arm around my lower leg and pulled themself a little more upright. "Maybe Gid could, too? He loves the ship, after all."

I blushed a little. "I love the ship, but I don't think I can help with illusions."

"You might be able to," Ora turned to look at me. "Your power can reflect and amplify emotions, maybe it can do it with magic as well?"

"I have absolutely no idea," I said, shrugging. "But maybe? I feel like you'd know better than me."

"I think Solomon would know," Ora said. Then they yawned and rested their head on my knee again. "Or he could find out."

Ora's curls looked soft, so I gently stroked them, making Ora hum happily.

Tate sighed and paced the length of the cabin again. "Let's

imagine this works, we can get the Kelpie into port and no one notices. What then? Ezra and I can't step foot off the ship. Gideon will be recognised…"

"It doesn't matter if I'm recognised," I said. "I want to speak to my father, so. It's fine. I'll say you let me go, and I've arrived unharmed on a merchant ship, or something."

"They won't recognise me," Ora said. "I can go with Gid."

There was a moment's silence and Tate smiled. "That does make me feel better."

"Me, too," Zeb said, lazily. "No one knows me on Kingston except as a cat."

"No one will recognise Solomon, either, come to that," Ezra said, his tone sardonic. "But let's say it all works and Gid can see his father, then what? You think he'll just blithely let you sail away again whenever you want?"

"No, I… well, no, I don't, but maybe once I've talked to him about Mother. Let him see that it's all right to grieve her and let go, maybe he'll let go of me as well."

Even as I spoke the words I knew they sounded weak. It wasn't much of a plan at all, and the idea of getting Father to listen to talk of emotions… well, it sounded even more impossible. But I had to try. I wanted to try, and I had promised my Mother.

"It'll be fine," Zeb said. "I can sneak him out of the house no problem at all."

"You can?" Ezra looked down at the huge man half sprawled in his lap. "Have a lot of practise with that, do you?"

"Yes," Zeb said. "Although, usually what I was sneaking out of a big, fancy house was a fillet of salmon, or a side of beef."

Ezra rolled his eyes and pushed Zeb off his lap. "Gideon is slightly larger than a fillet of salmon."

"And I'm larger in this form than I am in cat form," Zeb said. He sat up and glared at Ezra. "I can do it."

"All right, no need to fight," Tate said. He sighed, looked at me with a question in his eyes. I knew what he was asking.

Do we really have to do this?

I nodded, my chin up and my teeth clenched. *Yes, we do.*

"Right, then. I'll go talk with Solomon, and see what he thinks he can manage by way of tricks and illusions."

"I'll come with you," Ora said.

Solomon had largely stayed below deck for the first few days since we sailed from the Splintered Isles. Tate visited with him a couple of times a day. When I asked why he didn't spend more time down there, he replied that Solomon was used to his solitude, and had been finding the cramped living quarters irritating. Tate had helped him move into the brig, which at least was a bit more private than the crew's quarters, and the presence of the locking cell doors had comforted the crew, even if they weren't actually locked.

Ora had also been visiting with Solomon. As a long time resident of the waters near the Splintered Isles, Ora seemed to understand more of the loss Solomon was experiencing.

I was glad that they seemed to have formed a friendship. I myself was aware that my presence was still somewhat of an aggravation for him, and I was happy to keep my distance until he was more settled.

CHAPTER EIGHTEEN - IN WHICH GIDEON LEARNS WHAT IT'S LIKE TO HAVE TWO MASTERS

*T*ate and Ora left the cabin and let the door swing shut behind them. On the bed Ezra and Zeb were looking at each other with a certain intensity. Almost as if they were exchanging angry words but inside their heads.

I cleared my throat and tried to get their attention. "Perhaps we ought to-"

Zeb's hand shot out towards Ezra's throat, fast as he was in his cat form. Ezra caught his arm by the wrist and his eyebrows drew downwards.

"Careful, cat," he said. "You don't want to start something you don't have a hope of winning."

The words sounded angry, dangerous even, but I could see the telltale tug at the corner of Zeb's mouth. The flash of something in Ezra's eyes that said although he meant what he said, he meant it in the context of a game.

My heart sped up. Maybe I could get myself in the middle of this game... sure, I had work to get done but Ezra and Zeb battling for dominance was exciting me in all sorts of ways. I got up from the chair and crossed to the bed.

"Are you two all right?" I asked, although neither of them had broken eye contact.

"Sometimes the top cat needs to be challenged," Zeb said, his voice a low growl.

"Challenge all you like," Ezra said. "I'm top because I'm the best at it. I don't mind showing you all over again, if you need the lesson."

I licked my lips. Yes, I definitely liked the way this conversation was going.

Zeb bared his teeth and hissed a challenge. Ezra twisted his wrist and forced Zeb down and back, moving swiftly to straddle his waist.

"I will not," Zeb bucked under him and reached for his other hand, determined not to be subdued. "I will not be your pet."

"Gideon, the supplies," Ezra growled. Pleased to be involved even in this capacity, I went to the sea chest that held the sugar sack of bondage paraphernalia Ezra kept. Having no idea which items he wanted, and wishing to get quickly back to his side, I took the whole sack and brought to the bed.

While my back had been turned, Zeb had turned the tables somehow, and now he was pressing Ezra back against the wall of the cabin, one claw filled hand caressing at Ezra's throat, the other pinning his hands.

I'd never seen Ezra overpowered by a lover before, and it sent a curious mix of arousal and sickening wrongness through me. Ezra was my Master, he was always in charge. Although in some ways I'd like to take a turn being the one in power, I wasn't sure I was ready for that yet.

Ezra's mouth was twisted into a smirk, and when he saw me over Zeb's shoulder he licked his lips. "I have a better idea than fighting, Zebulon," he said.

"Just because I'm winning," Zeb said. He scratched one claw down Ezra's jaw, and I shivered with anticipation.

"You're not winning," Ezra twisted his arms, breaking free of Zeb's hold and shoving him onto his back with both hands. "But what if we both work out our frustration on Gideon? I don't mind sharing power, I just won't give it up."

Zeb huffed and looked over at me. I'm sure my face showed all my arousal and desire, and his mouth split into a wide grin.

"Go on then, let's see if we can't have him screaming."

With that they both let go of each other and reached for me.

I tried to back away, get away from their grabbing hands, but of course I wanted to be caught - getting involved had been my plan the entire time, and my cock was already straining against my breeches at the thought of both of them dominating me.

"Who says I'm going to let you do that?" I teased, although my voice was breathless.

"You can always say no, pet," Ezra said, his voice a low growl, his face a predatory smile as he advanced on me. I dropped the bag of supplies and backed away. "But I don't believe you want to."

Zeb skirted the cabin, positioning himself between me and the door.

My cock pushed against the fabric of my breeches, aching for touch.

"I don't wish to say no," I said softly.

Zeb's hands caught my waist and I stopped moving, my breath coming fast.

Ezra picked up the bag and sorted through it, pulled out an item I'd not paid attention to before, but which I had surely seen although I didn't remember it. It was a wide, flat piece of leather with a handle.

"What is that?" I asked, as Zeb's pulled me back against his chest and pulled my shirt open, hands roughly stroking over my chest.

"Paddle," Ezra said. "Bit more interesting than spanking with the flat of my hand."

I swallowed, pressing myself back and feeling Zeb's hardness against my rear.

What have I gotten myself into this time?

Zeb's teeth closed on my shoulder without warning and I gasped, half moaning and half protesting at the sudden pain but, reliable as the sunrise, my body took the pain and translated it to arousal and enjoyment.

Ezra grinned, pulled out a coil of rope as well, and while Zeb gripped me hard, keeping me still, he pushed my shirt off my shoulders, and started to loop the ropes around my body, making a tighter, rougher version of my leather harness.

"Move your feet apart, pet," Ezra said. I shuffled my feet a few inches wider apart.

I was already panting hard. Ezra went to his knees, opened my breeches and shoved them down my legs. I stepped out of them, one of my hands moving up to caress Zeb's hair as he bit at my shoulder and up my neck.

I had expected Ezra to lick my cock, but instead I felt rough rope looping between my legs, and he coiled it through the rope around my waist and tightened it.

"What is that?" I asked, shifting my weight from one foot to the other as Ezra ran his fingers down between my legs and adjusted where the rope sat. Finally he was satisfied with the way the rope sat with my genitalia wedged in between, chafing and tugging at me in a new and strangely enjoyable way.

That was when he chose to lean in and lick at me, and I felt myself melting into Zeb's arms.

"Uh-uh," Zeb mumbled in my ear. "You stand up straight and let us play with you."

He pushed me a little off his chest and I dropped my hands to my sides, trying not to fidget as Ezra licked at me.

Zeb scratched his nails down my back, here and there they caught on the ropes webbed around my torso and when one tugged, it sent a chain reaction through all of them, cutting in on my sides, teasing at my testicles and rubbing at the sides of my cock.

I felt the pain and discomfort sparking golden magic through my blood vessels and moaned with happiness. I had wanted to get in between them and I'd definitely managed that. I buried my hand in Ezra's hair as he took the length of me in his mouth, let my head drop down to see his lips touching the rope at the base of my cock.

He pressed his tongue to me as he withdrew, shaking his head free of my hand.

"No touching without permission," he said, his eyes dark. "You need to be punished."

"I thought you were going to spank me anyway," I said. Zeb curled his fingers against my skin between my shoulder blades, wrapping his hand around the knot of ropes and tugging so that it cut in all over my body.

"Good pets don't talk back, and they don't touch without permission," Ezra said. He stood up and glared down at me. I felt myself quail a little under his gaze. "And they address their Masters appropriately."

"I'm sorry, Master," I said, quickly. "I don't have my collar on, I didn't realise it was-"

"Quiet, I don't want to hear excuses," Ezra said. "Zeb, please would you put *our* pet into position for his punishment?"

Zeb's hand, gripping the ropes, propelled me towards the bed.

He shoved me roughly down on it, face first and I scrambled to get my knees under me, thinking he wanted me on hands and knees.

Instead I felt his hand between my shoulder blades again. "Flat on your front, pet," Zeb said. I shivered to hear him use that word for me. Ezra had said masters, plural, and Zeb certainly seemed to be taking to the role. He had of course, been dominant like this with me before - most notably on the day when I was tied to the mast - but this felt like another step into something new I hadn't experienced before. Something that suited Zeb very well indeed.

I lowered myself down as he demanded, then found I didn't know what to do with my hands. Lying them beside me seemed incorrect, so I reached them up beside my shoulders, palm down. I wasn't sure that was comfortable though.

"Restrain his hands?" I heard Zeb ask Ezra. Ezra, where had he gone? I tried to look over my shoulder to see but Zeb's hand pressed down on my head.

"I think so," Ezra said. Then Zeb let go of my head and pulled my hands behind me, folding my arms so I was holding my own elbows, and bound my arms together and to the rope harness there.

Since neither of them was interested in consulting me, I felt a wave of rebellion wash through me, and struggled a little as Zeb bound me. I was rewarded by Ezra gripping my arms and holding them in place as I was bound.

Thoroughly restrained and overpowered, I moaned, dropping down into that place where I could focus entirely on the hedonistic enjoyment of whatever my lovers chose to do to me. The hands let go, as the last knot was secured.

Just as my body relaxed, there was a sound thwack on my rear. The paddle. The flat leather connected squarely with the skin of my rump and I felt it must surely have left a large red mark where it had landed.

I groaned and Ezra rubbed his hand over the mark, making me hiss with the sting of it.

"Is that all right, pet?" He asked, his voice low. Checking in, making sure I was enjoying it and not becoming frightened.

I nodded. "Y-Yes, it's... intense, but... yes."

"Good, it's meant to be punishment after all." I felt them moving about on the bed and then I was being dragged sideways onto Ezra's bended knee, my ass in the air and my head down in the bedclothes.

Zeb pushed my legs apart and I heard the telltale sound of the coconut oil pot. I groaned and prepared myself for the feel of that, when the paddle hit me again, making me tense.

"Let's see if you can take five," Ezra said, hitting me again, rather harder than the time before. I cried out at the hit, which seemed to compile heat onto the already stinging skin and amplify it all until I could only concentrate on that.

Until, that is, Zeb's slick finger slowly pushed inside me.

Then I was in a strange conundrum, stuck between the sudden and unpredictable smack of the paddle and the gentle, insistent push of a finger teasing me open.

I whined and whimpered, squirming against the ropes and closing my eyes tight over the tears that threatened. Not that I was sad, or in unbearable pain, it wasn't that. The tears were from the overwhelming need and desire building inside me.

I'd lost count, but vaguely thought that Ezra had done far more when he put his hand in the small of my back, leaned forward over me.

"How are you holding up, pet? Think you can take another five?"

I hardly knew how to answer. I needed release, but with two masters I knew it was far too soon to ask for such a thing. I whined and swallowed, wanting to please him was battling with the fiery demands of my magic, which wanted more of everything. I could hardly concentrate on the question, as Zeb was now teasing me with two fingers, curling them to hit a spot inside me that curled my toes and made me gasp even more. I had to answer him though.

"Yes, I can," I gasped, my voice rasping. "Master."

"That's a good boy. Ask me for them." I could hear the echo of a laugh in his voice, he must have known how hard talking was becoming for me.

I squeezed my eyes shut and gritted my teeth. "Please, Master," I grated out. "Please hit me with the paddle."

The fingers inside me ceased moving and I groaned with the lack of it.

"Ask me, too," Zeb demanded.

"Please, Master," I puffed. "Please keep spreading me open."

"That's a good pet," Ezra said. "You'll have what you want." The paddle landed on my rear at the same time Zeb spread his fingers and I was reduced to a moaning mess.

I lost track of how long this stretched out, but there were more strikes, and I begged for them, until finally Zeb declared I was ready, and Ezra's hand pressed on the small of my back - no more blows landed.

I sucked in a deep, ragged breath as Ezra's moved from beneath me, and waited for what was next, hardly knowing what to expect.

"Which end would you prefer to use?" Ezra asked Zeb, almost as formally as if he were enquiring after table settings at a fine society dinner.

There was a muffled sound, I cracked open one damp eye to see the two of them kissing, which seemed awfully unfair to me. Here I was bound and ready to be used however they wanted, and they were taking pleasure in each other?

I turned my head a little more to watch as they undressed each other, hands moving all over each other's bodies, and I saw Ezra's hand stroking Zeb's cock. I moved my hips, rutting against the bed as I watched them, needing so much that I was whimpering.

"I think our pet is ready for use," Zeb said, his voice a lower register than normal - the deep predatory timbre that showed his own arousal.

He moved between my legs and pulled my hips up, pressing his cock between the ropes to my stretched and wanting hole.

"Oh, thank the Lord," I mumbled.

"Now, pet," Ezra said. "The Lord isn't here, you should be thanking both of your masters."

"Sorry," I said. "Thank you, Master Zeb!" The last word became rather more of a shout than a word as Zeb shoved his cock deep inside me. He was large, and although he'd stretched me for some time, I felt I was adjusting to him even more than usual. The tug and delicious sting of it flushed my face even redder than it had already been, if such a thing was possible.

"Better," Zeb said, his hand came down with force on what was undoubtedly a red mark left by the paddle and I cried out in surprise at the pain of it.

"Now, lift your chin," Ezra said, his fingers caressing my jaw.

I lifted it as best I could to find him kneeling in front of me. I opened my mouth in anticipation.

"That's a good pet," he said, pushing his cock inside me with a moan of his own.

I went to work licking and caressing it, wishing I was somehow in a better position to watch his face as I pleasured him.

Soon they were both moving their hips and rocking into me, taking pleasure as if I were nothing more than a toy that existed for them to use. I could hear them talking every now and then.

Filled with Zeb's largeness at one end and tasting the delicious tang of Ezra in my mouth, my arms bound and my body wrapped in ropes, I felt my magic flowing into both of them. I could feel their enjoyment of me, heightening what I was already feeling.

My eyes rolled back and I shivered below the both of them, moaning around Ezra's cock.

"I'm close," Zeb grunted, shoving his hips against mine. I slackened my jaw, so that my teeth didn't scrape on Ezra.

I could feel him throbbing against my tongue and I wanted so much to taste him.

"Ready, pet?" Ezra's hand fisted in my hair and held me still. I moaned my approval and he was throbbing and coming in my mouth. I swallowed down every drop and licked him clean as he eased out.

Zeb slammed his hips against me, jolting me hard against Ezra's lap, and then again before he cried out and filled me. He pushed so far inside his hips were tight against my rear, pressing against the hot skin where Ezra had paddled me.

I gasped and bucked against him, yearning for more friction than the rope and the bed, although I wasn't at all sure that I wouldn't just reach completion if Ezra told me to, I hoped I'd feel a hand or mouth instead.

Zeb stroked his hand gently on my hip and came to a rest, easing out of me.

"What now?" Zeb asked.

"We could just leave him," Ezra said, rubbing his fingers through my hair. "It is a punishment... leave him for a bit, come back and do it again."

I groaned - because honestly, I would have let them do it. I wouldn't have called him back or begged him to let me go - because the idea of being left, fucked out and ready for more, ready for any of my lovers to come and find me, it intensified my need and my arousal.

Just waiting, in this impossible predicament, hot and needy for someone to come and use.

Zeb chuckled, then they both flipped me onto my back. Zeb's hand closed around my cock and Ezra's tongue flicked my nipple, his hand teasing at the other one.

"Please, oh please please please, Masters, may I come, please?" I begged, the words falling out of my mouth without bypassing my brain at all.

"Yes, come," Ezra murmured against my chest as Zeb tugged on me extra hard. I came the instant I had permission.

The intensity of it was such that my back arched and my hips shoved into Zeb's hands, my heels dug into the bed and I cried out loudly.

When I relaxed again, I'd somehow ended up back on my front with my face in the sheets. Ezra was already untying my arms, and there was a soft, damp cloth cleaning me - must've been Zeb.

I found my voice after a few minutes. Ezra had removed the ropes from between my legs and was gently unravelling them from my body. Zeb's hands gently massaged my upper arms, which felt absolutely divine.

"That was... incredible," I said, with vehemence.

Ezra chuckled and tugged the last of the ropes free. "Glad you thought so. Wasn't exactly a standard training session, but you did well, pet. And you Zeb."

"You didn't do too badly yourself," Zeb said, and Ezra laughed a little louder.

CHAPTER NINETEEN - IN WHICH MAGIC IS DISCUSSED, AMONG OTHER THINGS

*T*ate's talk with Solomon, or perhaps his request for help had changed something on the ship. Solomon was more often up on deck now, and I even felt emboldened to approach him, even if just to say good morning.

He was often talking to Ora or Zeb, his face relaxing from a furious scowl to a more genial aspect as the days passed. Or rather, as the Grey Kelpie put distance between us and the Splintered Isles.

One such morning he was seated at the prow of the ship, talking to Ora, who was lying in the netting at the bowsprit, enjoying the waves.

I approached him, making sure I wasn't walking softly on the deck so that he'd not be surprised by my speaking. I shouldn't have worried, Ora sensed me and called out.

"Good morning, Gid!"

Smiling, I moved to the bow, leaning against the railings a couple of feet along from Solomon and waved down at Ora. "Hello, Ora! Did you sleep well?"

They beamed up at me, waving happily. Their tail was stretched out full, the deep grey scales catching the morning sunlight and seeming almost to sparkle.

"Yes, very well, found a school of tuna in the night as well, I brought a couple aboard to cook later. How about you?"

"Oh, I'm very well," I said. I cleared my throat and looked between Ora and Solomon. "Actually, I was wondering, hoping really, if I could have a word with Solomon?"

Solomon turned to me and sighed heavily. "Yes, I suppose it's overdue, isn't it?"

I flushed a little, uncertain as to what he was implying, but happy that he'd agreed to speak at the very least.

"I had some questions for you, mostly about magic," I said. "Did you want to uh, go somewhere private or is out here all right?"

Solomon frowned and shook his head. "Here is fine, I don't mind if Ora joins us as well. They have a lot of insight on magical things."

Ora flipped their tail, considering and then shook their head. "No, I think you two need to clear the air with some alone talk."

"Right," I let go of the railings and turned to Solomon. "How to start?"

"Sit first," Solomon said. He went to the low benches we usually used at meal times and sat down. I tried my best not to hesitate before joining him, not wanting to crowd him and make him regret agreeing to this.

"So, uh," I started, then swallowed, this was not the time to get tongue tied, but it also wasn't the time to fall back on my etiquette training and get overly formal. Uncertain of what to say with those two options ruled out I blurted the first thing that came to mind. "Tell me about magic?"

I dropped my eyes and sighed as Solomon's eyes widened and he let out a surprised bark of a laugh.

"I suppose I'm curious as to what you want to know," he said, slowly. "Seems to me as if you're well versed enough in your own powers."

"Perhaps." I swallowed and looked up at him. "You can walk in dreams, you can give people certain dreams, ones that make them want to stay asleep... you were in touch with the Navy while you were trapped on an island, I..." I shook my head. "How does any of that work?'

Solomon met my gaze and held it, his unnatural ability to stare and not blink making my heart rate increase as if I was in danger. I didn't believe I was, but his gaze was so piercing I found myself unable to look away. My body tensed.

He blinked and I was released, I breathed deeply and tried to relax.

"When I first started to use magic, I was a child," he said. "I won't bore you with the details, but small elemental tricks and walking in dreams were my skills. My first toys to play with."

"That must have alarmed your parents," I ventured, uncertain to how much Solomon wanted to share with me. This could easily have been prying. He shook his head.

"My mother was a witch, it was expected. As I grew, I learned more of what the dreams meant, and how to walk in them." He relaxed a little, leaned his arm on the railings of the ship and gave me a soft smile. "The rest came with time and with access to the source of power at the Splintered Isles. The Naval communication system, well. It wasn't set up by me, that was other witches, one assumes the Navy commissioned it from local witches. I was able to see what the network was, and use it for my own means."

He looked away, and I followed his gaze to Tate - standing at the helm. His hair loosened, blowing gently in the wind, his white shirt half open to show his expansive chest. Even though I was used to him, and how handsome he was, it still struck me with how he looked like the description of the pirate hero in one of my favourite romance stories.

"I'd do whatever I could to get him back, too," I said, softly.

"You already did," Solomon said. "More than once, I believe. The Trinity Royal and then the Isles…"

"Oh," I blushed. Two times I had thwarted Solomon's plans. I swallowed, feeling all elbows and knees as I adjusted how I was sitting.

How awkward to bring that up.

"Is that all you wanted to ask me?" Solomon said, not unkindly.

"No, I suppose…" I took a breath and tried to gather my thoughts. "I suppose I wanted to ask what you thought it meant to have magic inside you. I didn't grow up with it, it's only in the last month or so I've come to understand the truth about myself, my heritage. I don't know what it means, for me."

I thought for a moment, to how he would have responded to this question previously, back on the Isles where his darker emotions were amplified by the magic there, by the Isles own unknowable desires to hold him. But this wasn't then.

He pursed his lips, tipped his head back and shrugged. "I really don't know. I'd have to take a look through my books, or perhaps you'd like to. Coming into a fae power is… well, it's not entirely unheard of, but it's very unusual. The merfolk are fae, obviously, and there are other sorts. I've heard of selkies and kelpies around the coast of Ireland and Scotland. But in human society, so rare as to be impossible to find."

"You should have been a scholar," I said, impressed by his knowledge and vocabulary and not afraid to say so.

He chuckled and swung his head back around to look at me. "I would have loved to go to university, but my family didn't have the money or the connections."

I bit my lower lip. "Maybe… depending on how things go with my father, perhaps we can do something about that."

Solomon shook his head and looked out at the ocean. "If I've learned nothing else from my time on the Isles, it's that isolation is a bad state for me, it allows certain things to fester. I should like to stay close to Tate, as long as I'm able," he said.

I smiled, feeling affection grow in my chest. I couldn't help but admire him, he had adjusted quickly to life on the ship, and his dedication to Tate was impressive. More than those two things though, I genuinely commended the work he had done on his own mind. Or perhaps, his attitude to himself.

I could only imagine how easy it could be for him to assume that the rest of us were beneath him, or that his actions had been justified. But Solomon had chosen the far less easy route, and examined himself with a critical eye. Now he was opening himself up to us, and to new experiences.

"That's a good decision, I think," I said. He looked at me sharply and shook his head.

"I cannot understand how you have so little jealousy in you," he said. "I've struggled with it, when it comes to you. It hurt to have been replaced, but... you don't seem to have any concern at all."

"Because I don't," I said. I took a breath and tried to frame my thoughts in a way that would make sense to explain. "I suppose it could be the incubus part of me, or it could be my nature, I'm not sure. But I can see how much love Tate has in his heart. I can see that his loving me doesn't rule out love for you, or for Ezra, or Ora, or Zeb. He has the capacity to love so much, so many. It feels... it feels it would be selfish of me to demand that he kept it to himself, or just to me."

Solomon stared into my face as if searching for something, then finally he nodded. "Yes, it does make sense. As an incubus you have a lot more sensitivity to love and to the feelings of others. If that's what you see, then I accept it."

"It is," I said, simply. And without considering, I put my hand on his forearm and gently squeezed it.

He didn't flinch away, although he did tense under my

fingers. He inhaled sharply and then let it out in a slow breath out his mouth.

"Thank you, Gideon," he said slowly. "I'm truly sorry for the ways I hurt you. I know it'll be some time before you can forgive me, but please know that I'm trying to change for the better."

"I know you are, and I do forgive you." I pulled my hand back and pushed it through my hair, meeting his gaze. "I understand what happened, and I don't blame you for how you acted."

He shook his head impatiently. "It's too soon to forgive me, Gideon."

"Well, you can pretend I didn't say it, if you like," I said. "But I do."

His eyes widened and he took another slow breath. "You really are incredible. I can understand a little of how you've managed to create a workable situation with four lovers now."

It was an odd compliment, to be sure, but it was a compliment all the same, and I couldn't resist smiling. A compliment from Solomon? I might only ever get a handful of those in my entire lifetime.

"Thank you. I hope that in some way we can eventually be friends."

"Perhaps," he said, but his tone didn't hold a lot of hope for me.

CHAPTER TWENTY - IN WHICH THE ROYAL NAVY IS EVADED

$\mathcal{A}$s we left the waters surrounding the Splintered Isles, the problem of the British Navy came up again. No sails had been sighted, but Ezra and Tate felt it was only a matter of time and none of us could disagree with them.

"There's no way to Jamaica that won't take us into the path of the Navy," Ezra said. "It's a colony, they're always patrolling, or shipping back and forth doing whatever they do."

Ezra, Tate, Sagorika and I were in Tate's cabin, maps open on the desk and little time to make a decision. Sagorika paced up and down the cabin, her skirts swirling around her legs every time she turned.

"Maybe there's something Solomon can do," Tate said, uncertainly. "I'll go and get him."

I went to look at the map myself, purely for something to do - I was certain there was nothing Ezra would have missed, but just in case...

Tate reappeared with Solomon, who was wearing what appeared to be one of Ezra's old shirts.

"I'm not sure why you've dragged me up here," he said testily. He looked around all of us and the map. "You all look absolutely beaten down. That should make me happy, but somehow it doesn't any more."

I thought I saw the ghost of a smile around his lips, and looked back down at the map so he wouldn't see my corresponding smile.

"We need to get to Kingston undetected," Ezra said. "For *some reason* the British fleet have been a step ahead of us lately, and we don't wish to have any run ins."

Solomon folded his arms and bared his teeth at Ezra. "How very odd."

"Are you able to tap into the network, the uh, the witch message system the Navy were using?" Tate asked.

Solomon pursed his lips, narrowed his eyes and then tapped two fingers on his chin. "I would say yes, of course, I know how it works and I can get into it easily, but that was when I was on the Splintered Isles. I don't have access to that power any longer."

"Wait, why are we using the witch message system?" Ezra asked, looking between Tate and Solomon. "I don't think an order from us saying to stand down and not attack the Kelpie is going to work."

Tate frowned. "Perhaps if we could get a message to Governor Keene?" he said. He turned me with one hand on my shoulder. "Do you think that would work, Gid?"

I tried to imagine Father receiving some message from me, saying I was all right and not to worry, through a magical communication network and shook my head. "He still believes you kidnapped me, he'd think it was a ruse or something."

"Solomon could visit him in a dream, he could take you with him," Tate said.

I chewed on my bottom lip. "He's... I don't think he'd set much stock in dreams, even what appears to be magical ones," I said, slowly. I hated that these easier approaches didn't seem to be feasible. I hated that I felt like I was shooting down their solutions. "I really think I need to be there with him. Look him in the eyes."

Ezra sighed and Tate dropped his hand from my shoulder. "Right. So we have to get through their lines."

There was a long stretch of silence, everyone trying to come up with some kind of solution that would solve this particularly thorny problem.

"Solomon, you made us believe that there were Naval ships chasing us," Sagorika said, finally. She twisted her mouth to the side and her eyebrows drew together. "Could you make our ship appear to be a Naval one?"

"I don't have the same power I did on the Isles," Solomon said, folding his arms. He sighed. "If I did, I could simply cloak the ship in an illusion."

"But we have others on the ship with magic," Tate said. "What if you all cast something together, would that work?"

Ezra shrugged, folding his arms.

Solomon made a considering noise, a sort of long drawn out 'hmmmm.'

"Assuming they trust me enough to let me guide them in a spell," Solomon said slowly. "Perhaps it might work."

"There's Gideon, and Ora, of course. Who else?"

Sagorika raised a hand. "I have some power, mostly only trained in the healing arts, but..."

Solomon crossed to her, one hand raised. Sagorika pulled a knife. "What are you doing?"

"I was going to test the level of magic residing in you," Solomon said. He let his hand drop to his side. "Wasn't it obvious?"

"It wasn't," Sagorika said. "How do you check?"

"I'd have to look into your mind. I can do it with a touch and a little time."

Ezra moved his weight from one foot to the other, his hand going to the hilt of his sword.

Sagorika slowly sheathed her knife again. She hadn't broken eye contact with Solomon and it felt like there was a communication happening between them, something unsaid, some kind of power play.

"How would they know if you were doing something untoward?" Sagorika asked, her eyebrow raising elegantly.

"Ora would know," Ezra said immediately.

"Gid?" Tate put his hand on my shoulder and squeezed. "Would you know?"

I bit my lip and shrugged a little. "I can sense magic being used, so... maybe?"

"We could just wait for Ora," Ezra said.

"No, it's fine," Sagorika snapped. "Do it. I'm not afraid of him. Go on then."

She tilted her chin up and stared into his eyes. Solomon, almost tentatively, lifted his hand and placed his first two fingers on her forehead.

I felt *something* but it wasn't the same as the hexes or control spells I could remember Solomon doing.

I put my hand on Tate's, feeling the link we had and letting the love stir my magic a little. Then I felt more clearly the *intention* of what Solomon was doing. It was nothing more than what he'd said. He was sensing what was inside Sagorika, and I thought I heard, or perhaps I just imagined that I heard, the slight sound of Sagorika's magic responding to Solomon.

My mouth went dry. I had no idea I was capable of that...

Solomon pulled his hand gently away and Tate let go of me at the same moment. Solomon turned to Tate and I saw a smile that must surely have been the echo of the smile he'd won Tate's heart with all those years ago.

"You know, I think this might work," he said, almost sounding excited.

. . .

So that night, under the light of the crescent moon, we gathered on the foredeck. Ora held my hand, reassuring me silently, although for once I didn't feel worried. I felt curiously serene about our plan, quite confident that Solomon would do as he said.

Sagorika had brought out some candles and sturdy candlesticks and lit them to make a diamond shape. Tate watched carefully, like all sailors he was very wary of naked flame on the wooden deck.

The rest of the crew were watching as well. Rumours had spread across the ship like the fire Tate feared, and everyone knew that the goal of this ritual was to cloak the ship to make it unrecognisable to the British Navy.

I didn't myself know exactly how that would happen, but Solomon had spent several hours reading and planning it out, and now we were gathered to do it.

"Sagorika and Gideon you take the East and West points," Solomon said. "Ora and I will take North and South, respectively."

I squeezed Ora's hand and they walked to their appointed place, standing just behind the candle.

"What about me?" Zeb asked, yawning as he sauntered up.

Solomon blinked at him, tilted his head and frowned. "Yes, all right."

We'd all sort of forgotten about Zeb - he must've been napping somewhere, possibly up in the crow's nest. But of course, he had magic of his own now. It was somehow gifted from Solomon but he had control of it.

"Into the middle of the diamond," Solomon directed. Zeb shifted into cat form and took his place in the centre. I moved to my spot and smiled at Sagorika. She winked at me.

The crew were murmuring and moving about and Solomon turned, his eyes blazing. "Silence! If you're going to watch you can keep still and your mouths shut."

As one the crew went still and silent. Not from a magical effect, it was just a natural response to Solomon's intensity.

"Focus your attention on the candle in front of the person opposite you, Zeb, you just... do what feels right," Solomon said, turning back to those of us in the ritual. "Let it fill your mind, and when I speak the words, repeat them."

I breathed out slowly, let my eyes drop to the candle in front of Sagorika and did as Solomon said.

Look at the fire, the fire is all that matters. Flame, flickering, fragile but dangerous.

Solomon spoke a strange word, and I repeated it. I heard Ora and Sagorika do the same. Zeb mewed softly.

Then I sort of lost sense of time. I was focused so strongly on the flame, and I could feel my magic unfurling within me, responding to Solomon's words, and the words I was speaking. I could see the links between us in the diamond, a soft shimmering green fire - Solomon's - which was the strongest. Then there was a sparkling silver, emanating from Ora's end of the diamond, twining through Solomon's. I saw a golden light, which was mine, I recognised it from all the times I'd seen it in my mind's eye. It wasn't as strong at first, as it flowed from me, but when it touched Ora's it gained strength.

Sagorika's seemed for a moment as if it wouldn't emerge, but with a particular word, which Sagorika said louder than the rest of us, sounding annoyed, her warm bronze magic came out with a powerful burst.

Zeb's power didn't appear to me, but I felt him in the middle - almost anchoring the spell, the centre point of all the power.

Once we'd repeated the occult refrain seven times, all of our magics tracing the outline of the diamond and intersecting it, over Zeb's head, Solomon spoke in English.

"They shall not recognise this ship as the Grey Kelpie. It will be an innocent merchant ship, nothing more and nothing less. Certainly not anything to stir any suspicion, or any attention at all. Any who may wish harm on any soul on this ship shall see this ship and think nothing of it. So mote it be."

Instinctively, I repeated the final phrase. "So mote it be."

The others repeated it, too, and I was surprised to hear the crew murmur it too, even Ezra.

The magic lines of light abruptly vanished, and I found myself looking up from the candle flame. The spell was done, and I felt the weight of it settle over the ship.

"Did it work?" Tate asked. "I feel I hardly have to ask, but..."

Solomon shrugged. "I believe it did, but we won't know until it's tested, I suppose."

CHAPTER TWENTY-ONE - IN WHICH THE GREY KELPIE TAKES A SHIP

*W*e were five days from the Splintered Isles, making good time for Kingston, when Anton came running into the captain's cabin. Tate was tidying his beard with a straight razor, his face covered in foamy soap.

Zeb was stretched out on the bed, refusing to wake up, and I was at Tate's desk, making some notes and updating the ship's log.

"Yes, Anton?" Tate asked, raising his eyebrows. "You should really knock."

"I could hear that you weren't uh…" Anton flushed, looking at me and then at the bed. "There weren't any noises coming from the room, so I knew you weren't busy. With… things."

"What is it?" Tate asked. He set his razor down and picked up a towel.

"Ezra sent me to tell you there's a sail sighted, from the West. Flying a Spanish flag. Looks to be La Tortuga Voladora."

"Ah!" Tate wiped the soap off his face with the towel, which made me cringe, since it would no doubt be my job to wash the thing, and then grinned wide. "And is it sitting low in the water?"

"Too far off to say for sure," Anton said, grinning back at him. "But I'd wager it is."

"Excellent. Have Ezra prepare the Jolly Roger and we'll see if we can't make some money today."

"Aye, aye, Captain!" Anton said, and fled the room. Tate smacked his lips and clapped his hands together once.

"Gid, is there space in the hold for some treasure?" Tate went to the chest where he kept his clothes and pulled out some items.

"I.. uh, there's less space since we picked up Solomon, but yes, there is," I said. I blew on the wet ink and stood up. "Are we attacking the Spanish ship, then?"

"Aye, lad. If we're lucky she'll be heavy with gold we can relieve her of. Zeb, wake up!" He leaned over the bed to say this to Zeb, who startled awake and looked up at him with wide eyes.

"What *is* your problem?!" Zeb grumbled.

"We're taking a Spanish galleon," Tate said. "Your prowess in battle is required."

Zeb stretched and yawned, as if pretending he hadn't been woken a second before. He sniffed and examined his fingernails. "Yes, I think I can help."

I laughed softly. It was incredible to see them together, so comfortable. Tate appealing to Zeb's ego because he knew that was how to get him to agree. Watching them interact, I saw how much they cared for each other, how much they knew each other.

Privately, I was sure there'd be no way to keep Zeb out of the fight anyway, but it was still lovely to see.

Tate turned to me. I saw a slight hesitation in his face, a moment when he considered telling me to stay put. I felt a wave of... not exactly concern but more like a flash of fear off him, which was immediately put aside.

"Gideon, it's up to you if you want to be involved or not," he said. Then he smiled. "I won't lie, I'd be happier if you stayed safe in here, but it's up to you. I won't hold you back or lock you in."

"Thank you," I said. My heart thumped with pride. "I know I can't kill anyone, but the idea of sitting here and not knowing what's happening to any of you while the battle rages is unbearable. So, maybe I'll come out, but sort of hang back a little, if that's all right?"

He leaned in and kissed me on the lips. "Sounds good to me. Now, help me with my coat."

"With pleasure."

I held his most impressive grey brocade coat out for him and he slipped into it. Reaching up, I tugged it on his shoulders so it sat correctly and stepped back with a nod. "Very impressive."

"Got to look the part," Tate said.

"I'd surrender to you," I said. Tate winked at me and picked up his pistols and sabre.

Zeb jumped to his feet. "Come on, let's fight!"

As we approached the Spanish galleon, it became clear even to the naked eye that it was riding low in the water. Weighted with treasure.

Once we were close enough that they couldn't run, Tate gave the order to run up the Jolly Roger - warning them that we intended to attack and they could surrender or fight.

Ezra was at the helm, a hardness to his expression that for a moment made me sympathetic to the poor Spanish sailors, they were about to come up against the crew of the Kelpie and I hoped that they would surrender, rather than fight.

"What's happening?" I turned to see Solomon approaching from below deck.

"Spanish ship." I pointed.

"Ah." Solomon's face lit up and he went to stand beside Tate. "Do you want me to do something to subdue them?"

Tate glanced at him and then looked back at the ship. "No, I don't think it'll be needed, but... well, if the battle goes badly..."

"Of course."

Ora caught me around the waist and squeezed me. Their chin resting on my shoulder. "You're going to fight?"

"Well, not... not in the main attack," I said. I tried not to feel like it made me a coward, but I knew it was the right decision for me. "I can't kill someone, even if it comes down to it, and I'd rather not be someone others have to be looking out for."

Ora kissed my cheek and let go. "Good choice, but I'll be looking out for you anyway."

"Thanks, Ora."

We armed ourselves from the ship's supply of weaponry, and gathered as Tate addressed the crew. He emphasised that if someone was surrendering, we would let them. That the goal was the treasure, not the number of people killed.

The Spanish ship opened fire on us with its cannons, but Ezra had already angled the Kelpie to avoid the firing.

As we had a fair bit of speed up from the approach I wondered if his plan was to ram them, but we angled further and ropes were thrown over to the La Tortuga Voladora to secure them to us. This way they couldn't escape, and we wouldn't be chasing them further. The Kelpie's crew were quick and frighteningly efficient, especially since it had been weeks since we'd attacked any ships at all. However, all of them knew their role and the job was done in mere seconds. The momentum of the Kelpie threatened for a moment to tear us away from the Tortuga, but the ropes held, and it was dragged with us for a moment before but the ropes held.

Gangplanks were laid between the two ships and secured.

Tate led the charge, dangling from a rope secured to the yardarm of the mast, he swung from the Kelpie to the La Tortuga Voladora with a frightening war cry.

The Spanish captain shouted orders to his crew, and rushed

to meet Tate, their swords clanging together. Tate bore down on him, and then I lost sight of them. The Kelpie's crew flowed over the gangplanks and dove into a frenzy of battle with the Spanish.

They were not a military ship - that much was clear - but they fought valiantly, with fierce passion. However, from my safe vantage point on the Kelpie I could see that they were outnumbered and outmatched.

Zeb cut a swathe through the enemy with little difficulty, howling like a demon from the pits of Hell.

I caught sight of Ora, tackling someone to the ground and a brief, aborted cry of their victim.

My heart was pleased at least, that Ezra had chosen to stay back and man the helm, so I didn't have to worry about him. I kept my eyes on the others and on the gangplanks, if any of the Spanish tried to board the Kelpie, it would be up to me to fend them off.

I heard a cry and a curse. Recognising the voice, I struggled to find Sagorika in the melee. Finally I found her, running a man through, her left arm hanging to one side, blood soaking her shirtsleeve.

"Retirarse estamos! Superados en número!" the captain cried out.

There was swearing in Spanish but the men fighting all dropped their swords and raised their hands.

"Stand down!" Tate roared over the sound of the clattering steel. He had his own sword to the throat of the Spanish captain, who was eyeing him in fear and anger.

He grinned at the man, then turned his attention to the others. "Round up the prisoners and keep them at the stern. Zack, James and Zeb you guard them. Ora, take Sagorika back to the Kelpie when... when you're done. I'm going to see what this ship holds in its belly."

Anton hurried along with Tate. I shook my head as two people joined me on the deck.

"He always tries to go alone," Ezra said, tutting his tongue against his teeth.

"I'd have thought he'd have learned better by now," Solomon said. "Ridiculous."

I went to the gangplank to help as Sagorika climbed up from the Spanish side. Ora, with a smear of blood over their mouth, boosted her from behind.

"I'm fine," she said, testily. "It's hardly even a scratch." But she took my hands and leaned on me as she climbed down.

"It looks like a lot of blood," I said, and slipped my arm around her waist. She leaned on my shoulder with her good arm.

"I can take care of that," Solomon said. He held a hand out. Sagorika looked at it warily.

"Take care as in amputate? Enslave me with a sample of my blood? What is it you intend to do, exactly?"

I could feel Sagorika trembling against me, her usually firm grip weak and her fingers scrabbling at me. Solomon rolled his eyes.

"No, I was going to clean and bind it, put a healing on it so you stop losing blood."

"I don't trust you, sea witch," Sagorika said.

"Let's just, go into your cabin and see what Solomon can do," I said. "He's not done a thing to hurt any of us since he joined the ship, after all."

Ezra cleared his throat and Sagorika looked at him. "You can't tell me you trust him," she said.

"Well, no, I don't trust him," Ezra said. "But he's the best magic user on the ship, including yourself, and Ora's a little busy with... what Ora does after a battle, so you might as well give him a chance."

"I'll be with you," I said. "And I love you Sagorika, like a sister, and that should protect you from any wrongdoing anyway."

"Well?" Solomon rolled his eyes and crossed his arms. I had the feeling he was about to rescind his offer.

"Fine," Sagorika said.

Solomon was as good as his word. Sagorika's wound was deep and ragged, far nastier than she had claimed it was, but Solomon cleaned it carefully with a damp cloth, then spoke some words over it. I thought I recognised them from hearing Sagorika use them herself in the past.

I didn't feel anything strange in the magic atmosphere, just the power Solomon had, being used to bind up sinew and blood vessel. Then he carefully wrapped the wound in a clean bandage and tied it off.

"Don't strain it for a day or so," he said, as he sat back. "It might tear the magic off it. Try not to sleep on that side, either."

Sagorika's expression had slowly relaxed as he had worked. Sagorika's own magic was nothing like as strong as Solomon's but surely she could have sensed it in the same way I did.

He had kept his word, and helped and healed her.

"You did well," she said. "Thank you."

Solomon nodded and washed his hands in the water basin before picking it up. "I'll dump this overboard. Rest if you can, it will help to seal it in."

She nodded and rose as well, moving to her bed as Solomon left the room.

I helped her into bed and made sure she was comfortable before following him out. Ezra caught my eye as I stepped back out onto the deck, there was a question there. I nodded and gave a half smile.

"She'll be fine, Solomon healed it nicely."

There were shouts and laughter from the Spanish ship, and I

saw that chests had been brought up to the deck, the crew were working to haul them up to the gangplanks and over to the Kelpie. Ezra and I went to assist with lowering them to the deck on our side.

Tate appeared, carrying a chest on his own, his face flushed and beaming. "Treasure ship, lads! We're rich!"

CHAPTER TWENTY-TWO - IN WHICH TATE AND GIDEON CELEBRATE

The Spanish ship was relieved of its treasure chests, a few barrels of wine, and sides of pork before Tate ordered the crew of La Tortuga Voladora below deck. He locked them in the brig with the key nearby - near enough to reach if they worked together. He ordered the ropes loosened and gangplanks retrieved and we cut ourselves free.

The crew of the Grey Kelpie celebrated into the night, singing and drinking and cheering - recounting their daring deeds and close shaves with enemy steel.

Solomon retired first after only a little time of celebration. I couldn't imagine how hard it was to adjust to such a large group of people after being alone for so long. I hoped it wasn't too loud below deck.

Once the stars were all out, Tate pulled me tight against his side. "With the treasure we took today, we're well on our way to retiring," Tate said. "We can buy whatever we want in Jamaica. What do you want, Gideon?"

"I want..." I stretched my legs out, trying to think. Obviously Tate wasn't talking about our bigger problems, he wanted to know if he could buy me a new coat, or some pretty bauble. I couldn't think of anything much I needed. "Hmmm."

"Anything you want, my love."

"Our house on the cliff, overlooking the sea?" I asked, looking up at the stars and thinking fondly of my dreams. "We'd have to have it larger than I thought, make room for Solomon, maybe he could even have a separate wing?"

Tate kissed my cheek hard, smushing my face a little until I giggled. "You're so selfless. That house, with room for Solomon, that's something you want for all of us. What do you want for you?"

Selfless, I'm not sure if that's the word for me, but if he wants a selfish wish then I'm sure I can oblige.

My mind wandered to the bedroom, and I thought of the delightful session I'd had with Ezra and Zeb. But not that... I didn't want that again. Time alone with Tate would be nice. Just the two of us.

In fact, maybe this is the time for something I've been wishing for... something I've imagined on and off for a long time, but never quite managed to obtain.

"I see a smile full of promise," Tate said.

"How would you feel about a little time alone, just you and me," I said slowly. I turned so I could murmur into his ear. "I'd like to try something with you we haven't exactly done."

Tate pulled me closer with his hand around my waist.

"That's what I was hoping you'd say, Gid."

He stood up, pulling me with him. I almost spilled my cup of wine. "Whoops!"

"Give it to me," Zack said, laughing. He was already flushed with the wine, and Anton had his arm around him, singing softly. "I'll take good care of it for you, Gideon."

"Goodnight, fair crew of mine!" Tate said, raising his cup of rum and downing it as the crew cheered. "You've made us all rich today, and you deserve to celebrate! And so do I. Please excuse me, as I take my cabin boy to bed!"

The crew cheered again and I flushed with happiness,

laughing along with them. Tate tugged me into the cabin and locked the door behind him.

"Right, love, we're alone, as requested. What did you have in mind?" His hands were tugging at my shirt, unlacing the front of it.

I licked my lips. Now that we were here, alone, I felt a little flutter of nervousness. But Tate was in a good mood, I was sure he'd agree.

"I'd like to try and, uh, be in charge of you," I said, feeling embarrassed not because of what I was asking but because my words had largely failed me. I cleared my throat and tried again. "Like Ezra does with me, when he's my master. Ever since we first..."

"Fucked," Tate supplied. His eyes were twinkling, and my heart fluttered.

He's going to say yes!

"Right, yes, since then, I've wondered what it would be like to have you tied down, under me. Letting me have my way with you."

Tate nodded and kissed me softly. "Absolutely. I can't promise I'll be any good at it, but I trust you, Gid."

"And uh." My mind raced, thinking back to the things Ezra said to me. "You can say no at any time, and we can stop, or I can stop what it is that you don't like."

Tate nodded and smiled, pushing my shirt back from my shoulders and reaching down to undo my breeches.

"I understand. So, how do we start?"

I licked my lips, nervous and excited that he'd given me permission, that he'd agreed to let this happen. "You should take your clothes off, then get onto the bed."

"Right." Tate stepped back and started to strip. I stepped out of my breeches and left them pooled on the floor with my shirt. I went to the sea chest where Ezra stored the supplies and opened it.

For a moment, I hesitated, the range of things there was a little confounding. Then I thought of the saddlery in Tortuga where all these supplies came from, and Ezra saying the thick collar was too big for me, but maybe for Tate?

I went to my knees and took my time sorting through the stuff. I pulled out the heavy, black leather collar. There were leather cuffs that matched, so I took those too, and some chains and padlocks to connect them.

Feeling a little more confident, I got up and went to the bed, pleased to see that Tate was sitting on the bed, his legs crossed and utterly naked. His face was warm and trusting, smiling softly.

"I suppose it feels a bit strange," I said, in order to get the awkwardness out of the way up front. "I know I don't look like Ezra, I don't have his build, and I'm definitely not bigger or stronger than you..."

Tate shook his head. "But I know you're an incredible lover," Tate said. "And I trust you to make this amazing. I'll do what you say."

I knelt on the bed in front of him and fastened the collar around his neck. Ezra had been right, it looked amazing on him. The black echoed with the black swirls and waves of the tattoos on his shoulder and down his arm. The size of the collar suited the breadth of his chest and shoulders and I felt myself salivating as I looked at him.

"How does it feel?" I asked, again, thinking of how Ezra spoke to me when we did this kind of thing.

Tate nodded, reached a hand up to touch the leather and smiled. "Strange, not bad but... unusual."

I hooked a finger through the loop in the collar and pulled him in for a kiss. It was one of the things Ezra had done to me once or twice, and I wished he'd do more. Tate made a surprised noise, but kissed me back with a moan.

"Now, lie back and reach your arms up over your head." I

said, feeling a little more confident. He obeyed, laying down on the bed. I watched the muscles in his arms ripple as he reached up and then relaxed, his arms over his head.

"You're so beautiful," I breathed. Then I realised I ought to be terse and vaguely angry like Ezra was when he was my Master. I cleared my throat and straddled his middle, leaning up and over him to secure the cuffs on his wrists.

It was awkward leaning over him like that, and I fumbled a little, buckling the cuffs on him.

Maybe I should have done this before I told him to put his arms up? That would have made it easier on me, anyway. Ah well, remember for next time.

"You look very serious," Tate said, leaning up to kiss my nipple, which was easy due to where I was leaning over him. I gasped in surprise, and then leaned into his mouth because it felt absolutely divine.

"Ezra's always serious when he does it," I said, my voice breathless and not at all gruff.

"You're not Ezra," Tate said. His arm went around my waist and he pulled me close against him, kissing me hard.

I whined softly as I kissed him back, because of course he was right. The thing I wanted wasn't to become Ezra - it was to have Tate under me, squirming and helpless while I fucked him.

I bit my lip, pulled back from the kiss and grinned at him. "You're not supposed to touch me without permission."

"You didn't say that was a rule," he said. We shared a quick laugh, and then I took hold of his wrist and pinned it over his head.

Working as quick as I could manage, and leaning in to press my chest against his face, letting him lick and suck and pleasure me as much as he wished - because it felt like an indulgence. Like I was using him as something purely for my own enjoyment. Like Zeb and Ezra had used me.

I moaned, looped the chain around one of the posts at the

head of the bed, and locked the cuffs to the chain. Reluctantly, I pulled back from his mouth and grinned down at him.

"Can you get away from that?"

Tate tipped his head back to look at how he was bound and then tugged against it. I could see his biceps and the muscles in his chest move at the strain of it, but he stayed bound.

"No, I can't, Gid."

A heady powerful feeling filled me and I ground down on his hardness with my rear until he moaned. "Good. Sit tight while I get the oil."

It was never far away from the bed, these days, but I still had to get off him to reach it. I took my time, letting him wait, before I turned back, oil in hand, and climbed up between his legs, hitching them so his feet were flat on the bed and his knees in the air.

I dipped my fingers into the oil, moved in close and started to tease at him, my eyes roaming all over his body as he gasped and struggled.

The thrill of seeing such a huge, muscular man bound and at my mercy shot something deliciously dark through me. I felt my cock throbbing with need and my mouth splitting into what had to be a wicked grin to rival Ezra's.

I slipped my finger inside him, taking my time to stretch him open.

Tate arched his back, tipping his head against the bed and whined. "Gideon, please, more," he gasped.

The feeling of power spiked and I felt my magic flare in my stomach. Apparently the fae blood enjoyed being the one in control as much as I enjoyed giving my control up to my lovers. I felt Tate's need and my heart sped up.

His pleasure is mine to give or withhold.

I slipped another finger inside him. "More like that? Was that what you wanted?" I teased, leaning in to bite his jaw, scraping my teeth on his skin.

He groaned, closing his eyes. I kissed him, pressing down hard and using the kiss to dominate at the same time I curled my fingers inside him, making him moan.

Unable to resist the heightened emotions and need I felt from Tate, I rutted against his thigh, groaning at the friction on my cock.

"I... I want to feel you inside me," he gasped. I pressed into him with my fingers and then slowly withdrew them, teasing him as much as I could.

I took a generous amount of oil and slicked my cock. Tate opened his eyes and watched me. I could see the hunger in his eyes, and feel the desire pulsating off him and enveloping me, spurring me to tease him more.

My hand slowed on my cock and I pushed myself further up on my knees so Tate could see more of what I was doing. His eyes watched my hand go up and down, and I moaned loudly, exaggerating my noises just to see how he'd react.

It was blissful, he arched and moaned and I felt his desire tugging at me. Finally, I took pity on him and pushed my cock inside him, agonisingly slow.

At this point, I was torturing myself as well as him. I felt sweat bead on my forehead. I exalted as I pushed deep inside him.

"Thank fuck," Tate groaned. I leaned in and bit his lower lip.

"Mind your language, prisoner," I teased, emphasising my words with a shove of my hips.

"Ohhhh fu-" Tate swallowed. "Gideon, that feels so good. Please can you touch my cock, please?"

"Not yet," I said. I felt a little lightheaded. "I'm using you for my own pleasure."

Tate groaned as if I'd stroked his cock and I felt how much he was enjoying it through the way his body squeezed and pulsed around me. I could feel it through his emotions as well, the magical connection, heightened by my excitement over being dominant, echoing his pleasure over mine.

"Do you want to come?" I asked, leaning in to bite his shoulder and exalting in the shiver I drew from him.

"Yes, God, please, Gideon, please, please let me come!"

His voice cracked with need and I felt a wave of indulgent affection for him. This massive, dangerous man bound and begging for me. I almost came myself in that moment, but I bit down again to hold it back.

"Just a little longer, my darling," I said. I pushed my hand between us and stroked his cock, feeling it slick with his anticipatory spending. I gasped with my own need. "Come now!"

Obediently, he bucked and his cock throbbed in my hand, spurting wetness between us. His body squeezed my cock and I couldn't have held back if I'd tried. I arched my back, tossing my head as I filled him and moaned my pleasure.

We kept moving for a few more moments, Tate milking the last of my orgasm out of me.

Finally I pulled out of him, both of us groaning with the loss of connection and the way my magic ebbed away the intensity of the orgasm.

"How was that, love?" I asked, almost feeling shy now that it was all over. I leaned up to undo the bindings before snuggling into his side.

"Absolutely incredible," he said. "You can do that again whenever you want. Ezra's taught you some pretty fun things, hasn't he?"

"He has." I kissed his jaw and cheek, then nuzzled him the way Zeb nuzzled me. Then a thought occurred to me and I swore quietly.

"What? What's wrong?"

"Nothing, I just realised. I should have left you bound and called Ezra in to have fun with you."

Tate moaned softly and I saw his softening cock twitch once. "Maybe you should have. He'd have enjoyed that, and I'm sure I would have as well."

"Next time, that's a promise," I said. I pushed myself up on my elbow to kiss him on the lips and seal the promise. "I love you Tate."

"I love you too, Gideon, you marvellous treasure."

I chuckled. "You're just using that word because of all the gold we took today."

"No, you're the greatest treasure," he said, and kissed me again.

CHAPTER TWENTY-THREE - IN WHICH GIDEON IS REACQUAINTED WITH KINGSTON, JAMAICA

*a*s we approached Jamaica, and the Port of Kingston I felt a wave of something I hadn't expected. Homesickness.

Although I had long since come to think of the Grey Kelpie as my home, apparently some part of my heart was still attached to Kingston and I felt a curious hope in my chest. The familiarity of the buildings on the waterfront, the smells and the trees... it was all part of who I was. Who I had been.

I heard Tate shouting for everyone to be on guard. Confused, I scanned the ships moored at the marina. There - the familiar hull of the Trinity Royal. I caught my breath. The Trinity Royal meant Captain Thornton was in town, and he might well be dropping in on my father to share news.

That might put a dampener on our plans.

I hoped the illusion on our ship would hold true but now would be when we found out for sure. I glanced forward, where Solomon sat at the prow of the ship, his back flush to the railings and his legs spread out in front of him on the deck. He had a piece of string in his hand that had several knots in it. His eyes were closed, and a soft green glow played about his hands.

Ora had helped with the initial spell, and from what I could understand, some of the knots in that string had bound Ora's spell to Solomon's, allowing it more strength. When I had attempted to help, my fingers hadn't been able to tie the knot needed. Solomon had shaken his head.

"Not the right kind of magic, then," he'd said. "Ah well, perhaps your magic will help without intention, all the same."

I turned my attention from Solomon to the Trinity Royal again.

Although I couldn't make out anyone on deck, I had no doubt that there were Naval men on it watching and waiting for a ship such as ours, or perhaps exactly our ship.

I turned and found Ezra approaching me.

"What do you think?" I asked.

Ezra folded his arms over his chest, his eyes narrowed as he took in the sight of the Trinity Royal.

"I suppose we will find out for sure if Solomon was as good as his word," he said. His voice low.

I leaned against Ezra with my shoulder until he put his arm around me. "You still don't trust him?" Ezra sighed and squeezed me to him.

"No, I don't. But I trust you and I trust Tate, and Ora trusts him, too, so. If he proves himself while we're here, perhaps I'll consider trusting him."

"That's very generous of you," I teased.

"Careful, pet," Ezra said, digging his fingers into my side and pulling me closer to him. "I could still make you wear your leather harness under your clothes. I could lock something around your cock so you can't even wank until you see me again."

I shuddered against him, both afraid and intrigued. "You wouldn't..."

"Don't tempt me." He let go, spun me around and kissed me soundly. "This mission is too important to interfere with, but I absolutely would in other circumstances."

I kneaded my fingers in his shirt, hardly knowing what it was I wanted. "You're a cruel monster, Ezra."

"I know." He kissed me once more, cheerfully, and then looked me up and down. "So this is the outfit you're going with, peacock?"

He knew I'd agonised over what to wear, so I was confident he was teasing me again but I nodded. "Yes, clothes from my old life so it doesn't look as if I've been living well." The old red coat would have been the perfect addition, especially as waterlogged and ruined as it was, but Ora had long since lost it in the ocean. Or possibly gifted it to another merfolk. They refused to tell me. As it was, I wore my old trousers and a stained shirt. My hair hadn't been cut since I'd first left Kingston, so by leaving it out I imagined I'd look more rough than I felt.

Ora came out of the Captain's cabin. Dressed in a long skirt from Nassau and a simple white shirt, a scarf tied over their hair, Ora passed for a slim young woman with no problem. They were also wearing the leather slippers we'd purchased in Tortuga, and were pouting over it.

"Don't like shoes," Ora grumbled.

"Unfortunately, they're not optional." I kissed their cheek. "You look lovely, Ora."

Ezra had turned to watch as we sailed in to a free mooring. The crew's eyes were all on the Trinity Royal, but they hadn't appeared to notice us. There was no shout from the marina, no gathering of men in uniform with weapons.

Anton and James leapt onto the marina and the Grey Kelpie was soon moored and anchored.

Zeb strode out from the cabin, wearing a pair of Tate's grey trousers, his white shirt, one of Ezra's grey vests was over the top of the shirt, and he'd borrowed a long coat from James, to complete the look of an honest merchant, the captain of the made up ship we were passing the Kelpie off as.

I gave Ezra a quick hug and a kiss, then went to do the same with Tate. On my insistence, we'd agreed not to draw out our farewells, because otherwise I'd start crying. I had to look as if I had come through some hardship but not as if I was recently upset.

I shouldered the satchel of things I wanted to bring with me to my father's house and with a tight chest, waved goodbye to Zack and Sagorika and nodded to Zeb and Ora.

"Right then, let's go."

With my heart in my throat, I took the gangplank down to the wharf. I didn't look back, I didn't have it in me to look back. If I'd looked back and seen Tate or Ezra I might have changed my mind and gone back onto the ship.

Instead, I looked forward, and inhaled the familiar smells of the street food cooking in the market and the tangy perfume of the flowering bushes and trees.

The streets here were so familiar to me it was almost shocking. I'd travelled so far, and learned so much since the last time I was here. Although it was barely six months since I'd got up before dawn to run away from home, I felt like the boy I was back then was years behind me. Now I felt embarrassed at how naive I had been, and how reckless to have joined the first ship I'd seen.

In fairness, it had worked out remarkably well, but it could so easy have gone terribly badly for me. If I had joined a ship loyal to the King they might have returned me to my father as soon as they heard word from the Navy. If I'd joined a less friendly ship, I might have been beaten or thrown overboard.

Instead, I chose to thank my mother for looking out for me, for guiding me to the ship. Or perhaps I should have thanked Zeb, since he had led me there as a cat.

I glanced back at him and smiled. He smiled back, but he was largely busy sniffing the air.

"Is that salmon I smell?"

"Almost certainly," I said. "But we don't have time to linger in the markets and taste fish. I'm sure to be recognised soon, and then word will get to my father. It's best if we head straight to his... to my old house."

Ora took my arm, companionably, no doubt feeling the wave of fear and uncertainty that had swamped me as I spoke about seeing my father. Thankfully, as they were dressed as a woman, it wouldn't be shocking for anyone here to see me walk arm in arm with them.

I patted their hand and gave them a grateful smile.

Zeb grumbled a little, but largely he seemed to be remembering his role as a ship's captain, and kept his head up, his expression stony.

I had trodden the path from the market to the old villa on the hillside so many times I didn't need to think of it at all, my feet knew the way and they carried me there. As we got closer my heart filled with a grey sort of dread.

Why am I here? What was I thinking? Father will never concede to my wishes, I'm foolish for even trying.

But I had made a promise to Mother. And I could no sooner cut out my own heart than break that promise.

My breath caught in my throat when the house came into sight, and I coughed as if I were choking on my own breath. I stopped walking to rub my chest, trying to ease some of the tightness there. It felt hard to take a breath, as if I had forgotten how.

Ora dropped my arm and rubbed their hand on my back, making soothing noises. "It's all right. We'll be with you, and you'll be safe no matter what happens," they crooned softly. "The Grey Kelpie's in harbour, and no one will hurt you."

With a Herculean effort I took a breath and let it out slowly. I closed my eyes.

Ora doesn't know what they're saying. Father can hurt me with a look, with a word. I can't stand up to him, I never could. This was a mistake.

I shook my head. *Mother. I have to remember what Mother said. She believed I could help, that I could somehow ease Father's suffering. I have to try.*

I swallowed and straightened my spine. "It's all right," I said. "Thank you, Ora. I'm all right."

"That's the spirit," Zeb said. "You'll be fine. You can always scratch his eyes out, if things get difficult."

That piece of advice was strange enough that it snapped me out of my panic a bit. I shook my head slightly at Zeb. "I won't be doing that."

"Well, it's an option is what I'm saying," Zeb said. "You never know."

We resumed walking. I swallowed a few more times, but my feet kept on carrying me and inevitably I ended up at the front door. It seemed wrong somehow to let myself in, so I lifted the door knocker and let it fall.

Ora looked at me and smiled encouragingly. I squeezed their hand and then dropped it, turned to Zeb and gave him a grateful smile as well.

As I heard footsteps inside some new questions sprung to mind.

How intelligent was it to bring the two members of crew who aren't human, and don't understand society's rules?

How was Ora going to get to the ocean to sleep?

What if Zeb forgets, and shape shifts in front of my father, or really... anyone in the house?

My heart rattled alarmingly as I imagined with sickening clarity all the ways that this visit could go wrong, and then the door opened.

"Young master Gideon!" the maid cried. I tried to remember her name, but to my horror it was lost to me in that moment.

"I, uh, yes, it's me," I said. "Uh, is my father in?"

"Yes, yes of course, come in." She stepped back, opening the door wide to allow us access. "He's in his study. Gideon, sir, we thought you were dead!"

"Right, uh, no. I'm not dead," I said, feeling all the stiffness of my formal education and etiquette coming back to me. "Thank you so much for your concern. I'll go directly up to his study. Please would you prepare rooms for my guests? This is Captain Zebulon of the Flying Turtle and Mistress Olivia, his wife."

The maid tore her eyes from me and seemed to startle, as if she hadn't noticed that I had two companions with me. She nodded.

"Yes, of course, I'll arrange it immediately. Will they be attending on your father with you, or shall I see them to a sitting room?"

"They'll come with me for now," I said. "Thank you."

With that I turned and headed up the stairs, trying to feel confident and capable, trying to feel like the man I was on the ocean and not the frightened teenage boy who cowered when his father so much as glanced his way.

It was nearly impossible. The stairs were just as I remembered - the third one creaked when a foot landed on it. The hand railings were polished and smelled of beeswax. The stairway itself was lined with framed paintings of buildings in London and when I reached the top of the stairs, there was the heavy wooden door of my father's study.

The last time I had been here, this his study, I had lied to him. Told him I would find a wife and marry her, settle down to learn to be governor of Kingston. This time it would be a negotiation.

I knocked on the door as boldly as I could manage, checked that Zeb and Ora were still with me, and waited.

Shortly, I heard my father's voice.

"Enter."

I took a deep, steadying breath and pushed the door open. The study was as I had remembered. A huge set of floor to ceiling windows on one side - closed tight against the fresh air and scent of flowers from the garden.

Father's recessed bookshelves on the other wall, partially covered in books but mostly with souvenirs and trophies from his travels in the Navy.

"Gideon?"

I looked up at him, realised I'd been avoiding looking at him in order to scan the room, and met his eyes.

"Yes, Father, I'm back," I said. "And these are my friends, Captain Zebulon and his wife, Olivia."

Zeb strode through the room with no fear. He stopped in front of the desk, eyed my father then nodded.

"Hello."

"I don't understand." Father got up from the desk and walked around it, seeming to decide to ignore Zeb for the moment, and hastened to me. He took hold of my hands and gazed into my face. "Gideon... they said you were kidnapped by pirates, but we never got a ransom note. I don't understand, how are you back here now? Are you hurt?"

"No, Father, I'm all right." I was taken aback by his apparent concern for me, it was very unexpected. Maybe this was going to be easier than I had imagined?

"You look different," he said, reaching to touch my hair where it hung down on the side of my face, almost tenderly. "Older."

Ora moved, making a floorboard creak, and Father straightened up, dropped his hands and looked at Ora and Zeb.

"I assume I have you to thank for the safe return of my son," he said. It was phrased as a question but delivered quite coldly.

"We happened upon the wreck of the Grey Kelpie," Ora said, reciting the script Tate and I had come up with. "They'd come under fire from another pirate we think. Gideon here was clinging to a bit of wreckage, so we took him aboard."

Father blinked and then nodded. "Ah yes, there is no honour

amongst thieves. It was truly a miracle that you happened by in time to save his life."

"It was. I have invited them to stay in the house, until they're ready to sail again," I said. "I hope you don't mind, Father."

"Of course, of course," he waved his hand. "I'll have Betsy arrange one of the guest rooms."

Betsy, of course, how awful of me to have forgotten her name.

"I've already asked her," I said. "She let us in."

"Very well." Father turned on his heel and went to sit at his desk once more. "I expect you're wearied after your voyage. Please, take to your rooms and rest. We can talk again at dinner. Served at seven sharp."

I knew a dismissal when I heard it, even if it did rather take me by surprise so quickly after he'd seemed happy to see me back.

It reminded me of how Captain Thornton had treated me as well on the Trinity Royal. The strict control on his own emotions, the lack of empathy. I half expected Father would insist on locking my room.

"Perhaps we can speak together privately, Father," I said, hating how timid I sounded.

"Yes, we'll arrange an interview once you've rested," Father replied. His eyes on the paperwork on his desk, his attention elsewhere.

How I want to ask you how you're feeling, talk to you about Mother. Ask why exactly you have so much hatred for Ezra... but now is clearly not the moment.

I turned and nodded to Ora and Zeb, indicating the door.

"After you, Captain," I said. Zeb made a harrumphing noise and led the way out of Father's study. Betsy was in the hallway, a bundle of clean linens in her arms.

"I was just preparing the Lilac room," Betsy said. "For the visitors."

"Wonderful, thank you so much, Betsy," I said. I offered my arm to Ora. "It's this way."

Once they were shown the guest quarters, and Betsy had given them the linens and excused herself, I gave Ora and Zeb a quick kiss each.

"I'd better go to my room, wash and change. I don't want Father to suspect anything."

Ora nodded. "Seven for dinner, we'll be there."

I backed away and hurried into my room, shut the door and looked around the room I had grown up in.

CHAPTER TWENTY-FOUR - IN WHICH A CAT IS SEATED AT AN AWKWARD FORMAL DINNER

*M*y bedroom had obviously not been opened in weeks, perhaps not since I was last here.

I went to the windows and threw them open. The room was layered with dust, and the smell was musty. My bed was in disarray, the blankets thrown off as if I'd just left that morning.

I set my satchel down on my desk and pulled out the portrait of Mother, setting her where I'd always had her before.

"Well, here we are," I said to her. "Father almost seemed happy to see me, didn't you think? I'll have to try and find some time alone with him and see if I can't get through to him. Talk about you a little."

She smiled back at me, and I remembered her voice telling me she heard me when I spoke. "I love you," I added.

I stripped off my clothes and went to my wardrobe, flinging open the doors and seeing my range of clothes. It was like being reunited with old friends. The cedar wood of the robe had kept them fresh and moth-free, and I ran my hands over the various articles of clothing fondly.

"What to wear for tonight?" I pulled out one of my pale blue linen shirts and pressed it to my chest. "I missed you."

When it was time to leave, I was definitely going to bring more of my clothes along with me.

A little before seven I was ready. I'd washed, I'd combed out my hair and tied it back at the nape of my neck with a black ribbon. Dressed in my blue shirt, and a loose pair of deep grey trousers, with a matching waistcoat over the top. I left the top buttons of my shirt unbuttoned, because although I wanted in some way to blend in here, I couldn't entirely let the loose way of dressing I'd adopted on the ship go.

I made my way to the Lilac room and knocked on the door.

Ora opened it, eyes wide. "Oh, it's you, Gideon. Come in. You look delicious."

"Thank you, Ora. I came to let you know, it's almost time for dinner," I said, and walked into the room. Zeb was sprawled crossways over the bed, snoring. I went to stand over him, and grinning, slipped my hand between his legs to goose him.

Zeb startled awake, swiped at me with one hand, grumbled and fell back on the bed.

"You need to change for dinner," I said. "The other outfit you brought along, Ora? You'll need to put that on instead."

Dinner was a formal affair. Far more formal than any meal I'd had for months. And too late, in fact, not until we were in the dining room, did I realise that this meant that Zeb and Ora would never have been to such a formal dinner.

My skin went cold and clammy and my stomach plunged. Surely there'd be no way we could pull this off without my father noticing something strange.

Father stood at the head of his table behind his seat. Zeb sat down where Betsy had shown him his place was set. I hesitated, and Ora watched me. For a moment we stood like that, before I indicated, as subtly as I could with the hand hidden from Father, that Ora should sit.

"Oh! Sorry," Ora said, and took their seat. They blushed as Father and myself sat as well. Zeb looked between us, bewildered. I shook my head at him and pressed my lips together, hoping he'd get the hint to stay quiet.

"How nice to have company for dinner," my father said blandly, as if it were Ora and Zeb's presence that was unusual, rather than my sudden reappearance.

Betsy and one of the footmen Father employed brought in plates of food and set them in front of us.

Why didn't I remind them both to eat using the cutlery? I'm such a fool.

I picked up the knife and fork and cleared my throat. "How have things been, Father?" I asked, before catching both Ora and Zeb's gazes and looking pointedly at my plate as I cut my food into small pieces. I hoped that they would take my hint and follow suit. My stomach clenched and I exhaled slowly, knowing I couldn't eat if I got too nervous.

It was tuna steak with steamed vegetables, which was good. At least both Ora and Zeb would enjoy the fish.

Father made a harrumph noise then sighed. "The same. I'm glad you're home. I've already organised a dance to be held tomorrow."

I almost choked on my piece of carrot and had to clasp my napkin over my mouth. Father continued as if I hadn't responded.

"Obviously, it won't have the absolute cream of society - we haven't had time for that - but hopefully one of the young girls will catch your eye, Gideon."

I looked up at him in horror. "I'm sorry, what was that?"

"You're not getting any younger, and certainly none of the girls are," Father said. "Now that you're back here, you need to settle down. We've no time to lose."

Zeb was tucking into his fish using his fork, but not the knife. Ora was doing their best with the cutlery, but was listening to the conversation.

"I've... Father, I've only been back in the house for a few hours, I don't understand what your rush is."

Father straightened in his seat and gave me the look that had appeared in my nightmares. I stopped moving almost entirely, save for the shallow breaths I was taking in.

"Gideon. It's not appropriate for you to argue with me in this manner, especially in the presence of our honoured guests, to whom we owe your very life."

"It was our pleasure, of course," Ora said, quickly. They gave a wide smile to Father.

Zeb sucked his fork clean of the last of the fish and looked around for more.

"I'm sorry, Father," I said, my voice quavering just the way it used to.

The rest of the meal passed with Father lecturing all of us about the recent successes the Royal Navy had achieved against the Spanish fleet, and I was grateful that he seemed to not have noticed Ora and Zeb's poor table manners at all.

I became aware of a dull headache as the third course was tidied away and realised I had been clenching my teeth.

I've only been here a few hours and I'm back to the way I always was with him. Afraid, on edge and waiting for the axe to fall. How far away and long ago waking up with Tate seems. And it was only this morning!

I decided to take a chance on a new conversation topic. "I expect you're surprised to hear that I've become acquainted with the Shearwater Pirate, Father," I said. I managed to sound almost detached as I mentioned Ezra, which was the goal.

Father's knife screeched against his plate and he looked up at me. "I hardly think your experiences with bloodthirsty pirates are appropriate dinner conversation," he said.

I opened my mouth but my response caught in my throat. I swallowed and tried again, summoning up the last bit of bravery I could muster.

"It is rather on my mind," I said. I hated how petty I sounded, but I forged on. "So much of what happened seemed to be because of an enmity between the two of you."

"Not now," Father said. He shook his head and gave me a severe look. I dropped my eyes.

"Sorry, Father."

Betsy brought out a tray of small tarts, heaped with fresh pineapple and drenched in sugar glaze. They looked absolutely delicious but my stomach was tight as a drum from tension.

"Your favourite, master Gideon," Betsy said, smiling. She gave me a wink as she set the plate in front of me before serving the others.

Father watched as I picked up my fork and took a bite.

"It's lovely, thank you, Betsy," I said.

Zeb looked at the tart and sniffed. He started to get up from the table when Ora caught his arm.

"Are you quite well?" Father asked, his attention drawn to the movement

"Yes, time to nap," Zeb said. He shook free of Ora's hold and promptly left the room.

Ora looked at me with wide, startled eyes.

"It was a long voyage," I said, quickly. "I hope you'll excuse the Captain, Father. He means no disrespect, he's simply tired."

"Hm, well." Father looked doubtfully at Ora who was gamely slicing into the fruit tart and taking a bite. "I suppose, once does get rather exhausted on a trip across the ocean."

Once I'd finished the tart, I dabbed at my mouth with my napkin and cleared my throat. "Perhaps we should all turn in early," I said. My voice sounded thin and wavering to my ear and I took a breath, hoping to steady it. "If there's to be a dance tomorrow, I should like to rest up."

"Of course," Ora said. They stood up abruptly, and the chair made a horrible screeching noise on the tiled floor. "Rest."

"Right, of course," Father said, his eyes wide. "Don't let me keep you, of course."

I offered Ora my arm as we approached the door, not needing another word from Father to make our escape. Ora took my arm gratefully and once we were up the stairs they wrapped their arms around me.

"That was just awful," they said. "Are you all right?"

"I hardly know," I said, shaking my head. My jaw and head ached still, and I felt like I'd never catch my breath, but being away from Father's presence felt better. Not to mention Ora's close proximity. But we weren't on the Grey Kelpie, and we couldn't be seen close like this.

I pulled back from the embrace. "Perhaps, later on, we could... have a nightcap," I said, struggling to find a reason to be in the same room together after dinner. I wasn't sure if any servants were nearby or not, but just in case they were.

"A nightcap?" Ora said, tilting their head to the side.

"A cup of tea, before bed," I said. "In my room, perhaps in a few minutes, and of course, you should bring your husband."

I raised my eyebrows and looked at my room as significantly as I could. Ora's face split into an understanding grin and they nodded.

"Of course, my husband and I would be glad to join you."

There was, of course, no way it was safe to indulge in anything more than a kiss and a cuddle, but once Zeb and Ora had come to my bedroom and shut the door the temptation was great.

I kissed them both and then we settled on my bed, one of them on each side of me, sitting up so that we couldn't get into too much mischief. They each held me.

"Dinner was strange," Ora said, nuzzling into my neck under

my ear. "I thought he'd want to know about where you've been, instead he just talked about the Navy."

"That's, well, I suppose it's sort of normal for him," I said. I sighed, because truly it was disappointing, but it wasn't surprising.

Zeb stroked my back and pressed his lips to my neck on the other side.

I felt myself stir and shook my head slightly. "We can't. You two have to go back to your room... it's too risky to try anything while my Father is in the house."

Zeb grumbled and pulled back. "But I want to sleep in here, with you."

I exhaled. He'd make a fuss if we didn't allow this. "You can sleep in here as long as you come and go in cat form," I said. "Go into your room as a man and then come back here as cat."

"All right."

"I suppose, you should probably go now," I said, reluctantly. I kissed Ora and then Zeb.

"I'll be back in a while," Zeb said.

"Leave the door a little ajar and I'll close it when you're in." Ora rubbed their cheek against mine, a habit they'd picked up from Zeb, I assumed, and we said goodnight.

CHAPTER TWENTY-FIVE - IN WHICH SELF-CONTROL IS TESTED

J was brushing my hair out when Zeb sauntered back in as a black cat and jumped on the bed, making himself comfortable right in the centre of it.

"Don't get too comfortable," I said. "You still have to share with me." I closed the door and changed for bed, before climbing in beside him. He shifted back when I tried to move him aside, and we had to wrestle a bit before we each had space on the bed.

Wrestling turned into kissing and hands stroking bodies.

"Zeb, we can't make a sound," I breathed. "It's too dangerous." His hand found my cock and stroked it, I bit down on my tongue so as not to moan.

"So you'll have to be quiet," he said, smirking against my jaw.

I shivered a little, wrapping my arms around his neck and pulling him closer to me. "Cruel," I whispered.

"Risk adds flavour," Zeb murmured, barely more than a purr. "Danger spices the enjoyment."

I knew he was right... My body was responding to the risk and the excitement was certainly heightened. I crashed my mouth against Zeb's to stifle the sounds I wished to make.

He kissed me back and then up my jaw, nipping at my skin, before pushing his lips against my ear.

"Let's see how well Ezra has trained you," Zeb murmured.

I closed my eyes and shivered, feeling even hotter and more in need of touching. The thought that Zeb wanted to test me like that, to see how obedient I could be... It inflamed me.

"Oh god," I breathed. This was either going to be incredible or disastrous, but Zeb's hand was still tugging and stroking my cock and I couldn't resist seeing which outcome we'd get.

Stupid fae blood.

Zeb's free hand closed over my mouth and I had to suppress another moan.

I opened my eyes to see him leaning over me, his expression one of fierce delight.

He's enjoying teasing me like this.

My hips bucked against his hand and he raised an eyebrow, sat up and licked his lips, letting go of my mouth. He pushed my legs apart and started to tease at me

I reached to touch his chest, caressing his muscles and teasing at his nipples with my fingers. The urge to moan was pressing, so I bit my bottom lip and breathed hard, hoping the panting would take the edge of the need a little.

Looking around, he saw some oil I'd used for my hair once upon a time, and picked up the bottle, shaking it out directly onto my hole. I hissed with the sudden coldness in such a sensitive place, but bit my tongue instead of my lip.

The pain of that took the edge off the need to cry out a little.

Zeb caught my eye and grinned, using his fingers to push the oil inside me and stretch me open, his teeth bared in a promise of more.

I spread my legs wider, tried to wrap them around Zeb's waist, trying to bring him closer to me, trying to urge him to be quicker.

He stretched me wider then pushed my legs wider, guided his cock inside and shoved hard.

I gasped, but remembered in time not to make a noise with it. Zeb pinned my wrists to the bed and rocked his hips deeper into me.

Shuddering, I made the softest noise I could, knowing that something had to get out. A sigh, almost, but one full of the joy of being filled.

Zeb claimed my mouth with his and we kissed as he rocked inside me.

This, this is what I need. Forget who I used to be, the boy who lived in this room had only dreams. I have the reality. I have my lovers, who know what I want, and give it to me, and surprise me with things like this. So much joy and bliss I can't barely handle it.

I kissed Zeb back and thanked him silently.

My magic played under my skin, in the base of my abdomen, I arched my back and felt it flowing into him where he was pushed inside me. His eyes lit and as I watched they became slightly more catlike, I saw the black points of his ears push through his hair and with a very low growl he let go of my wrists and wrapped his arms tight around me, rutting against me roughly so that I felt sure I'd scream with how overjoyed I felt.

I wrapped my arms around his shoulders and buried my face in his neck. I didn't need any touch on my cock to come from this. I felt Zeb nearing climax and my body pulsed in perfect time with his.

I came, screwing my eyes shut, breathing hard against his neck and stifling what noise I made on his skin. The hot wetness of his filling me up seemed to satiate my magic for the moment, and it went dormant as we came to a breathless stop.

"So good," he murmured into my hair. "You're so good, Gideon."

"Love you," I breathed. "Thank you, thank you for everything."

Zeb held me, stroking my hair and my side and softly purring until I fell asleep, utterly content and feeling like myself again.

CHAPTER TWENTY-SIX - IN WHICH PREPARATIONS ARE MADE

*F*ather spent the next day locked his study - clearly avoiding me. Part of me feared it was because he had somehow heard or discovered what Zeb and I had done the night before, but a realistic part of my mind said that if he knew that, he'd have thrown me out of the house.

Betsy found me dithering outside his study door in the mid-morning, and gave me a sympathetic look.

"He's not to be bothered today," she said. "And he asked me to say that if you asked after him, he'd see you tonight at the dance. It's to start at six."

I sighed, feeling my shoulders hunch up under my ears. I went to run a hand through my hair to soothe myself, only to find it tied back.

"Right, yes, of course." I gave her a smile I didn't particularly feel.

Betsy moved a little closer and lowered her voice. "He has a free morning tomorrow," she said. "If you join him at breakfast at eight, you can catch him then. Assuming, well..." She trailed off, looking embarrassed. "Sorry, I didn't mean to presume."

"No, it's fine, assuming what?"

"Assuming that catching him alone is your goal."

"It is, thank you, Betsy." This time my smile for her was more sincere. She returned the smile, which dimpled her cheeks in a sweet way. I felt myself relaxing.

We started walking together, both of us naturally wanting to avoid speaking just outside Father's closed study door. We reached the stairs and descended them before I brought myself to ask her something that had been preying on the back of my mind.

"How... if you don't mind my asking, how has he been? I mean, I want to ensure he's you know, treating you and the other staff well, before I..." I bit my lip.

Betsy looked at me sidelong and I got the feeling she had predicted what I'd been about to say. That I wouldn't be staying. That I had no intention of being here in a month, or even a fortnight.

"Oh, yes, Master Gideon-"

"Please, just call me Gideon," I said, quickly. "Master isn't... it means something... it's just not correct for me." I shook my head, there was no way I could explain any single aspect of any of *that* to Betsy.

"Gideon, then." She nodded. "He's been, well, he's been very isolated. He doesn't go out much or entertain guests, hardly at all. He's good to us in the staff, in his way. But he's been raging at the Naval officers who come to report to him."

"I can imagine," I said. I glanced back up the stairs, half afraid he'd appear and chastise me for fraternising with the help. It was ridiculous though, Betsy was a person, just as much as him or me. I sighed and looked back at her, hoping I could be of some comfort. "I'm hoping to resolve all of that which is vexing him." I bit my tongue instead of adding *before I leave.*

I didn't *truly* have a reason to trust Betsy to stay discreet, but she had been honest with me and my gut told me I'd have nothing to lose by being honest back.

"I want to make it right, and then I want to make my own way in the world."

I held my breath, but Betsy smiled. "I think that's a grand plan, Gideon." She sighed and wiped her hands on her apron before clasping me by both shoulders. "You've not been gone so long, but already you've grown into a fine man. Your dear, departed mother would be so proud of you."

I flushed with happiness. Of course, Betsy had known my mother. I couldn't remember much about when she started, but I suspected it had been soon after the house was finished and we'd moved in.

"Thank you," I said. "That... that means a lot. I've been thinking of her often, recently."

"I'm sure," she said. She took a look at me, and then nodded, seeming to decide something. "It's good to see you home, even if it's just for a short time. Now, I'd better get back to the kitchen and ensure the preparations are coming along."

"Of course, thank you, Betsy, for everything."

Ora and Zeb hadn't emerged from their room yet, so I went to knock on the door to the guest room.

Ora opened it, wrapped in a silky Japanese style dressing gown that must have been in the room's wardrobe.

"Good morning," I said. Looking past them, I saw Zeb in cat form, snoring lightly on the bed.

"I wasn't sure what to do," Ora said. "If we should come downstairs or not. I thought I'd wait until you came to find us, so that Zeb didn't ruin anything."

I beamed. "Thank you. Now, it's the dance tonight and my father is not to be disturbed, which means we have an excuse to go into town and buy you a new dress."

Ora's face lit up and they bounced a little on the balls of their bare feet. "Yes! Okay, I'll get dressed and we can go."

. . .

The afternoon passed pleasantly. Zeb, Ora and I went to several of the stores I frequented when I lived in the town, and purchased a few new pieces of clothing. Zeb wasn't particularly interested in the clothes, but Tate had apparently told him to watch out for Ora and me, and he was taking that rather seriously.

It was sweet, really, knowing he wanted to look after us in some way.

However, being in town and therefore closer to the wharf, created an exquisite sort of torture. Because I knew we were close to Ezra and Tate, but I couldn't go to see them. It perhaps would have been acceptable if anyone had seen Ora and Zeb going to the ship, but not myself. It would be noticeable to any of Father's friends, if he still had any. They might tell him, and he'd have questions.

I was determined to keep any questions at bay until I had some time alone with him.

Soon enough, we were back at the house. The French doors on the ground floor were all being opened, the windows too, and lanterns were being hung at careful distances to lend some but not too much light.

The tables were draped with white cloths, and there were a few musicians arriving as we did.

I hurried up to my room, for although I had no intention of doing as Father said and finding a bride, I enjoyed any reason to get dressed in my finest and show myself off.

I'm a peacock after all, that's what Ezra calls me. Time to embrace that side of myself.

CHAPTER TWENTY-SEVEN - IN WHICH A DANCE IS HELD IN GIDEON'S HONOUR

I went downstairs, following Ora and Zeb, who were well turned out. I had spent some time brushing Ora's hair and then styling it for them. Now their dark curls were piled on top of their head and kept in place with a few of my mother's old hairpins. Not the jewelled ones that Father would recognise, but the plainer ones.

Ora's new dress was a deep oyster grey - reminiscent of their tail - and featured a boned bodice, which Ora had surprised me by loving. They looked every inch a lady, and it gave me a secret thrill to think of the shock and consternation it would cause if my Father knew the truth of who and what 'Olivia' was.

I had insisted Zeb purchase a new outfit as well, breeches and hose, and shiny black shoes of the latest style. It looked odd to see him without his signature leather and heavy boots, but I couldn't deny the style suited him.

Walking behind both of them, I salivated quietly, and made a promise to myself to get them to wear these outfits again and then I'd…. I wasn't sure. Tear the clothes off both of them? Make them dominate me and keep me on my knees? Make love to me while still as fully dressed as possible? Possibly… all of those options. Perhaps not in that particular order though.

I swallowed and tried to focus as we reached the foot of the stairs. Ora and Zeb hesitated.

"It's this way," I said, leading the way to the largest room in the house, which had been set up for the affair. The room's doors and windows had been opened to let in the evening air and the scent of blossoms. There were already a few guests in the room, I recognised some of Father's old friends, and several of them had their daughters in attendance, wearing the newest, flashiest fashions.

They all looked at me as I walked in. I straightened my back and made my way directly to Father.

"Good evening, Father."

"Gideon, good to see you. Ah, and Captain Zebulon, thank you for joining us." He smiled graciously and Zeb nodded.

"Yes, I was told there'd be food," Zeb said. "Is that true?"

Father raised his eyebrows and then nodded slowly. "Indeed, the servants are serving a buffet in a half hour."

"Hm," Zeb said. Ora's arm tightened on his and I imagined they were keeping him from wandering off.

"Gideon, you know what your charge is for the evening. I'm sure the captain and his wife would excuse your company so that you can mingle with our guests." It was phrased politely, but the words held an order I knew I should at least appear to obey. For now. Finding a moment to speak to him would be a challenge, I knew, but I would try all the same. Perhaps later when he'd had a few wines to soften his mood.

"Yes, of course, please excuse me," I said, and nodded to Ora and Zeb, before turning to see who I should talk to.

The nearest cluster of folks seemed the best option, I vaguely knew the man as someone Father had to dinner perhaps once a year.

I made polite small talk with him and his admittedly charming daughter, Suzanne. I was pleased to realised after a few sentences that she had as little interest in me as I had in her.

Once I had established that she certainly wouldn't complain if I excused myself quickly, I did exactly that.

I walked up the hall towards the front of the house and looked out at the driveway, where a carriage had just pulled up.

A young lady sidled up to me as I looked out the window. "Gideon Keene, I presume?" she asked.

"Indeed," I turned to her reluctantly and gave her a polite bow. "It's my pleasure to meet you, miss...?"

"Iliana," she said. She held her hand out to me delicately, so I took it and brushed my lips against the back of it.

"Ah yes," she said, looking past my shoulder and out the open window. She flicked open a fan with a flourish and fanned herself. "The Lady Caroline. No doubt she's the one your father hopes you'll choose this evening."

I turned to watch as the Lady Caroline descended from the carriage gracefully, pulled her parasol out and shading her eyes from the last of the Jamaican sun before it set.

Her dress and slippers were of the latest fashion from Paris, and I was sure Iliana was right about Father's wishes. Unfortunately for her, that wouldn't be an option, but perhaps one of the other young men attending the ball would make her happy?

I cleared my throat, looked back at Iliana and gave her a rueful smile. "I fear he is destined to be disappointed in that regard."

"Is that so?" Iliana moved a little closer and smiled behind her fan. "Did I make good by being bold and introducing myself to you before she had a chance?"

"Ah, no, I'm afraid you will also be disappointed," I said, as carefully as I could. "For despite whatever my father may have said, I have no intention of making a proposal this evening, or indeed, at all."

She dropped her fan to her side, her eyes widening and her smile turning from coquettish to intrigued. "Is that so? How very interesting. Honestly, these dances are getting utterly boring for those of us charged with making a match. Do tell..."

"I, uh, it wouldn't be appropriate to go into details," I said. "Please, accept my apologies. I'm sure you're a perfectly lovely person, Iliana, but I simply...."

"Oh, please," she said. "Let's dance, and you can tell me all about it. I promise I'm the soul of discretion, I'm just looking for a little diversion."

"I..." I swallowed, because I did feel for her. She was in the same situation I could have found myself in if I hadn't run away from home. In fact, she had even fewer opportunities to escape such a life. "I'm sorry. Maybe later? I need to be seen to be mingling, after all."

"Of course, I'll put your name on my dance card." She winked and gave me a smile. "Have a lovely evening until then."

She swept off and I watched as another carriage drew up to the front door and footmen hurried to let out whoever was inside.

How am I going to get through this interminable night?

"Gideon?"

I felt a hand on my elbow and turned, recognising the voice, but not quite able to place it immediately... It was Oscar Carroll.

"Oh, Oscar, I mean, uh, Lieutenant Commander Carroll," I said. "What a pleasant surprise." My old etiquette training kicked in again and I was glad of it. I had no idea what to say to him otherwise.

"How kind of you to say. Please, call me Oscar if you wish to." His face was relaxed, open, and his eyes wide as he smiled softly at me, almost shyly.

"Well, uh. Hello," I managed, confused by his expression and feeling my heart speed up as if I were in danger.

"It's so good to see you safe," he said. I became aware that he still had his hand on my elbow, his thumb rubbing gently on me. I cleared my throat.

Why was he still holding my arm?

"I was so worried we'd let you go to your doom." He shook his head, raising his eyes to the Heavens before refocusing on my face. "You have no idea how pleased I was when I heard the news of your safe return to Jamaica."

"Oh," I said. "That's kind of you. But really, you needn't have worried. I wasn't harmed by Capt... by the pirates."

"I almost fought the Captain," he said. "But I realised if I were court-martialled I wouldn't be able to find you again."

"You... were court-martialled?"

"When we didn't pursue the Grey Kelpie immediately, I could have been." His hand tightened on my arm a little. "But the best way to find you was by staying on the Trinity Royal. And look, now I have, and in your father's house as well. Almost as if it were fated."

My head spun, trying to make sense of all of that, but I wasn't sure I could. *Fought the Captain? Just to pursue me?*

"As I said, there really was no need, I wasn't harmed. Thank you for your concern, but-"

"I can hardly believe that," he said. "After the state you were in when we found you, and they were doing such..." he paused, his cheeks went quite red, and his fingers dug into my arm briefly. "Unspeakable things to you, I just. I couldn't stop imagining, once you were recaptured-" He cut himself off, his hand flying to his mouth.

Oh. Oh. I think I know what's happened... That night on the Trinity Royal when I... when I could see how to flatter him, make him like me. I used my magic so it was as if he were smitten.

As delicately as I could, I pulled my arm out of his grasp.

"Really, you don't need to uh, trouble yourself, with imagining any of that."

"Oh, no, of course, I wasn't." He dropped his hands to his sides, shifted his weight from one foot to the other and looked down, blushing. "I didn't mean..."

Time to make my excuses, then. I can feel my own cheeks warming.

"I'm sorry, I'd better go and speak with my father, I think I heard him call my name," I said, lying. "Please excuse me."

"Oh of course," he said. "I'd like to speak with you later though, perhaps privately? Tonight?"

My heart was racing now, and a sensation of cold fear trickled down my spine, I started to walk away, speaking over my shoulder. "Uh, I'm sorry, I'm not sure if that will be possible."

I made my escape, unsure if I had truly felt, or simply imagined the brush of his hand on the small of my back, caressing...

Oh Mother, what have I done?

I had no idea that my powers could do such a thing. I'd had no inkling when I'd pushed at him, those many nights ago on the Trinity Royal, that I would have any lingering effect at all. I had no idea what to do about it now, either.

For this moment, some distance between us would certainly serve. I had to collect my thoughts together and I certainly couldn't do it while I was staring him in the face.

Without particularly meaning to, but perhaps because I had said it out loud so my feet had listened, I found myself approaching Father. He was deep in conversation with a fashionable gentleman I didn't know.

Straightening my spine, I approached and cleared my throat, waiting for Father to notice me. The strange man observed me first.

"Ah, this must be the young man himself," he said, smiling politely. Father turned and nodded. He took a step back to include me in the conversation.

"Yes, this is Gideon. Gideon, it's my pleasure to introduce you to Sir Gabriel Durant. I've heard he's been the toast of London society, but he's out here to explore investment opportunities."

Sir Gabriel held his hand out to me and I shook it politely.

He was a tall man, definitely muscular under his fine silk suit, the coat hanging open to display the intricate embroidery on his waistcoat. His face was undoubtedly handsome, clean shaven, with piercingly bright hazel eyes that appeared almost golden in the lamplight.

His skin was more tanned than was strictly fashionable but he carried it off with confidence. I noticed his hands were more calloused than I might have expected of a gentleman, although if he had served in the Navy that wouldn't be unusual.

"It's a pleasure to meet you, Sir Gabriel," I said, as politely as I could manage. Handsome he was, but after my encounter with Oscar, I didn't want to feel or project any sort of attraction or allure. "What sort of investments are you investigating?"

"All manner, really," Gabriel said. "Perhaps land, if I can find anything suitable to build on. Perhaps goods, I'm really open to any sort of business, if it comes down to it."

Father made an approving noise. "Very entrepreneurial of you, I'm sure there's plenty a fine man such as yourself could do around this island."

"That's very kind of you to say. I'll be in touch with your permission, Governor." Father nodded, smiling blandly. "I'm sorry, I see someone I need to speak with. Please, excuse me," Gabriel said, and bowed slightly before moving away.

"Right, Gideon," Father said. He put his hand on my shoulder. "Come and meet Lieutenant Ford and his daughter, Chelsea. She's very well accomplished, and some say one of the beauties of the island."

"Father, I was hoping we could discuss my future," I said, as he guided me across the hall to another one of his old friends.

"We are securing your future, tonight," he said. "Now come along."

CHAPTER TWENTY-EIGHT - IN WHICH GIDEON HEARS SOME GOSSIP AND THE PARTY COMES TO A CLOSE

A few hours later, I went out into the garden for a moment to myself. Father's insistence on this confounded ball was wearing on me. Lady after lady had been introduced to me, and each of them so hopeful - expecting something of me. Expecting me to fall instantly in love and ask for their hand in marriage.

It was insufferable.

"Pardon me," a French accented voice said. "I don't mean to interrupt your reverie..."

I turned to see a charmingly dressed lady with dark, elegantly curled hair. "Oh, it's nothing, you're interrupting nothing at all, Miss..."

She held her hand out to me and I dutifully kissed the back of her hand. "Michelle, de la Burt. I only thought you might like to know there's a somewhat more lively party a few houses down the way. Might be a little more to your taste, I think?"

My eyebrows shot up and I cleared my throat. "Is that so?"

"Have you ever heard of the Hellfire Club?"

I swallowed. "I haven't, but it does sound truly intriguing."

"Well, if you can get away," she said. "I've heard Cedric Hale-

Harrington is there, and you know that anything he attends will be truly entertaining."

"Cedric?" I asked, feeling utterly confused. "I'm afraid I don't know who that is."

"Oh, you'd adore Cedric. He caused a scandal at the Ainsworth's masquerade ball a month ago. Rumour has it his father has insisted he return to London, as soon as possible, but of course... well, there are ways to avoid your parents, aren't there?"

I nodded, slowly, getting the sinking feeling that Michelle hadn't only seen straight through my ruse of going along with Father's dance, but that she understood a lot of why I'd been absent from Kingston society for months.

She produced a card and slipped it into my hand. "If you can liberate yourself from this party, see if you can come along," she said. She hid her mouth behind her fan and gave me a wink. "There may even be pirates there..."

With that she turned and was gone, vanishing through the trees of the garden and heading towards the driveway.

I was legitimately tempted to follow her. My interest was spiked by her inference and the name of the club. The card in my hand was shiny and black, with just the symbol of a flame embossed on it. Curiosity about this Cedric was piqued as well, but I knew I couldn't go.

Zeb and Ora were inside this hall, and if I were to leave the party who knows what mischief they'd get up to.

I pocketed the card and went inside, sighing a little. The hours passed in a whirlwind of polite introductions and gentle flirtations from the various ladies, not to mention a smattering of quadrilles, waltzes and various other dances.

Finally, I was gratified to see a number of people saying their goodbyes to my father. That surely heralded the end of the evening was near.

I made my way to the remains of the buffet, where Zeb was

picking at the fillet of salmon and Ora was chatting with a cluster of ladies.

"How has your evening been, Captain Zebulon?" I asked, moving in beside him. My stomach rumbled and I realised I'd had little time over the evening to eat. My father had been so efficient at ensuring I'd met all the guests. I helped myself to a piece of bread and a slice of salmon.

"Good salmon," Zeb said. "Ora's made friends."

"I can see that. You've been very discreet, so, thank you for that," I said. I took a piece of candied pineapple and popped it in my mouth.

"I know how to act around humans," Zeb said. "I'm almost considering being offended."

I smiled at him and then approached Ora. "Good evening, Miss Olivia," I said, a little loudly, by way of announcing my presence.

Ora turned, absolutely beaming. "Gideon, my darling! Come and meet my new friends, they're absolutely lovely."

Ora took my elbow and drew me into the group. "Er, hello," I said, bemused.

"This is Sara, June and Merabella," Ora said, gesturing with a fan to each in turn. Ora hadn't started the evening with a fan. I wondered where and how they'd got it.

"It's a pleasure to meet you," I said. The women all eyed me and giggled.

"The man of the hour," Sara said. "How has the evening been, Gideon, have you chosen a wife?"

"Sara!" Merabella said, and nudged her with her elbow. "You can't be so blunt, it's not becoming."

Sara blushed and shook her head. "I'm so sorry."

"But, have you?" June asked. "I mean, we're all here to try and win your heart, and then Olivia here says you're not even interested in an engagement."

"Oh did she?" I asked, giving Ora a look. They returned it with a wide smile.

"Indeed, I was telling them the story of how you fell in love with one of the merfolk," they said. I sputtered and felt my cheeks redden.

"Olivia! How could you..."

The girls dissolved into peals of giggles, Merabella and June clutched each other's elbows to hold each other up.

"With a response like that, one could almost believe her," Sara said, wiping at her eyes with an embroidered handkerchief. "She is convinced that you wish to return to sea, though."

"Well, that is not far from the truth at all," I said, relieved as the girls calmed down again. I was sure the noise they'd made had attracted some attention. I looked over my shoulder to see my father watching, smiling approvingly.

"Well, I should certainly like to hear more about the merfolk," June said. She smiled at me and did a sort of fluttering thing with her eyelashes. "Perhaps if you were to get an invitation to dinner you might favour me and my family with a story?"

"Oh, uh, perhaps," I said. I squeezed Ora's elbow. "How did you get to talking with such charming young ladies?"

"Oh, we were drawn to each other," Ora said, airily. "Aren't they adorable, couldn't you just eat them up?"

The women all giggled again and I stifled a groan. It sounded salacious to the ladies, and when one knew what I knew about what Ora liked to eat, it became rather alarming.

"Ah," June said. "My mother is approaching. I expect that means we're soon to be leaving. It was a pleasure to meet you, Gideon," she extended her hand to me, and I bent a little to kiss the back of it. A move I had made several times over the course of the evening.

"Thank you for coming," I said, as graciously as I could manage, though truly I was weary by that point in the night.

The girls said far more enthusiastic goodbyes to Ora, and they seemed to be exchanging cards to get in touch with them, there was even talk about afternoon tea.

Where had Ora found cards to hand out? Perhaps they'd dug up some of my old ones? More likely they were just handing out cards they'd already been given from other people?

I moved back beside Zeb, and wondered if there was any way I could get a hug from him without it looking strange.

There absolutely wasn't, but the evening did seem to be drawing to a close.

"Come along," I said to Ora once they had extricated themselves from the young women. "We can make our excuses to Father and turn in."

"This was a lovely evening," Ora said, threading their arm through Zeb's. "I could almost get used to shoes if this was a regular thing humans do. Weren't those girls lovely? I rather think they liked me."

"They definitely liked you," Zeb said. "Couldn't you smell it? They thought you'd put in a good word for them with Gideon."

I spluttered a little, then sighed. "That's probably for the best, I suppose."

Father looked over as we approached and raised his eyebrows. "Well, Gideon? You've met all the best that Kingston has to offer tonight, which girls particularly caught your eye?"

I looked around, saw that aside from Zeb and Ora, the last of the guests were bustling out the front door and to all effects and purposes Father and I were alone.

Perhaps it was the glasses of wine I'd used to fortify myself over the night, but perhaps my patience was simply wearing thin. The town thought I was looking for a bride, I'd played my part well enough not to stir any suspicions against that idea. Father wouldn't lose face, or be seen as a fool for holding a ball of this magnitude. But for now, I had the liberty to be honest.

"None, Father," I said. His expression turned quickly from

magnanimous to stern. I felt my courage shrivel, but I spat out the rest of what I wished to say. "Father, I have no intention of staying, marrying, or taking over your post as Governor."

His face turned a dramatic shade of scarlet. I could see him building up to a proper shouting match, but then he seemed to remember that Zeb and Ora were there. He cleared his throat.

"Gideon, I won't hear such nonsense. Not after I've gone to so much effort to make you happy. You will choose one of the ladies present tonight, or I'll choose for you and arrange the entire thing with her father. It won't be the first time such a match is made."

His voice was low, his words spoken through a clenched jaw, but I could hear the anger vibrating through each syllable.

Dread flooded my body, twisting my stomach into a knot as I swallowed - my mouth was dry now, and my heart fluttering like a hummingbird. "Father, if you'd just listen," I tried, although my voice was weak and reedy.

"You'd best go to bed," Father said. "Right now."

I didn't have to be told twice. Father's rages had turned violent in the past, and I had no desire to be involved in a fight with my father, especially since with Zeb ad Ora both being protective of me, it could turn seriously dangerous.

"Bed, right," I felt lightheaded as I replied. "Captain, Olivia, let us turn in."

I turned on my heels and led the way out of the room, taking the stairs two at a time to get distance between myself and my father.

Zeb and Ora hurried after me and I turned to say goodnight to them on the stairs.

"Best if you stay in your own room tonight," I said to Zeb. "I'll attempt to talk to my father in the morning, alone."

Ora kissed my cheek, squeezed my hand and whispered. "Be strong, you can do this."

Zeb enfolded me in his arms and I relaxed against him,

grateful for the comfort, the warmth of him. "I mean it, Zeb, no sneaking in tonight."

I half expected him to argue but he purred softly and nodded. "I understand, Gid."

With a heavy heart I went to my room, closed and locked the door and settled in bed alone.

I couldn't sleep though. My mind was so full of how I could possibly make Father understand.

Mother had said he was sad, that he missed her... how could I use that to get through to him.

I tossed and turned, kicked my blankets off and then pulled them back over me, sighing with frustration.

Finally I went to sleep, and when I woke I had the answer.

CHAPTER TWENTY-NINE - IN WHICH GIDEON SPEAKS TO HIS FATHER

I washed my face, pulled on one of my old shirts and a pair of breeches, ran my fingers through my hair and tied it back loosely at the nape of my neck. I retrieved one of my leather bound notebooks from the things I'd brought from the ship, then I left my room and went downstairs to join my father for breakfast.

Betsy had said eight in the morning, and I was slightly early, but there he was. Seated at the dining table, his bowl of porridge before him. The same meal I could remember him eating all through my childhood. It struck me as suddenly terribly sad that he never tried anything else, that this would be his breakfast for years to come with nothing changing.

My heart ached for him, seeing him morning after morning alone in this room with his porridge.

Mother's voice echoed in my head. On waking, I'd realised how I had been approaching things entirely in the wrong way. I had to be open and truthful, and I had to use my heart. It wouldn't be easy, I knew that for certain, but I had to try all the same.

I sat in my usual seat. Betsy hurried in with a pot of tea and poured me a cup.

"What would you like for breakfast, Gideon?"

"Uh, toast please, and some fresh fruit would be absolutely lovely, thank you Betsy." I smiled warmly at her, she returned the smile and bustled out.

Father narrowed his eyes at me. "You shouldn't allow her to speak to you so informally, Gideon, it sets a bad precedent."

Right, so, we're starting off as we mean to go on. Time to trust your gut and listen.

"I disagree, Father," I said. "But that isn't what I wished to speak to you about."

"If this is about-"

I held up my hand and cleared my throat. "Father, please just listen for a moment. Please. I need to explain some things to you, and I know they won't be easy to hear."

He inhaled, picked up his cup of tea and then nodded.

"First of all, I wasn't kidnapped by pirates. I ran away from home, and somewhat by accident I joined a pirate ship."

"If you expect me to believe that tripe, you are deluded."

"Here." I pushed the journal towards him, my heart in my throat. I had hoped on some level I wouldn't need it, but I could see... no, I could sense, I could feel his obstinate determination to ignore me and what I was saying. I had to break through the wall of his anger somehow, get him off-footed so he would actually listen to me. If it had to be this way, then so be it.

He eyed the book distrustfully, then opened it and flipped through a few pages.

"What is this? A journal?"

"Yes, Father. It's a journal I've made, an account of all I've done while I've been on the Grey Kelpie. A lot of it is written from memory since I only got the journals a few weeks ago, but it's quite detailed."

I watched as he flipped to one of the pages where I detailed the extensive sexual encounters I'd had with Tate and Ezra. It was the first journal, Ora came into the second one, and Zeb was in the third. Father's eyebrows raised and his complexion paled.

"Gideon, this is outrageous," he said. He slammed the book shut and pushed it away from himself. "Scandalous and disgusting. I don't understand why you'd show me something like this."

"Because I want you to understand something about me," I said, boldly. Betsy walked in with a tray of breakfast for me and set it down. "I want you to understand why I won't do what you say, and why I won't be the son you want me to be. Which I'm sorry for, by the way. Genuinely, I'm sorry I'm a disappointment to you."

I swallowed then, surprised by the tears welling up. Betsy set the food in front of me, the plates rattled in her haste. "Thank you, Betsy."

She fled the room.

"What do you want me to understand?" Father asked. "That you're a... I don't even know what. A sinner? Or worse, that this is all fiction and you're trying to use it to make some obscure point?"

"I'm not trying to trick you, Father," I said. I took a deep breath, because his words still hurt, even if they were things I had battled with internally myself, things I had hated myself for. I picked up my knife and buttered a piece of toast. "This is going to be hard to understand. I found out something remarkable about my mother, about your wife, she was... she had magic in her. Real magic."

Father sputtered before shouting, loud enough to startle me so I dropped my knife. "Your mother wasn't a witch!"

"No," I clenched my teeth together. *If only he would listen!* "No, I know she wasn't. She had fae blood. Real fae magic, buried inside her, and I inherited it from her. I've learned... so much about myself, and I've even spoken to her."

That shocked him. He had been starting to get up from his

seat, to do what, I had no idea, but he fell back into his seat, one hand on his chest.

"What?"

I swallowed and nodded. "Yes, she's... well, she's not a ghost, she's in a different place-"

"Heaven, your mother is in Heaven."

"Maybe," I shrugged. "I went to the Splintered Isles, and O... uh, one of my lovers, they took me to the source of magic there. Mother spoke to me, she told me... she told me that you wouldn't give up on getting me back. That you'd continue to send the Navy after the Grey Kelpie because you miss her, and you won't lose me too."

Father picked up his teacup and drained it, then shook his head. "This is ridiculous. Your time away has clearly addled your mind. I'll have to see about getting a doctor..."

"Father, no!" I stood up and shouted. I think I surprised myself as much as I surprised him. I had never said such a thing in such a way to him. But I knew I was right, that hard as it was, he had to hear this. "I spoke to her. She loves you, I love you, God help me, and we both want you to be happy, but you have to let yourself grieve her first. You have to release your sadness over it. You have to be happy that you had that time with her, and you have to let me go and be happy myself. I have found my path, and it's not here."

"Gideon," Father said. His eyes narrowed and his jaw clenched and he started to stand up. I stood my ground. "You are speaking improperly, it's utterly unacceptable for you to talk to me like this. You don't know what you're talking about."

I closed my eyes and thought of love. The love I'd felt from Mother. The love I still had for Father, despite everything. The joy and pride I felt when I was with my lovers, the acceptance and love they gave me.

My fingertips tingled as my magic flooded through me. I opened myself up to him, let my heart feel what he was feeling.

It was surprisingly easy to feel it. Anger, yes, rage more accurately, but it masked such fear. He ached with the fear and under that, fuelling the fear, was loneliness. It was like a punch to the gut, feeling the power of that loneliness.

I pushed my chair back, moved closer to him with one hand raised. He was standing now and eyeing me uncertainly. "Please, I know you're afraid," I said, fearing retaliation of some kind, I pushed through the resistance and put my hand on his chest. Under his shirt I could feel his heart pounding. "I feel it too. You don't have to hide that. You don't have to pretend things are all right when they're not."

For a moment we stood like that, me looking up at him with my hand on his chest. Him looking back at me, a muscle in his jaw jumping with tension, his face red now, his eyebrows drawn down and together.

With all the desperation and yearning for my mother I could summon, I pushed my magic into him. Willing him to feel the love I had for them, hoping he'd feel the truth in my words, the need I had to be free to go with them.

Hopefully this will do something like it did with Solomon, and it will break through that damn wall of his.

I felt it working, in some manner. I could feel the heat of my love flowing from me into him, the way the fire of my magic showed itself in my mind's eye.

But then my flames hit something, something strange and indefinable. A barrier? An actual wall? How could that be?

I thought of my mother again and a devastating sadness and loss seemed to reflect off the barrier somehow and I gasped at the raw pain of it.

Father recoiled from my grasp and I let go of him, my magic sputtered out.

Certainly *something* had happened, but I had no idea what it was, it certainly felt like the barrier - the sadness? Had stopped my magic from working the way it had on Solomon.

As I tried to understand what had happened, Father raised a hand and backhanded me.

It was such a hard blow it knocked me into the table. The edge of the table bit into my side, making my ribs ache, but the real pain was in my cheek, where I felt sure he'd have bruised me. My hand had flown out with the impact, and crashed into the teacups and plates, shattering some of them on the floor.

I took a deep breath. "Hitting me won't keep me here," I said, as fiercely as I could manage. "And it *won't* bring her back. You don't have to be lonely unless you choose to."

"Quiet!" he shouted.

"Listen, we could still have a relationship, but if you don't stop sending people after me, if you won't see reason and let this go, then I could take those journals to one of the printing presses and get it published."

He paled then. "No one would publish that smut, that filth!"

"I could pay them to, I have money of my own, now." I stood up and checked my hand for china shards, but there was nothing there. "Someone would publish it, and distribute it."

"I'll burn it!"

"You can't burn it out of my memory," I said. "I can write it all over again."

"Your threat is meaningless," Father said. "It's fiction, pornography, it wouldn't mean anything."

"Yes, Father, it would," I said. "My name, which is also your name, would be printed on the cover. At best, your friends would think your son has a wicked imagination and perverted tendencies. At worst, they'd believe it was a true account and they'd know both of those things are true."

He stumbled back against the wall and clutched his chest. For a moment I feared he was suffering a heart attack but then he shook his head. "You wouldn't dare, your reputation would be ruined as well."

"I don't care about my reputation." Some of the fire of my

anger died, and I sighed instead, because although my claim had the effect I wanted it to, it wasn't the way I wanted this conversation to go. I adjusted the way my shirt sat and swallowed, looking into his eyes.

"Father, *please*. I'd far rather leave on amenable terms. If you wish to train someone to take your place, perhaps you could mentor one of the men from the Trinity Royal. If you wish to have closer friends, then you need to open yourself up to them in some small way. But you can't hold me here and force me to be something I don't want to be."

"You're my son," he said, low.

"Yes, but the problem isn't me. You aren't allowing yourself to feel anything, you're trying to control everything instead of feel... You have to grieve your wife. You have to grieve Alison, we both do, and then let go of those feelings. You can honour her memory, and you can love her still, but you can also live your life in her honour. She wants you to be happy." I blinked away tears, not wanting to look weak while I talked about something which undoubtedly made Father feel weak himself.

Father stared at me and for a moment I thought I had got through to him. But then he pulled himself up to his full height, closed the distance between us and gripped me by the arm.

"You will go to your room and think about how you should address your father with respect," he said.

"I won't!"

He started to move, propelling me before him with one hand on my arm. "Father, I'm not a child, don't be ridiculous!"

We were at the base of the stairs when he really let loose with a bellow. "I am your father! I am the master of this house! I will have your obedience!"

He gripped me by both shoulders and shook me. I was overwhelmed, feeling the rage and sadness that warred within my father. My eyes streamed with tears now, as the sadness flowed out of me, compounded by the beloved memories I had for my mother, and my frustration at his unyieldingness.

There was a noise at the top of the stairs and we both looked up to see Zeb and Ora descending the stairs. Zeb was in his black leather trousers again, shirtless, showing off his gloriously muscled chest. Ora was in a nightshirt, and had a certain inhuman cast to their skin, shiny and silver. One could instantly see that Ora had no womanly curve to their chest, and that they weren't an ordinary human.

"You should take your hands off Gideon," Zeb said, his voice a warning growl.

"Captain, this is none of your concern, please go back to your room while I deal with my rebellious child."

"I'm not a child," I said. Reaching to try and dislodge Father's grip on me but finding it impossible.

"You'd better let him go," Ora said. They came down the stairs with eerie grace. "Or you won't like what happens next."

"Ora, no, Zeb, it's all right." I held my hand out to them palm out, signalling them to stop. "Please, I can handle this."

"How dare you address the Captain and his wife that way," Father said, obviously ignoring what was actually happening to fall back on etiquette. Something I must have learned from him, after all.

"They're not.. Father, please listen. They're not who I said they were. Ora is one of the merfolk, they took me to the magic place where I spoke to Mother. Zeb is… well, Zeb used to be a cat, but now he can shift forms into a human when he chooses to." I swallowed, looked up into Father's face. It felt like my last chance to get through to him, so I took hold of his hand. "I know it's hard to understand, but please, please try."

This time I didn't focus on my feelings for Mother, although they were certainly still present. I thought of the love I had for Ora and Zeb, how flattered I was that they had come to look after me and protect me.

My thoughts turned to Tate and Ezra, and I missed them with a fierce ache but I focused on the love I had for them. Then the rest of the crew of the Kelpie, all my friends and how they had enriched my life. Sagorika and her fierceness, balanced with love and kindness, Zack and his quest to be himself as truly as he could. Anton, James, all of them...

My magic flared up inside me and it flowed down my hand and into Father's hand.

Do you see? I asked him, silently, locking my eyes to his. *Do you see how much love there is in the world? Do you see who I am and how happy I've been? Do you see me?*

I felt the barrier, the anger and the sadness. It was so powerful, it had been there for so many years after all, I realised.

I felt something new from my father, something there behind the barrier, something different. Gently as I could, I pressed my magic against the barrier, trying to get through it. There.

Loss. Father's belief that the universe had taken something from him, which it had, of course. That he was the victim.

I took a deep breath and let the warmth of my magic course into him, pushing through the barrier, warming it and melting it almost. He'd lost his wife, and it was a tragedy, but he'd held onto that feeling of being victimised over everything else. The only thing he'd let himself feel was protecting him from everything else. Anger to hold out the joy and the love and the wonder.

It felt like it was working, almost. I blinked, my mind racing for what the missing piece of the magic connection could be.

Then I found it. My love for my father. I set aside the fear and the anger I felt towards him and focused on how much I loved him instead. How I accepted his flaws, his denial of me, and loved him all the same.

My heart felt broken open and I gasped, Father breathed in a rasping, hoarse noise as if he hadn't taken a breath in years and was unaccustomed to it.

"That's it," I said. Father pulled his hand from mine and shut his eyes, his hand flying to his chest again.

Ora thundered down the stairs to my side, half stepping between me and Father.

"It's all right," I said. I put my hand on Ora's shoulder and moved past them, closer to my father. "Father, it's all right."

He looked at me with horror, his eyes wide, uncomprehending, tears leaking out. "I don't understand, this is.. This is monstrous. What did you do?"

Father turned on his heel and stormed up the stairs, pushing past Zeb, who sort of lunged at him, but let him pass. We listened as his steps thundered up the hallway and the door on his study slammed shut.

Ora slipped their arm around my waist and rested their chin on my shoulder. My heart was pounding and I was unsure - should I follow my father, and keep trying to talk to him? Or should I give him some time to process all that I'd said?

I had no idea.

I took a deep breath and glanced sideways at Ora. "Thanks for appearing when you did. I think he was going to lock me in my room and force me to marry Lady Caroline."

"Any time," Ora said, and kissed my cheek. "What happens now, do we pack up and leave?"

My heart sunk, because, yes, maybe that was the wisest course of action. "I need my journal back first. Are you two hungry? Betsy will make you breakfast, I think."

We went back into the dining room, and I went to the kitchen to find Betsy, she was cowering a little behind the kitchen table.

"Father's in his study," I said. I gave her a sad smile and she relaxed a little, straightening her shoulders. "If you don't mind, we'd like to continue breakfast, me and my guests."

"Of course, Gideon," she said. "What would they like?"

"If there's any salmon leftover from last night, or bacon I'm sure that would go down well." She nodded and went to the ice box. "Betsy, I expect you overheard all of that," I said, feeling suddenly shy, despite all that had happened. "I hope you don't think less of me."

She turned back with a fierce smile on her face. "Not at all, Gideon," she said. "My sister is the same. I figure love is just love, no matter who it's between."

I relaxed and let out a breath I hadn't realised I'd been holding. "Thank you, Betsy. That means a lot."

"I'll be out in a moment with some things to eat. How about kippers?"

"Definitely, thank you so much."

CHAPTER THIRTY - IN WHICH GIDEON AND HIS FATHER TALK FURTHER

Ora and Zeb were in the Lilac room, packing up what little they'd brought from the ship, and the new clothes we'd purchased.

"Give me a bit of time," I'd asked them. "There's a few things in my room I need to decide whether to bring or not."

Then I'd pulled out my mother's old suitcases from the storage cupboard, opened them on my bed and started the difficult process of packing.

I lined the bottom of one of the cases with the rest of my books I'd left behind the first time. Then I'd gone to the wardrobe to decide which of my clothes to bring and which I could live without.

The suitcases would only take so many items, so I found my absolute favourite pieces and started with those. A brocade coat of dusky green, an embroidered waistcoat... I was trying to choose between two linen shirts when the door to my bedroom opened.

"I told you I'd need a bit of time," I said.

"I wasn't aware of any such thing," my father replied.

My heart skipped and I turned to look at him, dropping both shirts onto the bed. "Father?"

"It looks as though you're leaving," he said, almost blandly. The anger had gone from his voice, and from him. When I tried to sense what he was feeling I felt only sadness now.

"I expected you didn't want to see me again."

"I wasn't sure what I wanted," he said. He took a seat at my vanity and looked me up and down. "This is a lot for me to take in, I'm sure you're aware."

"I am." I closed one of the suitcases, moved it to the side and sat on the bed. "It's an incredible amount, and I'm sure I do sound utterly mad to you."

He rubbed his fingers over the bridge of his nose and closed his eyes. "I did think... but then you touched me and I felt... I felt something I haven't felt in a long time. It made me think of your mother so much, and then when I thought about her, of my Alison, and the way she made me feel." He swallowed and I realised he was fighting back tears. My heart leapt with excitement.

Oh, Mother, did it work? Did I get through to him?

"How she made you feel?" I prompted, moving a little further down the bed to get closer to him. "What do you mean?"

"When we were first courting," he said, slowly. He dropped his hand to his lap and twisted his fingers together, keeping his gaze on them. "She had many suitors, many vying for her attention. She was so... so alive. Her eyes would shine like stars, and her smile." He shook his head, smiling himself now. I felt a wave of affection and excitement off him, it must have been how he felt back then. "When she spoke to you, you felt like you were the most important, the most interesting person in the world."

"I remember," I said, smiling a little myself now. "Like whatever you were saying, she wanted to hear it, she wanted to hear me."

Father looked up at me, his expression softer than I'd seen it for years.

I remember when I was a little boy. Him taking Mother and me on a rowing boat, around to a secluded bay. We had a picnic on the beach and bathed in the water. He was so happy then, Mother sang a song...

"She always made me feel like that. I knew I had to do anything I could to win her over, and somehow, it worked. She chose me, although she could have had her pick of any of the bachelors in London society, young, old, any of them."

I felt his joy, as it had been then, the echo of it as he felt it. The excitement and pride of being the one.

"You were so happy," I breathed.

"I was." He sat up straighter and took a deep breath. "Then we married. I knew how lucky I was, I knew she chose me, and that I had her. I think I knew, on some level, she was more than just another girl."

"She was your true love?"

"No, that she had some kind of magic about her."

I stopped breathing for a moment. I had no idea Father had ever known such a thing. To hear him say so now was enough to stun me into silence. Father seemed like his old self again, remembering Mother this way. I dared to hope, although I was still utterly confused by his apparent change of heart.

"I never pursued it, never asked her about it, in fact I have no idea if she was aware of it herself, but when you get to know someone the way you do when you're married... I could see the effect she had on people. Even total strangers. She made them better. She understood their emotions, what they needed, without being told."

He looked over at the portrait I had of her on the bedside table and smiled, his eyes crinkling in a way I hadn't seen since before Mother got sick.

"Then, later, after she died. I could see her in you."

A scratchy lump formed in my throat and I swallowed against it, feeling tears pricking at the back of my eyes. "You could?"

"It wasn't just your hair, or the shape of your face, although those are certainly hers. It was the way you understood people. It wasn't as... you coming back, saying those things to me this morning. I can see it. I see you have her same charm, the magic, whatever it is."

"Father..." I said. I got up and moved off the bed, moving to stand in front of him. "Thank you, you have no idea how much it means to me to hear you say that."

His vulnerability had put me entirely at ease, and I felt nothing for him now but love. I wanted to help him through this.

"You ... whatever you did downstairs, with your hands... it unlocked something in me. I was afraid..."

I went to my knees and took his hands in mine, showing him I was with him, helping him through expressing something that was clearly difficult.

"But your words, I kept hearing them. That I'd stopped myself feeling anything at all, and you were right. So, here I am. I'm sorry, Gideon. I know I've been very hard on you, and I haven't listened. Please understand, I was doing what I thought was right."

"I know you were," I said. I squeezed his hands and he gently squeezed back.

"I can't approve of your choice to go to sea with... with those pirates."

My stomach turned over and I sat back on my heels. "What?"

"I can't approve. But I thought about your mother, how she loved you and wanted you to be happy, so I can't stop you, I won't stop you. But you are still my son, and I can't have you known as a pirate."

I swallowed hard. It half sounded like he wanted me to follow my heart, but also he couldn't let me?

"I'm afraid I don't understand, what are you saying?"

"They're pirates, Gideon, they're the enemy."

"They're not what you think they are," I said. "They're actually very good men. Tate takes slave ships and releases the slaves, he leaves them enough money to survive and gives them the ship. It's good work. And well, we steal from the Spanish too, but they're the enemy of England. They don't rape, they don't abuse their power over their prisoners. They kill when they have to, but so do the men of the Navy."

I bit my lip, uncertain if any of what I was saying would get through to him.

His face had closed off into a frown. His mouth a thin line. "The Shearwater, though..."

"I don't know exactly what happened between the two of you," I said. "Perhaps if you could explain?"

"He made me a laughing stock. Took my merchant fleet, thumbed his nose at the Navy. I was a Captain and he stole them right from under my nose, stole my first mate even..." He sighed and shook his head. "But after everything that has happened since then, it all feels less important somehow. Perhaps it was a way to feel *something*..."

"Do you think..." I swallowed, the hope in me desperate and wanting him to agree so badly. I cleared my throat. "You're the governor, you have the authority to grant pardons, don't you?"

Father looked at me, one eyebrow raised.

"I just think," I started. I cleared my throat once more, feeling shy but, well, if I'd already told him this much, I might as well ask for everything at once. The worst he could do was lock me in my room and never let me out again... and realistically, Zeb and Ora would break me out.

"If what you're worried about my going with pirates, well. If you pardoned them, said there was a misunderstanding, perhaps issued Tate with a letter of Marque... then you could tell your friends I was making my way as a privateer. It'd be a lot more acceptable wouldn't it? Especially after I failed out of the Navy."

My father sat back in the chair and folded his arms. "Gideon."

I swallowed but didn't respond. I could feel his uncertainty, but there was a spark of hope there too. Maybe he'd consider my plan?

There was a knock on my door, and both of us jumped. I got to my feet. "Come in!"

I expected Zeb and Ora but it was Betsy. "Gideon," she said, then she saw my father and visibly stiffened. "I'm so sorry to interrupt sir, but there's someone here to visit Gideon."

"There is?" It wasn't like I was expecting anyone. A thrill of fear went through me - it couldn't be Tate or Ezra could it? They wouldn't be so rash, I hoped.

"Indeed, if you'll come downstairs? Or I could tell him you're not taking visitors."

"No, I'll see him," I said, quickly. "Father, you can think about what I've suggested, perhaps? I think... I think it would be mutually beneficial."

He looked up at me, but didn't respond. I leaned in on impulse and kissed him on the cheek. "I love you," I said, because whatever happened, I may as well be as honest with him as I could. I was feeling his emotions, and I hoped he could feel mine too. The hope, and the love, in particular. The relief I felt that he was actually talking and listening, I hoped he felt that as well.

"This way, then," Betsy said, her eyes wide as she watched this interchange, and then she led the way out and downstairs.

CHAPTER THIRTY-ONE - IN WHICH THERE IS AN AWKWARD CONVERSATION

"*H*e's just in the parlour," Betsy said, nodding at the door. "Go on. I'll bring tea."

"Thank you, Betsy," I said. I was now rather certain it was somehow Tate, maybe Solomon had disguised him magically, or maybe he had just gotten bolder. I was excited to see him again, because I missed him, so there was a spring in my step as I pushed the door open enough to walk through.

It wasn't Tate. Oscar Carroll stood near the unlit fireplace, dressed in his formal Naval uniform.

My heart sank.

Oh, yes, he said he wanted to speak with me privately, and then I didn't see him again last night.

"Lieutenant Commander Carroll," I said. I wished I had put on a waistcoat or something, I felt my stomach turn over, unpleasantly. There were footsteps behind me, I turned, expecting Betsy, but Zeb walked in.

"We're ready to go," Zeb said. He looked at Oscar. "Who's this?"

"Lieutenant Oscar Carroll, of the Trinity Royal," I said, formally. "This is Captain Zebulon of the..." my mind blanked on the made up ship name we'd invented for the fake ship. "Ship I came in on," I finished.

"Oh, right," Oscar said. "How lovely to meet you. I uh, I apologise for the bluntness, but this was to be a private conversation."

"Uh, with all due respect," I said quickly. "There's nothing I don't trust Zeb, I mean, Captain Zebulon with. You can speak freely with him here."

Oscar cleared his throat and raised his eyebrows. "You're quite sure?"

I swallowed, my heart sinking. This didn't sound like it could be good.

Betsy came in with a tray of teacups and a teapot. "Please excuse me," she said as she set the tray down and started arranging the tea things.

Oscar looked at her and then at me, his expression perplexed. I nodded at him. "Go on, you had something you wanted to say?"

"Gideon..." he approached with three quick strides and took my hand. He peered into my eyes as if I were a puzzle. "Gideon, I love you."

The room was utterly silent. My stomach roiled and I swallowed. "No," I breathed. He ignored me.

Zeb barked out a laugh, then I heard him call out. "Ora! Come see this!"

Oscar's cheeks had two points of redness on them and he squeezed my hand harder. "I love you, and I want to ask you to marry me. I know it won't be a legal wedding, we probably can't do it in a church, but I'd like to spend the rest of my life with you and this is the best way I can think of."

I tried to pull my hand back but his grip was strong.

"No, Oscar, I don't think, this isn't a good idea," I said, stammering and falling over my response.

I heard footsteps, looking over my shoulder I saw Ora arrive in the doorway, wearing their old clothes. "What's happening?"

"This Naval man wants to marry Gid."

"He what?" Ora's eyes widened.

"I know it's against the normal way of things," Oscar said. I could see a sheen of sweat over his forehead and I felt absolutely wretched. "But please, Gideon. I must have your answer."

I shook my head. "No, Oscar, I can't, I don't love you. You don't even love me, you've just been... uh." I didn't want to tell him what I'd done. It made me feel dirty and wicked, and not in a fun way. It made me feel like I'd done something awful. "Confused," I finished, like a coward.

I slipped my hand out of his and took a step back.

"I'm not confused, Gideon. I knew it on the Trinity Royal, and I knew it again last night at the dance. I hated the thought of you choosing one of those girls."

I took a deep breath and rubbed my forehead, conscious that I was mirroring my father.

Ora chuckled behind me.

"Oscar, I know what you feel is real, but please, it's magic. There's magic involved, and I don't. I'm so sorry, I had no idea that it would have this kind of effect on you. I feel awful, really. I never intended -"

Another set of footsteps. I turned to look, seeing that Betsy was still in the room as well. She'd moved back to the wall and was just watching, blatantly.

Father was in the doorway. "Gideon, who is... Oh, hello, Lieutenant Commander Carroll. How nice to see you again."

Out of the misery swamping me, a panicked idea came to mind. "Father, Oscar Carroll would be a wonderful candidate for you to take under your wing, don't you think?"

"I, what?" Oscar asked, perplexed.

"I beg your pardon?" Father said, apparently as perplexed.

Their confusion bolstered my idea, made me a little more confident in the wisdom of it.

"As I'm planning on going back to sea," I started, speaking slowly. "And Father will need someone to help with his work, someone to train to take over eventually as Governor, perhaps he could speak with Captain Thornton on your behalf. Then you could further your career," I said to Oscar.

"Going back to sea?" Oscar echoed.

"Indeed, it's the best idea. Far more practical than what you were suggesting," I said.

To my consternation, I felt an arm around my waist and stiffened. Zeb leaned in and rubbed his cheek against my forehead, staking his claim as if he were still a cat.

Oscar's eyes widened and his mouth dropped open.

I didn't look at Father. Instead I gently pulled away from Zeb and cleared my throat again.

I have to do something to break the enchantment. Maybe I could push at him with my magic... It had worked with Solomon and Father. Just... try and feel nothing, try and break the attraction he had for me.

I took a breath and went to put my hand on Oscar's elbow, which seemed like the least intimate way I could touch him. I summoned my magic and let it flow through my fingers and guided him towards my father.

Stop loving me, I'm nothing special, I thought. His body stiffened, either from my touch or from the magic, I couldn't guess.

"What do you think, Father? Could such a thing be arranged for such a promising young lieutenant?"

Father seemed as if he knew something was out of the ordinary, but he didn't seem inclined to find out what it was. He looked Oscar up and down.

"Yes, perhaps, if such a thing is of interest to Carroll?"

Oscar's breath hitched as I let go of his elbow, and he swallowed hard. He glanced at me, and then back at Father.

"I, yeh," he cleared his throat. "I mean, uh. Yes, sir. It would be my honour to be singled out in such a way."

"Wonderful. How about we all leave you two to work out the details between you, I'll see the Captain and Olivia back to their room, to finish their packing," I babbled. "So sorry, Oscar, but good luck!"

I'm not entirely sure if that worked or not. It could be that he's still in love with me and using this opportunity to ingratiate himself to my father. But he's not actively trying to marry me so that's something of a win.

He did seem to stutter, perhaps it did work?

Before anyone could protest, I bustled Ora and Zeb out of the room, followed by Betsy. Father cleared his throat and started talking logistics and permissions from the Navy, and I breathed a sigh of relief.

CHAPTER THIRTY-TWO - IN WHICH
THE CREW IS REUNITED

*S*everal hours later, I stood in the entranceway of my
father's house. He stood between me and the door.

"This all seems very fast," he said. "Will you come back and
visit?"

"Will... uh, would all of my friends be welcome in the
house?" I asked.

Father's expression shot through aggravated and afraid and
then settled on accepting. "It won't be easy, and you'll each have
your own rooms, but yes. I think I can make that concession."

"Then I'd love to come back and visit."

He handed me a few pieces of paper and I slipped them into
my satchel. Zeb carried my suitcases down the stairs.

"I'm sorry for springing all of this on you so fast," I said.
Then I hugged him. He hugged me back and I felt affection and
love flow between us. I could hardly believe things had worked
out in this way.

"Keep honouring your mother," he said, softly. "I'll ensure
Carroll isn't... uh, bereft."

"You will?" I pulled back to look at him.

"I'll give him so many things to read, he won't have time to
think of you."

I breathed a sigh of relief and nodded. "I think he'll stop caring anyway, I tried something, but..."

"You're not easy to forget," Ora said, taking my hand.

"Right, thank you." I shook my head and gave my father a smile. "Thank you for everything. I'll write, and I'll let you know when we're coming back to port."

"Travel well," Father said.

We walked into town together, Zeb, Ora and myself. There was a lightness to my heart that I hadn't felt in months, perhaps in all my years since I had realised I didn't want to marry a girl. The nagging worry at the back of my head was gone now.

"The oracle cards might help with Carroll," Ora said, thoughtfully.

"Oh, yes, maybe," I said, surprised. "I'd honestly forgotten about them. That's a good idea, I'll check them. Maybe Solomon knows how they work..."

The day was sunny and warm, and I could hear birds singing in the trees we passed on the way into town.

I couldn't stop smiling. Father had broken down his wall and opened his heart to me. He had embraced Mother's memory. I'd even noticed he'd taken a portrait of her out of storage and put it up in his study. It was a good sign. She'd be able to watch over him.

Although in some ways I'd have liked to stay a few more days and spend more time with him, I knew in my heart that some space would be good for him. He'd had a huge emotional breakthrough and although he'd managed well today, I felt he needed time to adjust.

Time to think through what we'd spoken of, time to actually grieve mother, with tears and memories, time to heal those wounds as best he could.

If I was around it could get in the way of that process. He

could feel my emotions instead of his own, or he could fall back on his own ways and insist I study or marry a girl again.

No, my instincts told me that I'd done enough for now, and that Father needed time. I was getting more and more confident in my skin, and in trusting my instincts.

I also knew I'd never draw on my magic to make someone attracted to me ever again.

Never, ever again.

We entered the town and the market smells of fresh food washed over us.

"To the ship?" Zeb asked.

I thought for a moment, considering Tate and Ezra, imagining what they looked like, and focused on how much I'd been missing them in the last few days. I got an image of the inn the sailors frequented - The King's Court.

"I know where Tate and Ezra are," I said. "Let's go and surprise them."

The King's Court wasn't a place I'd ever ventured into before. But I knew where it was. I sped up as we got closer, feeling anticipation building in my stomach.

I'm going to see my Captain and my Master!

My soul exalted.

The inn was much nicer, cleaner and more respectable looking than the ones in Nassau and Tortuga we'd been to recently. It was relatively busy, with various ensigns and low level sailors from the Navy occupying some of the tables, along with merchants and what must be corsairs or privateers taking up the rest of the tables.

Zeb made a beeline for a table in the back corner where Tate sat beside Ezra, with Solomon on his other side and Sagorika sitting with her back to us. They appeared to be playing cards and drinking.

Ezra saw us right away and his eyes met mine. My heart thumped and my cock stirred a little, anticipating the promise of being reunited with him.

Tate caught sight of me soon after and his face lit up in a bright smile. "We heard there was a party at the Governor's house," Tate said.

"Did you choose a bride?" Ezra asked. "Everyone's just dying to know." He propped his chin on his hand and grinned at me, wickedly.

"That's rich coming from you," I teased. "The only one with an actual wife." He stuck his tongue out in response, and I realised some of the giddy happiness I felt was reflected from him and Tate, not just my own.

"A lieutenant from the Navy did propose," Ora said, taking the seat beside Solomon and giving him a warm smile. Solomon raised his eyebrows but gave Ora a slight smile.

"He did?" Tate asked. "That sounds like a story."

"I don't want to talk about that right this moment, thank you," I said.

Zeb took the seat beside Sagorika and I sidled behind the table to wrap my arms around Tate and kiss him hello.

"It's so fucking good to see you again, Gid," Tate said. "Tell us what happened?"

"Well, first thing...." I pulled the papers Father had given me out of my satchel, checked them and then spread two on the table. "Official pardons for one 'Bloody' Tate Blythe - I don't think I knew that was your last name, it's adorable. And one for Ezra Jackson, also known as the Shearwater pirate."

Ezra frowned, grabbed the piece of paper with his name on it and pulled it towards him. "How did you... ?" he ran a finger over the wax seal next to my father's signature. "This is real?"

"Oh yes, it is," I said. "As Governor, and a former Admiral, he has the power from the King. And furthermore," I paused dramatically and pulled out the other piece of paper and set it on the table before them.

This piece of paper had a long piece of text on it and two seals at the bottom. One of them was from the admiralty court.

"A letter of Marque?" Tate asked, his voice utterly toneless. "It can't be."

"It is. Father has a handful pre-approved from the court, to use at his discretion."

"I wasn't aware such a thing was possible," Ezra said. He stood, leaning over the table to check over the signatures.

"Father has a fair bit of influence," I said, feeling quite proud of him. "And he wants us to come back and visit. If he didn't do these, then it would be rather hard."

"I expect he's putting word out through the witch network, too," Solomon said. "This is remarkable, really."

I sat down in the free seat next to Ezra and leaned over to kiss him hello.

"This is incredible, Gideon," Ezra said, kissing me again. "Very impressive."

"It wasn't exactly easy," I said. "He almost locked me in my room, but thankfully Zeb and Ora put an end to that."

"Thank goodness," Tate said. Then he smirked and winked at me. "We'd have had to steal you away in the middle of the night."

I shivered at the thought of that. That fantasy I'd spoken to Tate of once and he'd always remembered. "Hm, well, maybe we can pretend something like that anyway?"

"You got us pardons and a letter of marque," Tate said. He wrapped his arm around my shoulder and pulled me against him. "You can have anything you want, Gideon."

"Do you have rooms here?" I asked Tate, leaning my head on his shoulder, and feeling like now I was truly home.

"Indeed. Just upstairs."

"Then I think I know what I want."

CHAPTER THIRTY-THREE - IN WHICH GIDEON AND HIS LOVERS ARE REACQUAINTED AND CELEBRATE THEIR GOOD FORTUNE

*H*aving made excuses to Solomon and Sagorika, we ensconced ourselves in the room Tate had hired upstairs.

The anticipation was high, and I could almost feel my lovers' hands on me before they touched me. My skin felt electric. As soon as the door shut I started to pull off my clothes.

Tate shrugged off his shirt and then wrapped me in his arms, kissing me passionately. I melted against him, losing myself in the kiss, and feeling my magic flow up and into him, accentuating my excitement and eagerness and echoing off his passion.

I felt hands at the waistband of my trousers and realised I was being stripped further by Ora. They leaned in to kiss my neck just below my ear, making me shiver pleasantly.

Tate pulled back from the kiss and Ezra took his place, claiming my mouth in a possessive and invigorating way. I moaned and pressed my rear towards Ora, who slipped their hand down to tease at me.

Ezra broke the kiss to bite at my neck on the other side to Ora and I saw Zeb and Tate in a clinch, their hands roaming freely over each other as they kissed deeply.

I wanted to sink to the ground then and there but Ora's fingers were insistent and methodical in opening me up. Ezra's fingers found my nipple and teased at it, making it hard before flicking it with one finger so that I gasped.

Ora withdrew their fingers and wrapped their arms around my waist, leaning over my shoulder to kiss Ezra.

"I'm going first," Ora murmured into Ezra's mouth. He responded with a brief nod. Before I could ascertain what they were referring to, Ora had pushed their cock inside me, making me gasp. My knees buckled and threatened to give out. I found myself held up by Ora's hand, leaning my head on Ezra's shoulder, his arm around me as well.

"That's right," Ezra growled in approval. "Fuck our little wanton whore against me, I want to feel it through him."

Ora moaned and shoved into me harder. I lifted my arms to wrap them around Ezra's neck, my cheeks flaming from the name calling but unable to deny that at that moment all I wanted was to be their whore, to take whatever reaming they'd give me and beg for more.

Ezra seemed a little unsteady on his feet as well, with Ora pushing me bodily against him. Then Tate wrapped his arms around Ezra from behind and braced us all up with his sturdy stance.

Ezra's trousers were shoved down and his hand wrapped around my cock and his, stroking both at once. A high pitched keening noise erupted from my throat and I closed my eyes as the sensations threatened to overwhelm me.

"You're not to come yet, pet," Ezra growled. I heard the growl echoed by Zeb, somewhere behind me, behind Ora I had to assume, since I heard them moan louder and then thrust harder into me.

With my eyes closed I focused on the linking magic flame, an eternal chain linking me to each of my lovers and in my mind's eye I saw the way we were connected. Zeb fucking Ora, Ora fucking me, Ezra and my cocks stroked together and Tate teasing into Ezra's hole.

My eyes opened and I looked into Ezra's face... he almost never took a cock, in fact... I couldn't remember it ever happening. He always was the one fucking someone else.

"Ez," I breathed.

"If not with all of you then when?" he asked softly, pressing his forehead to mine as his breathing turned into a deep moan.

It sent fire through me and I wanted to reach completion then and there, but I remembered his words.

Ora bucked into me and cried out as they filled me and leaned their cheek on my back, their body reverberating with the pounding Zeb gave them.

I kept eye contact with Ezra, watching his expressions as Tate took him apart with his fingers, teasing and stretching and then the incredible moment when he entered him, and Ezra's face became a silent scream of happiness, melting into bliss.

"Please Ezra, Master, my love," I breathed, bucking my hips forward into his hand. "Please, I need to."

"More," Tate said. He clamped his arm around Ezra's chest and pulled him upright, impaling him on his cock. Ezra lost his grip on my cock and I whined softly, trying to follow. Ora's hands clasped on my waist and lifted me bodily. Ezra caught me, plunging himself inside me, my hole still slick with Ora's fluids, so that he entered smooth and easy, although the ease didn't lessen the sensation at all. I positioned my legs as if I was putting them around Ezra's waist, but Tate was right there, too, so I braced my heels on his hips.

"Yes!" I cried, reaching behind for Ora. Zeb pushed them both forward, one arm looping my waist as they pressed against Tate and Ezra's sides. No one wanted to lose the sense of connection, or the heightened bliss of my magic, emphasising each touch.

I felt undone, opened up and lit from within with the love I felt for all of them, the lust simply adding more to the experience.

"Now," Ezra groaned, his own cock throbbing inside me as Tate shoved up with a mighty thrust that must have lifted Ezra clear off his feet.

I didn't need to be told again. Like a comet arcing over the sky, or perhaps a bonfire raging on a beach, I gave myself over to the orgasm. Bucking and writhing and lost in the rapture of Tate's passion, Ezra's desire, Ora's adoration and Zeb's hedonism.

Sparks went off behind my eyes and I struggled to catch my breath as I soared through each of their varied but united feelings.

Finally, I came back to myself, found that we had at some point, collapsed to the floor. The soft Persian rug under my cheek was a welcome surprise. Each of my lovers was panting, moaning with satisfaction and residual enjoyment.

It was with a fair amount of effort we got up onto the bed, but it was exceedingly easy to fall asleep, safe with my lovers, back in the hearts I belonged to, who also belonged to me.

CHAPTER THIRTY-FOUR - IN WHICH WE HAVE AN EPILOGUE OF SORTS

Casting off from the Kingston, the mood on the Grey Kelpie was one of celebration. The illusion Ora and Solomon had placed on the ship had been stripped off overnight, since now the Grey Kelpie wasn't to be a pirate ship at all, but a privateer. Father had given us the official flag - the Union Jack with the white crest in the centre to fly.

I looked out over the marina and the town beyond it with a feeling of freedom. This happiness I had found didn't feel fragile at all, it felt reassured and solid.

"With the letter of marque, we can take the trade routes," Sagorika said to me. "Find more ships to liberate from slavers, more Spanish vessels to liberate of their coin."

I took a deep breath, the sea air filling my lungs and making me feel I was where I belonged.

"How long until we have enough coin to retire, do you think?"

"Hard to say," she said, grinning wide enough to show all her even, straight teeth. "But the crew used to be pirates. They may never feel they have enough gold."

I shrugged and laughed a little. "Well, we'll see about that. I have this dream about a house on a cliff, overlooking a harbour..."

"It's a nice dream," she said. "Maybe one day you can convince Tate to stay on land longer than a week."

"If anyone could, it's Gideon," Zeb said. He was coiling the last of the mooring ropes nearby. Once he'd done that he promptly sat beside them on the deck, leaning one shoulder on them and closing his eyes. He yawned. "Gideon could convince a whale it needed a top hat, if he tried."

I laughed and blushed. "That's... utterly ridiculous, but thank you, Zeb."

"Well now, I suppose I'd better make sure the crew are all pulling their weight," Sagorika said. She kissed my cheek and I kissed hers and then she turned to walk the deck.

I gave Kingston one last look, sending my love out on the wind to my father, and hoping that he didn't fall back into his old habits.

"Thank you, Mother," I said, softly. "I hope that did the trick."

There was a splash in the water below, and I looked over the railing to see Ora in merfolk form, swimming along in the wake of the ship. I waved at them, laughing as they leapt out of the water, dolphin-like.

They had spent a few days out of the water at my father's house, and I assumed that meant they needed a few days in the ocean now. That was all right, I knew they'd be close by, whatever happened.

I turned and made my way up to the helm, where Ezra and Tate were affectionately bickering. Tate's hands were on the wheel, Ezra was pointing at a map.

"I'm not sure you want to interrupt them, Gid," Zack said. He paused his mopping to wipe his brow and I saw a most welcome shadow on his jaw.

"Zack, I think you need a shave," I said, full of joy for him.

He ducked his head and nodded. "Aye, I reckon I might let it grow a while," he said. "Since I can."

"I'm so happy for you." I gave him a kiss on the cheek and a warm hug, which he returned happily.

"Get back to work!" Sagorika called, teasing the both of us.

"I'd better talk to the Captain, see if he has any orders for me," I said, letting go of Zack. I went to the helm, smiling as their bickering resolved itself into sentences as I got close enough to hear.

"You promised us the Americas," Ezra said. "If you don't follow through, the crew could mutiny."

"That was before the letter of marque," Tate said. "Now the whole ocean is open to us, we could make so much money! Just think, we could skirt Tortuga, up to Nassau and even Singapore. There's so much treasure to be found."

"Mutiny?" I asked, lightly, grinning as I ducked under Ezra's arm and pressed against his side.

"Aye, and I'll lead it myself. Chain the captain up and do what I like," Ezra said, a wicked glint in his eye.

"Oh, that sounds fun, let's do that," I said, grinning. "Then you can do it to me, too."

Tate rolled his eyes but his smile was wide. "Later, when someone else is at helm, please."

"If you're all quite done with flirting," Solomon said, drily. He appeared on the far side of Tate, the ghost of a smile playing about his mouth. "I'd like to talk to Gideon about the cards he showed me. I believe I found a book that will help decode them."

I kissed Ezra, leaned up to kiss Tate and then extricated myself from between them.

"Sounds wonderful," I said. "You two, no mutinies unless they're the fun kind. Cabin Boy's orders."

"Well, if the *Cabin Boy* is ordering it," Tate said, laughing.

"I promise nothing," Ezra said.

I went to offer Solomon my hand. "Please, show me the book." He eyed my hand, rolled his eyes and took it with a long suffering sigh.

"This happens once, and then never again," he said.

And as we walked to the Captain's cabin together, the ship left Kingston behind and sailed towards the West and the setting sun.

I felt my happiness and love grow large enough to encompass the entire ship and everyone on it, including my beloved merfolk swimming behind.

I didn't know what the future held, and I knew I had plenty still to learn about my magic, about the others on board and about relationships with each of my lovers, but it was a future I looked forward to with relish.

I knew whatever happened, I'd be strong enough to face it.

The end (for now)

Thanks for reading His Piratical Harem! Gideon and the crew will return later this year in the Further Adventures of the Grey Kelpie.

∿

If you enjoyed this book, please leave review on Amazon. Indie authors rely on star ratings and reviews to go up the algorithm and be seen by more readers.

∿

Sign up for Drake's newsletter for updates on new releases
https://www.subscribepage.com/q4c4no
Come join Drake's Crew reader's group to meet other fans and get exclusive content – maybe
you'll even get to name – or become! – a character in the next book
https://www.facebook.com/groups/1272511269588779/

∿

Find Drake online:
    Twitter: https://twitter.com/DrakeLamarque
    Pinterest: https://www.pinterest.nz/drakelamarque/
    Newsletter: https://www.subscribepage.com/q4c4no
    BookBub: https://www.bookbub.com/profile/drake-lamarque
    Instagram: https://www.instagram.com/drakelamarque/

ACKNOWLEDGMENTS

To my beloved Tate. You're the light of my life, and thanks for going on this voyage with me. I'd marry you again in an instant.

To my beta-readers, thanks for your patience, your feedback and your enthusiasm for these stories, this manuscript wouldn't be what it is without the two of you. Zeb cuddles for the both of you.

To the delightful members of Drake's Crew, thank you for all your support! I hope you've enjoyed spotting names in the dance sequence, I hope you'll all join me on my next adventures.

COMING SOON...

The Gentleman's Bounty – the next paranormal gay harem book, featuring Cedric, is coming out soon! Make sure you're following on Amazon or in Drake's Crew to get the news as soon as I release it

The Gentleman's Bounty, book one

Kidnapped by a Gentleman

Cedric's been kidnapped by pirates.
...they have no idea how much trouble they're in for.

Cedric was living his best life, partying in Jamaica, bedding whomever he pleased and trusting that his parents' money and affluence would get him out of any unfortunate scrapes. Not to mention mooning over his handsome but unfortunately proper tutor.

That was, until he was kidnapped by the fearsome pirate with an angel's name. Lucifer took one look at Cedric and saw ransom money, and now he intends to collect it all.

Now Cedric is trapped on a pirate ship with a dashingly handsome captain, a first mate who won't stop staring at him and a powerful need to find some fun.

BOOK ONE OF HIS PIRATICAL HAREM – CABIN BOY

Buy Now

I've never been what I was supposed to be. Wealthy sons of Port Governors aren't supposed to be ejected from the British Navy after less than a year, they're not supposed to like pulp romances or daydream about the handsome heroes of the stories instead of the heroines.

When my Father issued me an order to marry a woman, I knew I had no choice but to make my own way in the world, and I found a berth on the first ship out of Jamaica.

I didn't mean to join a pirate ship, and I certainly didn't intend to find myself the cabin boy to an incredibly charming Pirate Captain. Or that I'd also be attracted to the mysterious First Mate, or that both of them would show me all sorts of unspeakable and salacious pleasures while on board. How can I choose just one of them when I want both?

In addition to confusion on board the ship, there's also enchanting genderfluid merfolk, a cat which seems to understand a lot more than it should, an unseasonable storm and a sea witch with a serious grudge... and with all these complications, I am definitely in over my head.

--

Come and meet the crew:

Gideon: an innocent with a lot of forbidden desires and a lot of love to give

Tate: a huge, muscular ship's captain with a sweet side

Ezra: a dominant and closed off first mate

Ora: a genderqueer, curious and affectionate merman

BOOK TWO OF HIS PIRATICAL HAREM – FIRST MATE'S PET

Buy Now

Things were looking good, until the ship's cat became a man...

I didn't mean to join a pirate ship, but now that I'm here, well. Life is pretty good. Between the sexy and intimidating Captain Tate, the mysterious First Mate, Ora the merfolk and now Zeb the ship's cat I'm well entertained.

Rumours abound that the Royal Navy are searching for me at my father's order, and between that, an eventful trip to Tortuga (the famed pirate town) and maintaining the relationships with the crew... I've certainly got my work cut out for me.

Meet the crew:

Gideon: a well bred young man who is discovering his forbidden desires aren't necessarily a problem at sea
Tate: the impressive Captain with a sweet side
Ezra: the controlling and alluring First Mate

Ora: a genderqueer, sweet and mystical merman
Zeb: a cat shifter, who's learning about being human

MM romance, this is part two of a multiple book series -
working towards a HEA at the end of the series

BOOK THREE OF HIS PIRATICAL
HAREM – MERFOLK'S MATE

Buy Now

The British Navy caught up to the Grey Kelpie, and everything
I'd built for my life has fallen apart.

Tate and Ezra are headed for the gallows. Ora has disappeared
into an unwelcome sea and I have no idea what's become of the
ship's cat...

It's up to me to save them, but I'm trapped on the Naval ship, the
same as my lovers. If I'm to get us out of here, I'm going to have
to use all my wits, and maybe a little magic?

Meet the crew:

Gideon: a well-bred young man discovering a new side of
himself
    Tate: the sweet Captain with a dark past
    Ezra: a dominating First Mate who's slowly finding his
soft side
    Ora: a mystical merfolk who understands more than the rest

Zeb: an affectionate cat shifter who knows what he wants

MM romance, this is part three of a multiple book series - working towards a HEA at the end of the series - cannot be read as a standalone.

Content warning: some knife and blood play in one scene

Rival Princes by Jaxon Knight

There are three golden rules for new recruits at Fairyland
Theme Park:

1. No breaking character, even if you're dying of heat exhaustion
2. Always give guests the most magical time
3. No falling in love.

Nate's only been at work one day, and he's already broken all
three.

Fast-tracked into a Prince role, Nate's at odds with Dash, the
handsome not-so-charming prince who is supposed to be
training him. Nate doesn't know how he ended up on Dash's bad
side, but the broody prince sure is hot when he gets mad.

Dash has worked long and hard to play Prince Justice at
Fairyland. Now, instead of focusing on his own performance, he
is forced to train newbie Nate to be the perfect prince. Nate's
annoying ease with the guests coupled with his charm and good

looks could dethrone Dash from his number one spot ... so why does he secretly want to kiss him?

Fairyland heats up as sparks fly between the two rival princes. Will they get their fairytale romance before they're kicked out of Fairyland for good?

Find out in this standalone MM contemporary romance by Jaxon Knight, set in an amusement park where fairytales can come true.

ALSO PUBLISHED BY GREY KELPIE
STUDIO

Mischief and Mayhem by Jaxon Knight

Mischief

Protecting royalty at Fairyland theme park seemed about as far from Afghanistan as Cody could get. But the hot new rollercoaster brings up some unexpected trouble - and not the kind of trouble he knows how to handle alone.

Mayhem

Dean loves running the Spaceship Mayhem roller coaster - he gets to meet new people every day! When he sees a handsome, troubled security guard repeatedly fail to ride it, he sees an opportunity to help. And maybe they can be more than friends?

Cody reluctantly accepts cute, boy-next-door Dean's help and sparks fly between them, but between mischief, mayhem and miscommunication, can they ever make a relationship work?

Mischief and Mayhem is a slow burn, opposites attract MM

sweet romance featuring snark, foolishness, motorbikes, assumptions, the chicken door and a HEA

ALSO PUBLISHED BY GREY KELPIE STUDIO

Recipe for Chaos by Jaxon Knight

The recipe is simple:
    Charlie cooks an amazing meal
    Charlie impresses heir to the theme park Max Jones
    Charlie gets a promotion and a dash of control over his kitchen

But the perfect recipe becomes unpalatable with one wrong ingredient and Max Jones is not behaving how Charlie expected...

Max is meant to inherit the entire Fairyland theme park but he just wants to party, have fun and bed as many people as possible. That is, until he meets Charlie and falls for him so hard he can't even finish the delicious meal.

Charlie doesn't have time for clubs or helicopter flights over the city, but Max is accustomed to getting what he wants, and he wants Charlie.

Featuring one part Billionaire, one part sensible chef, six cups of attraction, a generous dose of snark and a freshly prepared Happy Ever After.

ALSO PUBLISHED BY GREY KELPIE
STUDIO

The Good, the Bad and the Dad by Jaxon Knight

Haru is a single dad, a widower, doing his best to balance his career and raising his little girl, Minako. Thankfully Fairyland theme park is a haven for both of them. However, when both a prince and a pirate start courting Haru, his balancing act gets a lot harder...

Cillian plays a pirate at Fairyland theme park and he loves playing the roguish character in and out of work hours. The last thing he wants is to settle down with a guy with a kid, so can't he stop thinking about handsome single dad Haru. And why can't he stop looking at pictures of Prince Magnificence and his stupid symmetrical face? And why does he keep running into both of them?

Grayson feels he's found his home in the role of Prince Magnificence, but he's more likely to run from love than seek it out. Until he meets Haru, that is. Christmas is complicated by Grayson's role being featured in a special Christmas celebration. Not only that, but his feelings for Haru, and his possible rival

Cillian keep on growing. Maybe it's time to stop hiding who he really is?

--

The Good, the Bad and the Dad is a sweet MMM romance featuring a single father, a rogue and a trans prince with a heart of gold. No cheating, just the tentative first steps into polyamory.